北京联合大学学科建设项目经费资助

北京市教委重点联合项目（2014-LH03）和面上项目（2015-MS194）结项成果

TOWARDS A PRAGMATIC STUDY OF
EUPHEMISMS IN *A DREAM OF RED MANSIONS*:
A RAPPORT MANAGEMENT APPROACH

人际关系管理理论视阈下《红楼梦》委婉语语用研究

刘晓玲　著

知识产权出版社

全国百佳图书出版单位

图书在版编目（CIP）数据

人际关系管理理论视阈下《红楼梦》委婉语语用研究=TOWARDS A PRAGMATIC STUDY OF EUPHEMISMS IN *A DREAM OF RED MANSIONS*: A RAPPORT MANAGEMENT APPROACH：英文/刘晓玲著.—北京：知识产权出版社，2017.8

ISBN 978-7-5130-1650-6

Ⅰ．①人… Ⅱ．①刘… Ⅲ．①《红楼梦》—言语交往—社会习惯语—研究—英文 Ⅳ．①I207.411②H131

中国版本图书馆 CIP 数据核字（2016）第 031660 号

内容提要

在中国，保全面子的工作是典型的防止冲突的机制，而关系管理理论的基础和核心内容恰好与中国人重视人际关系、关注面子的传统观念不谋而合。因此，本书以海伦·斯宾塞-欧迪（Helen Spencer-Oatey）的人际关系管理理论为框架，从语用学的角度对《红楼梦》人物话语中的委婉语进行探讨和研究。基于小说中复杂而严格的社会与家庭的等级观念和权势关系，本研究以权势作为变量，综合其他影响性因素如关系取向、信息内容、参与者之间的关系、交际活动以及关系管理的结果等，对于人物话语中的委婉语展开分析。

责任编辑：刘琳琳　　　　　　　　　　　责任出版：孙婷婷

人际关系管理理论视阈下《红楼梦》委婉语语用研究
TOWARDS A PRAGMATIC STUDY OF EUPHEMISMS IN *A DREAM OF RED MANSIONS*: A RAPPORT MANAGEMENT APPROACH

刘晓玲　著

出版发行：知识产权出版社有限责任公司	网　　址：http://www.ipph.cn
社　　址：北京市海淀区气象路 50 号院	邮　　编：100081
责编电话：010-82000860 转 8390	责编邮箱：sunsan-lin886@163.com
发行电话：010-82000860 转 8101/8102	发行传真：010-82000893/82005070/82000270
印　　刷：北京中献拓方科技发展有限公司	经　　销：各大网上书店、新华书店及相关专业书店
开　　本：720mm×1000mm　1/16	印　　张：14.25
版　　次：2017 年 8 月第 1 版	印　　次：2017 年 8 月第 1 次印刷
字　　数：180 千字	定　　价：39.00 元

ISBN 978-7-5130-1650-6

序

在刘晓玲的《人际关系管理理论视阈下〈红楼梦〉委婉语语用研究》一书即将出版之际，作为她的导师，我很高兴为此书作序。

本书的主要内容是：运用 Helen Spencer-Oatey 的人际关系管理理论，以"权势"作为变量，将《红楼梦》人物话语中的委婉语置于一个动态的语境中进行较为全面和系统的语用分析。

Helen Spencer-Oatey 的人际关系管理理论是以面子理论和礼貌原则为基础，以面子（face）和权利（rights）为核心内容构建起来的人际关系管理框架。面子包括素质面子（quality face）和身份面子（identity face），权利则包括公平权（equity rights）和交际权（association rights）。该理论关注人际关系和谐的一面，强调身份面子和交际权，即二者的社会性特征和意义。委婉语是一种语言现象，同时也是一种社会和文化现象，是维护和保全交际双方面子的重要语言手段，因此在人际关系中具有不可替代的协调作用。文学巨著《红楼梦》在展现高度礼教化和等级森严的封建社会的同时，也道出了中国传统的"和合"二字在人际关系中的重要性。小说人物在不同的权势关系中，使用了多种多样的委婉语，这为相关研究提供了丰富的语言材料。

本书的研究价值主要有以下三点：

一、本书在 Helen Spencer-Oatey 的人际关系管理理论、委婉语和《红楼梦》人物话语中的委婉语之间找到了一个有效的切入点，即这三者都是以人际关系为基础，以"和"为目的，因此具有一定的研究价值。迄今还没有人运用 Helen Spencer-Oatey 的人际关系管理理论对于中国小说中的委婉语及其所涉及的人际关系进行较为系统的研究，而这正是本研究最大的亮点。

二、本书在运用 Helen Spencer-Oatey 的人际关系管理理论对于《红楼梦》人物话语中的委婉语进行分析后发现，该理论所关注的身份面子和交际权得到了充分的体现，这印证了该理论的基础、核心内容及其面子和权利的社会性一面恰好与中国人重视人际关系、关注面子的传统观念不谋而合。同时，还验证了该理论对于小说中的人物如何选择和使用语委婉语具有较为强大的控制力和解释力，说明了该理论的必要性和可行性。因此，这一研究具有一定的理论和实践意义。

三、本书将"权势"作为变量，综合其他影响性因素，对于人物话语中的委婉语进行了系统的分析和研究，并得出有益的结论。一方面，对于红学研究起到了一定的丰富和补充的作用。另一方面，对于之后的各种相关研究具有一定的启发和激励意义。比如，后续研究还可以将"距离"作为变量，对于《红楼梦》人物话语中的委婉语进行分析，另外，还可以进一步运用 Helen Spencer-Oatey 的人际关系管理理论对于其他文本进行语用研究。

本书体现了刘晓玲较为敏锐的学术嗅觉、较为宽阔的学术视野、较为独到的学术见解和较为扎实的语言功底。

刘晓玲在上海外国语大学攻读博士学位期间，刻苦钻研，勤于思考，在指导她撰写博士论文期间，我见证了她从论文开题到论文答辩必经的每一个阶段，这是一个痛苦、曲折但是又充满挑战和喜悦的刻骨铭心的历程，最终她以第一名的成绩通过了语言学科的博士论文答辩，顺利获得了博士学位。毕业之后，她满怀热情返回工作岗位，全身心投身到英语教学与科研中，并取得了一定的成绩。

作为她的导师，我为她的持之以恒和不断进步而由衷地感到骄傲和欣慰，并衷心希望她在未来的教学和科研中潜心笃志，厚积薄发，迈上一个新的台阶。

俞东明

于上海外国语大学

2016 年 8 月

Acknowledgements

On accomplishing the present book, I wish to avail myself of this very opportunity to express my sincere obligation and appreciation for all the gracious and intelligent help that I have received along the way.

This book would have been impossible without the generous sponsorship of Beijing Union University and genuine support of Professor Huang Xiankai, Professor Xie Zhi'an, Professor Zhang Dian'en and Professor He Fang.

As the book is closely based on my PhD dissertation, I wish to acknowledge the following individuals for their wisdom, guidance and support in the whole process of the work.

I feel particularly indebted to my reverend supervisor, Professor Yu Dongming, for his illuminating direction, instructive comments, inspirational advice and invaluable suggestions. I have benefited enormously throughout the process of narrowing down the scope of study, culling the materials, collecting the cases in point and structuring the argumentation. Thomas' principle of expressibility reads, "Anything that can be meant can be said." My gratitude to Professor Yu can undeniably be meant yet can never be said in a maximally expressible way owing to my language inadequacy. As a profound scholar and earnest teacher, Professor Yu has set a perfect example to me in my future study and work.

Please allow me to extend my heartfelt appreciation to other professors of Shanghai Foreign Studies University, whose informative lectures, meticulous scholarship and constructive suggestions provide me with not only nourishment in intellectual growth but also enthusiasm for academic pursuit during my years of study and preparations for the dissertation. They are Professor Dai Weidong, Professor He Zhaoxiong, Professor Mei Deming, Professor Xu Yulong, Professor Li Ji'an, Professor Yu Jianhua, Professor Li Weiping and Professor Shi Zhikang.

I am equally obliged to Professor He Zhaoxiong, Professor Cai Jigang, Professor Wang Zhenhua, Professor Han Zhongqian, Professor Mei Deming, Professor Xu Haiming, Professor Zhang Xuemei and Professor Ge Yixiang for unsparingly spending their time, painstakingly reading, critically commenting and graciously advising so that further amendment and improvement can be made of this dissertation.

I am extremely grateful to Dr. Helen Spencer-Oatey, proposer of the theory of rapport management, for her enlightening ideas and brilliant exposition. My gratitude also goes to the authors whose works and research findings I have referred to in the present study. I owe special thanks to my former colleagues for unselfishly sharing my teaching load and kindly offering continued support.

Thanks also go to my classmates who have offered help and concern along the way and from whom I have appreciably benefited both academically and spiritually. Their names are alphabetically Han Shuying, Hao Hongyao, Huang Xiaoying, Liu Guilan, Shi Yunxia, Sun Hongyan, Wang Lei, Wang Suqing, Yang Li and Zhao Guiwang.

I am most grateful to all my family members for their unselfish love and support. I sincerely acknowledge that my husband has a claim to my achievements, if there are any. He has devotedly supported me for so many years with unfailing love, care, kindness, warmth and humor. Every progress I have made I owe to him, in part. My mother, a retired teacher over eighty, has always been a constant supporter along my "Long March". My daughter has also been an important source of inspiration and understanding. As a busy high-schooler four years ago she always spared time talking to me and inquiring about my weekly progress in the dissertation. At that time we both were students and friends in terms of "distance" rather than mother and daughter in terms of "power". The latter term found much favor in my dissertation but unfortunately fell out of it in our "alliance".

Finally I would like to say "thank you" to Intellectual Property Publishing House, especially its three staff members: Liu Linlin and Yin Yamin for their professional support in editing the book, and Shao Jianwen for the exquisite cover design.

The oral defence of my PhD dissertation was memorably in May. It so happens that my mother's birthday falls on May 31 and my daughter's May 28 (That's why her English name is May). For this reason the present book is specially dedicated to their birthdays.

摘　要

　　委婉语产生于禁忌，是一种间接性语言。同时，委婉语也是一种社会和文化现象，它是有效协调人际关系的润滑剂，也是保全交际双方面子的重要手段。因此，人们普遍认为，委婉语与面子和礼貌之间存在着密不可分的关系。关于委婉语的文献综述表明，长期以来，委婉语一直被作为一种修辞手段进行探讨和研究，因此，对于委婉语的定义也仅局限于修辞范围。近年来，对于委婉语的研究已经拓展到了社会语言学、语义学、语用学和认知语言学等学科领域，并且取得了长足的进步。

　　本书首先就委婉语的间接性以及与之相关的概念和理论，如面子、面子的维护、Grice 的会话合作原则和会话含义理论、Leech 的礼貌原则、Brown 和 Levinson 的面子保全论以及顾曰国的礼貌原则进行了全面的梳理。之后，详细分析了学者们在不同时期从不同角度对于委婉语所下的不同版本的定义，认为迄今为止邵军航所阐述的委婉语的定义最为全面和客观。同时，对于委婉语的产生做了简单的回顾。国内外对于委婉语的研究异彩纷呈。国外的研究集中在辞典的编纂和专著的出版，主要探讨委婉语的词源、发展、分类和使用情况。也有研究将语言学理论与文学作品结合起来，用以分析文学作品中的委婉语。国内的研究除了传统的修辞范畴、词典编纂和专著出版之外，则多受国外各种语言学理论的影响，陆续主要从社会语言学、语义学、语用学和认知语言学的角度对于委婉语的产生机制、社会文化因素、认知因素、使用原则以及构成手段等进行了有益的探讨和发展。

　　《红楼梦》是一部文学巨著，它展现了一幅高度礼教化和等级森严的封建社会的画卷，同时也道出了中国传统的"和合"二字在人际关系中的重要作用。其错综复杂的社会、家庭关系以及对众多角色的驾驭为小说语言艺术的分析提供了丰富的历史文化背景和语言素材。对于《红楼梦》语言艺术的大量研究多见于其修辞特色，因此对于作品中委婉语的研究也多从修辞的角度入手。另外，有不少学者从翻译学的角度对《红楼梦》原作与译作中的委婉语进行对比研究。近几年，也有学者尝试运用语用学的理论对作品中的委婉语进行分析和探讨。但是，迄今还没有人从语用学的角度对于《红楼梦》人物话语中的委婉语进行较为系统的研究。

Helen Spencer-Oatey 的人际关系管理理论是以面子和礼貌为基础，以面子和权利为核心内容构建起来的人际关系管理框架。在中国，保全面子的工作是典型的防止冲突的机制，而关系管理理论的基础和核心内容恰好与中国人重视人际关系、关注面子的传统观念不谋而合。因此，本研究以 Helen Spencer-Oatey 的人际关系管理理论为框架，从语用学的角度对于《红楼梦》人物话语中的委婉语进行探讨和研究。基于小说中复杂而严格的社会与家庭的等级观念和权势关系，本研究以权势作为变量，综合其他影响性因素，如关系取向、信息内容、参与者之间的关系、交际活动以及关系管理的结果等，对于人物话语中的委婉语展开分析。

本书属于理论研究与实证研究相结合，主要运用观察法对《红楼梦》人物话语中的委婉语进行客观描述。定性研究则是对于具有代表性的典型例子进行详细的分析。研究结果表明，人际关系管理理论对于《红楼梦》人物话语中的委婉语具有很强的解释力，即人际关系管理理论具有跨文化和跨时间的普遍意义。

本书尝试运用人际关系管理理论对于《红楼梦》人物话语中的委婉语进行分析，验证了该理论的必要性和可行性。因此，本研究具有一定的创新性，并且具有一定的理论意义和实践意义。由于将权势作为影响因素，将小说人物话语中的委婉语置于一个动态的语境中进行系统的研究，该结果有望在一定程度上补充和丰富红学研究。由于委婉语被广泛运用于人际交往中，因此在很大程度上依赖于语境。制约委婉语使用的影响性因素也是语用学的关心所在，因而本研究的结果也有助于验证和丰富语用学的相关原理。本书将《红楼梦》作为文本，以人际关系管理理论为框架，对人物话语中的委婉语进行了研究。经验证，该理论能够制约和解释小说人物话语中委婉语的选择和使用。这表明，该理论也可以用来对汉英语言中的其他文本进行语用分析。语言既具有普遍性，又是文化的载体，作为语言的一部分，委婉语反映文化传统和民族心理，但同时也受到文化传统和民族心理的制约。因此，本研究结果对于文化学和人类学的研究也具有一定的启发意义。

Abstract

Euphemism originates in taboo and manifests itself in a form of indirect language. As a social and cultural phenomenon, euphemism is used to effectively lubricate interpersonal relations and maintain the face of interactants. It is thus commonly agreed that euphemism relates closely to face and politeness. Literature review indicates that euphemism has long been a subject in the realm of rhetoric. Hence, the definitions of euphemism have also long been confined to the field of rhetoric. Recent years has witnessed remarkable progress in the study of euphemism with expansion into the domains of sociolinguistics, semantics, pragmatics and cognitive pragmatics.

The present study proceeds from a systematic literature review of indirectness of euphemism together with related notions and theories such as face, facework, Grice's CP (Cooperative Principle) and CI (Conversational Implicature), Leech's PP (Politeness Principle), Brown and Levinson's face theory as well as Gu Yueguo's PP. It is followed by an overview of a number of definitions, with a conclusion that the very definition proposed by Shao Junhang is so far the most comprehensive and objective. Then there is a brief retrospect of the origin of euphemism. As for the research that has already been done on euphemism, scholars abroad have mainly produced dictionaries and monographs with regard to its etymology, development, categorization and usage. Some researchers have investigated euphemisms in literary works with the help of linguistic theories and principles. Studies of euphemism at home are varied. Apart from the rhetorical investigation of euphemism, there have been dictionaries and monographs published. At the same time, influenced by a variety of linguistic theories, significant research has been done on the generative mechanisms, socio-cultural factors, cognitive factors, principles of usage and formational devices of euphemism mainly from such perspectives as sociolinguistics, semantics, pragmatics and cognitive linguistics.

As a literary masterpiece, *A Dream of Red Mansions* unfolds a panoramic picture of a highly ritualized and strictly hierarchical feudal society. At the same time, it highlights the important role that the traditional Chinese idea of "harmony and integrity" assumes in interpersonal relations. The complexity of the social and familial relations in the novel and its author's politic handling of a large cast of characters lend abundant historical, cultural and linguistic resources to the study of the art of language in the novel. So far great efforts have been made at the rhetorical characteristics of the novel. Therefore, it is no wonder that research on euphemisms of the novel has also been primarily rhetorical. Quite a few researchers have made comparative studies of euphemisms between the Chinese version and quite a number of English versions in terms of translation. In very recent years attempts have also been made at the euphemisms of the novel in light of related pragmatic principles. But up till now no systematic pragmatic study has been conducted on the euphemisms in the character utterances of the novel.

Built upon the notions of face and politeness, Helen Spencer-Oatey's rapport management is a theoretical framework for interpersonal relations with face and rights as its core components. As facework is typically a Chinese conflict-preventive mechanism, the theoretical foundation and core components of rapport management happen to be in concert with the traditional Chinese attachment to interpersonal relations and face. The present research takes Helen Spencer-Oatey's rapport management as its theoretical framework and investigates the euphemisms in the character utterances of the novel. Considering the complexity and rigidity of social and familial hierarchy and power relations, the study aims to take power as its major variable. Other influencing factors such as rapport orientation, message content, relational role, communicative activity and rapport outcome are by no means neglected. They are analyzed comprehensively with power.

The book is both theoretical and empirical. Observation is mainly conducted with regard to the objective description of euphemisms whereas qualitative method works mainly in the demonstration and categorization analysis of typical examples. The result of the study reveals that the theory of rapport management has a strong controlling force and explanatory power over the euphemisms in the character utterances of the novel. That is, the theory has proved to be largely universal in terms of culture and time differences.

There are some implications in the book. It has tentatively and innovatively verified the necessity and feasibility of the theory of rapport management in relation to the analysis of euphemisms in the character utterances of *A Dream of Red Mansions*. It is assumed that the study has both theoretical and practical implications. A systematic study has been conducted on the character utterances, in which euphemisms are put in a dynamic context with power being a major factor that influences the strategic use of euphemisms. The result of the pragmatic investigation of euphemisms in the character utterances of *A Dream of Red Mansions* is expected to supplement and enrich the unremitting nation-wide and even world-wide academic studies of the novel, namely, Redology. As euphemisms are found extensively abundant in interpersonal communication, they are largely context-dependent. The variables governing the use of euphemisms are also concerns in the field of pragmatics. So the findings of the study are supposed to help, to some extent, verify and enrich the related principles in pragmatics. The present study has taken *A Dream of Red Mansions* as its text and attempts to analyze the euphemisms in the character utterances of the novel in light of the theory of rapport management. The theory has proved to be capable of governing and explaining the option and use of euphemisms in the novel, which significantly indicates that the theory can also be applied to the pragmatic analysis of other texts in both English and Chinese languages. Language is both universal and culture-bound. As a part of language, euphemisms reflect yet are constrained by cultural traditions and national mentality. The findings of the present research are supposed to have some implications to culturology and ethnography.

List of Tables

Table 1   Contrasting X-phemisms   / 35

Table 2   Components of rapport management   / 56

Table 3   Chief characters in the novel and their relationships   / 97

Table 4   Specification of all the influencing factors   / 101

Table 5   Euphemisms used by Jia Zheng for the Imperial Consort's face and
          rights   / 103

Table 6   Specification of all the influencing factors   / 105

Table 7   Euphemism used by the Lady Dowager for the Imperial Consort's
          face   / 106

Table 8   Specification of all the influencing factors   / 108

Table 9   Euphemisms used by the attendant for Jia Yucun's face and
          rights   / 110

Table 10   Specification of all the influencing factors   / 111

Table 11   Euphemisms used by the doctor for face and rights of mistresses
           and Dajie   / 112

Table 12   Specification of all the influencing factors   / 114

Table 13   Euphemisms used by Lady Wang for face and rights of Jia Zheng
           and the Lady Dowager   / 115

Table 14   Specification of all the influencing factors   / 118

Table 15   Euphemisms used by the Lady Dowger for face and rights of
           Lady Wang   / 121

Table 16   Specification of all the influencing factors   / 122

Table 17   Euphemisms used by Jia Zhen for Qin Keqing's rights   / 123

Table 18   Specification of all the influencing factors   / 125

Table 19   Euphemisms used by Concubine Zhao for Baochai's and Lady

Wang's face   / 126

Table 20   Specification of all the influencing factors   / 129

Table 21   Euphemisms used by Lai Da for face and rights of his masters and

the ladies   / 130

Table 22   Specification of all the influencing factors   / 132

Table 23   Euphemisms used by Zijuan for Lin Daiyu's rights   / 133

Table 24   Lexicalization of the self-denigration maxim   / 162

List of Figures

Figure 1   Strategies to attend to face wants   / 26

Figure 2   Distinguishing X-phemisms   / 35

Figure 3   Classification of the main devices for constructing euphemisms / 36

Figure 4   Spencer-Oatey's framework of rapport management   / 68

Figure 5   Euphemisms for maintenance/enhancement of quality face / 138

Figure 6   Euphemisms explicated by the maintenance of quality face / 139

Figure 7   Euphemisms for maintenance/enhancement of identity face / 140

Figure 8   Euphemisms explicated by maintenance/enhancement of

identity face   / 141

Figure 9   Euphemisms for maintenance of equity rights   / 143

Figure 10   Euphemisms explicated by maintenance of equity rights   / 143

Figure 11   Euphemisms for maintenance of association rights   / 145

Figure 12   Euphemisms explicated by maintenance of association

rights   / 146

Figure 13   Grice's CP & CI, Spencer-Oatey's rapport and euphemisms / 152

Figure 14   Leech's PP, Spencer-Oatey's rapport and euphemisms   / 158

Figure 15   Brown and Levinson's conceptualization of face and

Spencer-Oatey's rapport   / 160

Figure 16   Gu Yueguo's PP and Spencer-Oatey's rapport   / 164

List of Abbreviations

CP	Cooperative Principle
CI	Conversational Implicature
DRM	*A Dream of Red Mansions*
H	Hearer
MP	Model Person
PP	Politeness Principle
S	Speaker
the Yangs	Yang Xianyi and Gladys Yang

Contents

Acknowledgements / I

摘　要 / I

Abstract / I

List of Tables / I

List of Figures / III

List of Abbreviations / IV

Chapter One　Introduction **/ 001**

1.1　Background of the Study / 001

1.2　Objectives / 007

1.3　Questions for the Study / 008

1.4　Significance of the Study / 009

1.5　Methodology / 010

1.6　Collection of Euphemisms / 011

1.7　Organization of the Book / 013

Chapter Two　Literature Review **/ 015**

2.1　Introduction / 015

2.2　Fundamentals Revisited / 015

2.2.1　Indirectness, Grice's CP & CI and Leech's PP / 016

2.2.2　Face, Facework, Brown & Levinson's Face Theory and Gu's PP / 023

2.3   Euphemism   / 029

  2.3.1   Definitions   / 030

  2.3.2   Origin of Euphemism   / 032

2.4   Studies of Euphemism in Retrospect   / 033

  2.4.1   Studies of Euphemism Abroad   / 033

  2.4.2   Studies of Euphemism at Home   / 038

2.5   Studies of Euphemisms in *DRM*   / 047

2.6   Summary   / 051

Chapter Three   Theoretical Framework:
Rapport Management   **/ 052**

3.1   Introduction   / 052

3.2   Components of Rapport Management   / 053

  3.2.1   Quality Face and Identity Face   / 054

  3.2.2   Equity Rights and Association Rights   / 055

3.3   Rapport-Threatening Behavior: Managing Face and

       Sociality Rights   / 057

3.4   Rapport-Management Strategy Domains   / 059

3.5   Factors Influencing Strategy Use   / 060

  3.5.1   Rapport Orientation   / 060

  3.5.2   Contextual Variables   / 062

  3.5.3   Pragmatic Conventions   / 066

3.6   Rapport Management Outcomes   / 067

3.7   Summary   / 069

Chapter Four   Description and Categorization of
Euphemisms in *DRM*   **/ 070**

4.1   Introduction   / 070

4.2   Conventional Euphemisms   / 071

4.2.1	Devil and Disaster	/ 072
4.2.2	Death and Funeral Affairs	/ 073
4.2.3	Disease and Ill Health	/ 075
4.2.4	Sex	/ 076
4.2.5	Excreta and Secretion	/ 077
4.2.6	Pregnancy and Birth	/ 077
4.2.7	Ageing	/ 078
4.2.8	Love and Affection	/ 078
4.2.9	Marriage and Concubinage	/ 079
4.2.10	Women's Jealousy in Love	/ 080
4.2.11	Address Terms for Interpersonal Relations	/ 080
4.2.12	Servants and Housemaids	/ 082
4.2.13	Personal Names Regarded as Taboos	/ 082
4.2.14	Moral Standing and Disposition	/ 083
4.2.15	Buddhist Practice and Buddhist Practitioner	/ 083
4.3	Situational Euphemisms	/ 084
4.3.1	Euphemisms with Semantic Fuzziness	/ 084
4.3.2	Euphemisms with Syntactical Devices	/ 086
4.4	Summary	/ 093

Chapter Five Demonstration Analysis of Euphemisms in *DRM* / 094
5.1	Introduction	/ 094
5.2	Power	/ 095
5.3	Social Power Relations	/ 099
5.3.1	The Absolute Royal Power	/ 099
5.3.2	Social Unequals	/ 107
5.4	Familial Power Relations	/ 113
5.4.1	Unequal Kinship	/ 113

5.4.2   Master-Servant Relations / 127

5.5 Summary / 134

Chapter Six   Discussions / 135

6.1 Introduction / 135

6.2 Rapport Management and Euphemisms in *DRM* / 136

6.2.1   Quality Face and Euphemisms / 137

6.2.2   Identity Face and Euphemisms / 139

6.2.3   Equity Rights and Euphemisms / 141

6.2.4   Association Rights and Euphemisms / 144

6.3 A Comparative and Contrastive Analysis of Related Theories and Principles / 147

6.3.1   Grice's CP & CI and Spencer-Oatey's Rapport / 147

6.3.2   Leech's PP and Spencer-Oatey's Rapport / 152

6.3.3   Brown & Levinson's Face Theory and Spencer-Oatey's Rapport / 158

6.3.4   Gu Yueguo's PP and Spencer-Oatey's Rapport / 160

6.4 Non-use of Euphemisms / 164

6.5 *Li* and Politeness / 167

6.6 Summary / 169

Chapter Seven   Conclusion / 172

7.1 Introduction / 172

7.2 Findings / 173

7.3 Implications / 185

7.4 Limitations and Suggestions / 187

Bibliography / 189

Chapter One

Introduction

·❯❯ 1.1　Background of the Study

Every language has a dual function of transferring information and managing social relations. There is more than one way of communicating: literal and indirect. Speakers are frequently puzzled as to which way to choose, or rather, in Blakemore's (1992) words, "Whenever a speaker communicates he must make a decision as to what he chooses to make explicit and what he chooses to leave implicit" (7). Although literalness costs the least linguistic effort, Sperber and Wilson (1986) argue that it is not necessarily the most communicatively efficient way of saying something. In other words, indirectness is deemed alternatively desirable and efficient in interaction.

As for the rationality of people's preference for indirectness, Thomas (1995) observes,

> Everyone (or, at least, everyone who is 'in the know') employs indirectness on certain occasions, even though to do so apparently costs them unnecessary effort... We are more likely to conclude that people obtain

advantage or avoid some negative consequence by employing indirectness. They may wish to avoid hurting someone else or appearing "pushy" or to show how clever they are (122).

Thomas goes on to point out another possibility, saying,

People may employ indirectness because they are prey to some superstitions or are avoiding a taboo word or topic. But whatever the underlying motivation for using indirectness (even if it is because of an irrational belief) the use of indirectness itself is perfectly rational, if it enables the speaker to achieve his or her goal or to avoid unpleasantness (ibid.).

Euphemism is first and foremost characterized with linguistic indirectness. Wu Liquan (2002) claims that any manner of speaking that leans towards indirectness may be a euphemism. This indirectness can also be put under pragmatic examination. Xu Haiming (1996) argues "The use of euphemism is quite a result of flouting the maxims (of the CP). Consequently, the hearer has to make efforts to get what is implicated behind the euphemism and infer what is truly meant by the speaker" (委婉语的使用恰恰违背了这四个次则。因此,听话人须从委婉语的背后领会"话外话",并推断说话人的真正意图。) (22). Being a type of indirect language, euphemism is intended to flout one or more of the maxims of the CP, which gives rise to CI.

What claims attention is that euphemism is also a communicative strategy in interpersonal relations owing to its relatedness to face and facework. Noticing the important role that euphemism assumes in maintaining face, Allan and Burridge (1991) rightly put, "A euphemism is used as an alternative to a dispreferred expression, in order to avoid possible loss of face: either one's own face or, through giving offence, that of the audience, or of some third party" (18). And in their 2006 work, *Forbidden*

Words: Taboo and the Censoring of Language, Allan and Burridge (2006) reinforce the paramount significance of face with regard to euphemism by pointing out,

> Social interaction is generally oriented towards maintaining (saving) face. Just as we look after our own face (self-respect), we are expected to be considerate of, and look after, the face-wants of others. Those who are skilled are said to have social *savoir faire*; they are said to be perceptive and diplomatic. In short, in Anglo communities, face is one's public self-image. That is, the way that one perceives one's self to be viewed in the eyes of others (33-34).

To a great extent, euphemism is deemed an effective way of protecting face and managing identity in communication. Furthermore, it is closely related to politeness. According to Brown (1980),

> What politeness essentially consists in is a special way of treating people, saying and doing things in such a way as to take into account the other person's feelings. On the whole that means that what one says politely will be less straightforward or more complicated than what one would say if one wasn't taking the other's feelings into account (114).

The primary concern of politeness for the other's feelings is in effect the care of his/her face. And the care of his/her face entails language as a means of communication which can be achieved "on the one hand through the speaker's use of intentional strategies to allow his utterances to be received favourably by the addressee and on the other by the speaker's expression of the expected and prescribed norms of speech" (Ide, 1988: 371). There is no denying that euphemism is a desirable linguistic strategy of politeness. Leech (1983) believes that "If we want to explain why many speakers prefer to use euphemistic words or phrases to substitute for those unpleasant ones in their interpersonal communication or to express their meanings in a roundabout way, the reason is for politeness" (46). Focusing on the matter of politeness in language behaviour as far as euphemism is concerned, Allan and Burridge (2006) maintain that a polite language behaviour "is at least inoffensive and at best pleasing to an audience. That which is offensive is impolite." (30) Naturally, euphemism is a linguistic way of actualizing politeness.

In effect, euphemism is found socially all-pervasive. In Hugh Rawson's (1981) words, "Euphemisms are embedded so deeply in our language that few of us, even those who pride themselves on being plain spoken, ever get through a day without using them" (3). Mentioning the importance of euphemism, Enright (1985) also states, "A language without euphemisms would be a defective instrument of communication" (29). In this sense, euphemism assumes, at least in part, an important role in ensuring successful communication.

Literature review couches the closeness of euphemism with indirectness, the CP and CI. And adequate study has been conducted on euphemism in light of the CP and CI. Again, euphemism is found to be a linguistic strategy of handling face and facework as well as applying face theory and PP in a favourable manner.

In fact, the study of face, facework and politeness has been extensively conducted in the realms of pragmatics and cross-cultural communication. For example, some specialists like Brown and Levinson (1978) intend their face theory to be universal in interpreting human interactions. Other researchers attach more importance to culture specificity and endeavour to account for human interactions in terms of cultural peculiarities (Matsumoto, 1988; Ting-Toomey, 1988; Gu, 1990; Zhan, 1992; Chang & Holt, 1994; Cupach & Metts, 1994; Penman, 1994; Scollon & Scollon, 1994; Ting-Toomey & Cocroft, 1994; Tracey & Baratz, 1994). Still a number of scholars take strong interest in the Chinese concept of face and work at a theory or principle that is totally characteristic of and well-grounded in the Chinese culture (Hu, 1944; Ho, 1976; Cheng, 1986; Chang & Holt, 1994).

With regard to the applicability of Brown and Levinson's theory of politeness or face theory to the Oriental culture as a whole, critiques are not few. One of the criticisms of Brown and Levinson's theory of politeness is that it is a highly rational model rather than a relational one (Matsumoto, 1988; Ting-Toomey, 1988; Gu, 1990; Chang & Holt, 1994; Penman, 1994). Ting-Toomey (1988) argues that Brown and Levinson's theory conceptualizes "positive face" and "negative face" from the individualistic culture framework. Matsumoto (1988) criticizes the theory in that the negative face want of preservation of individual territories seems alien to Japanese. Gu Yueguo (1990) holds that the model does not apply to the Chinese social interaction. Penman (1994) points out that both the negative face and the positive face are self-oriented. Finally, Chang and Holt (1994) find,

> Western understanding of facework is very much influenced by the idea of impression management, reflecting the dominant individualistic characteristics of Western cultures. This can be contrasted with the Chinese conception of *mianzi* which places more emphasis on the nature of the relationship (126).

Criticism is also posed by Scollon & Scollon (1994). They discover that while the Western facework is largely transactional there is a fundamentally moral dimension to the Eastern concept of face; face constitutes the Asian sense of being an Asian. They suggest that the concept of self is perhaps more applicable in looking at Western social interactions. This resonates with Ho's (1976) idea that "the Western mentality, deeply ingrained with the values of individuality, is not one which is favorably disposed to the idea of face, for face is never a purely individual thing" (882).

Another question is raised as to its neglect of social identity as a concept. Therefore, Brown and Levinson's conceptualization of face is accepted with reservations and challenge remains unsettled. Matsumoto (1988), Ide (1989) and Mao (1994) all argue for the importance of social identity as a concept especially in Japanese and Chinese societies. Matsumoto (1988) maintains,

> What is of paramount concern to a Japanese is not his/her own territory, but the position in relation to the others in the group and his/her acceptance by those others. Loss of face is associated with the perception by others that one has not comprehended and acknowledged the structure and hierarchy of the group... A Japanese generally must understand where s/he stands in relation to other members of the group or society, and must acknowledge his/her dependence on the others. Acknowledgement and maintenance of the relative position of others, rather than preservation of an individual's proper territory, governs all social interaction (405).

Matsumoto's criticism pinpoints the drawbacks in Brown and Levinson's conceptualization of face: overlook of interactional or social aspect of face and overemphasis of individual freedom or autonomy. Again, by truthfully examining the Chinese situation, Gu Yueguo (1998) argues it is not that concerns about autonomy, imposition and so on do not exist in Eastern cultures, but rather that they are not regarded as face concerns (qtd. Spencer-Oatey, 2007: 13).

Taking all these arguments into consideration, Helen Spencer-Oatey (2000, 2007) proposes a modified framework for the conceptualization of face and rapport. She maintains "Brown and Levinson's (1987) conceptualization of positive face has been underspecified, and that the concerns they identify as negative face issues are not necessarily face concerns at all" (13). Rather, she proposes that rapport management (the management of harmony-disharmony among people) involve two main components: the management of face and the management of sociality rights.

Guided by Helen Spencer-Oatey's theory of rapport management, the present study purports to investigate euphemisms in the character utterances of *A Dream of Red Mansions*. The remaining chapter presents the objectives and methodology of the study, collection of euphemisms, questions guiding the study, significance of the study and general organization of the book.

1.2   Objectives

The present study investigates euphemisms in the character utterances of *A Dream of Red Mansions* within the theoretical framework of Helen Spencer-Oatey's rapport management. In general, the study is intended to achieve the following purposes.

Firstly, based on such related notions and principles as indirectness, Grice's CP and CI, Leech's PP, Goffman's notion of face, Brown and Levinson's face theory, and Gu Yueguo's PP, the necessity and possibility of applying the theory of rapport management to the present research will be put under discussion. The theory's salient emphasis on the "socialness" of "face" and "rights" will merit adequate attention and effort in the study.

Secondly, by making an exhaustive literature review of the related research on euphemism, the main concepts and notions about euphemism will be discriminated and discussed. Facing the complexity of definitions of euphemism, the study is aimed to compare and contrast the strengths and weaknesses of each definition in order to arrive at a more advanced and comprehensive one, which is already there and which is so far supposed to be equal to the concept of euphemism for the present study within a pragmatic context.

Thirdly, universal as it is, language is also culture-specific. When the theory of rapport management is applied to a context that is linguistically, culturally, socially and psychologically Chinese, there must be both success and challenge as far as its controlling force and explanatory power are concerned. More importantly, inadequacy may arise in the applicability of the theory. Hopefully the findings of the present study will help further testify the theory of rapport management.

Fourthly, a tentative pragmatic study of euphemisms in the character utterances of *A Dream of Red Mansions* might contribute to Redology, which is nation-wide and perhaps even world-wide academic research of the novel.

1.3 Questions for the Study

The following questions are supposed to guide the whole study.

1) What are the general patterns of euphemisms in the character utterances of the novel?

2) How does euphemism as a linguistic strategy contribute to the management of face and rights proposed by Spencer-Oatey?

3) How does power as a variable influence the characters' choice of euphemisms?

4) Does the degree of indirectness positively correlate with power relations?

5) What types of euphemisms does an inferior tend to use when he/she interacts with his/her superior?

6) What types of euphemisms is a superior inclined to use when he/she interacts with an inferior?

7) Is the salient emphasis on "socialness" of "face" and "rights" in Spencer-Oatey's rapport management well exemplified in the characters' choice of euphemisms in *DRM*?

8) Does the theory of rapport management have a controlling force and

explanatory power over the characters' option of euphemisms in *DRM* ?

9) What is supposed to be the inadequacy of the theory of rapport management in the analysis of the euphemisms in *DRM* , if there is any?

10) Is there any room for the improvement of the theory of rapport management with the findings of the present study?

1.4　Significance of the Study

The present study is envisioned having both theoretical and practical implications.

1) Previously, a number of articles, MA theses and PhD dissertations discussed euphemism pragmatically in the case of either flouting the CP or observing the PP, or both. Some endeavoured to study euphemism in light of Brown and Levinson's face theory or Gu Yueguo's PP. However, this research contrives to pioneeringly and tentatively take Spencer-Oatey's theory of rapport management as its theoretical framework, which is relatively new and challenging in pragmatically interpreting the option and use of euphemisms. The attempt is also supposed to be one of the innovations of the present study. The study is to verify the feasibility and applicability of the theory in the Chinese context.

2) Generally, euphemisms in *A Dream of Red Mansions* have been approached in the following ways: euphemisms in the chapter titles of the novel; euphemisms regarding particular subject matters such as death, disease, sex as well as excreta and secretion in the novel; a comparative study of those euphemisms in the novel that are translated into English especially with regard to David Hawke's version and that of the Yangs. It is, however, a pity that euphemisms in the character utterances of the novel have not yet been comprehensively investigated. The result of the present study from the

pragmatic perspective may complement the unremitting nation-wide and even perhaps, world-wide research of the novel, namely, Redology, which has dominantly been literary-criticism-oriented and rhetoric-oriented.

3) As euphemisms are extensively used in interpersonal communication, more often than not they are context-dependent. The variables governing the use of euphemisms are also believed to be a concern of pragmatics. So the findings of the study may help verify and enrich the related principles in the field of pragmatics.

4) The present study takes *A Dream of Red Mansions* as its text and tentatively discusses the euphemisms in the character utterances of the novel in light of Spencer-Oatey's theory of rapport management in an attempt to find out to what extent the new theory is able to govern and explain the euphemisms in the character utterances of the novel. If it works, the theory can also be applied to the analysis of other texts in both English and Chinese languages.

5) There is no denying that language is universal, yet it is culture-bound. As a part of language, while euphemisms mirror cultural traditions and national mentality they are also constrained by such factors. The findings of the present research may have some implications to culturology and ethnography.

1.5 Methodology

The present study is both theoretical and empirical. Methodologically speaking, it is theoretical in the presentation of literature review and exposition of the theoretical framework. Empirically, while the method of observation is applied to the categorization and description of euphemisms, a qualitative method is adopted in the demonstration analysis of sample euphemisms in concert with the theoretical framework of rapport management. To facilitate the study, comparison, contrast, illustration, categorization, induction and discussion are thought to be appropriate supplementary methods. The method of comparison and contrast is applied especially when various approaches to the study of euphemism are discussed, compared and contrasted with Spencer-Oatey's theory of rapport management. As linguistic phenomena are best explained and comprehended with the help of examples, the method of illustration is extensively used throughout. Likewise, a comparative and contrastive study can never do without induction, so the method of induction is also found equal to the tasks of comparing, contrasting and summing-up of the euphemisms under discussion. In this study, verbal euphemisms are examined not only at the lexical level but also at the syntactical level because they both contribute to the pragmatic analysis of euphemisms in the character utterances.

1.6 Collection of Euphemisms

The present researcher quite agrees with Lan Chun (2007) as she narrates why she has chosen *DRM* as a text in her study:

Pragmatics is concerned with context in which language is put in use. Context in its narrow sense involves speaker, hearer, bystander, time, place as well as cause and effect. Context in its broad sense, however, includes the cultural traditions, social values and moral concepts behind the interlocutors. *A Dream of Red Mansions* abounds in vivid and lifelike dialogues, which suffice pragmatic analysis in both its narrow sense and broad sense (语用学研究关注语言使用的语境。狭义的语境包括说话人、听话人、旁听者、时间、地点、前因后果等，广义的语境则包括参与者背后的文化传统、社会价值、道德观念等。红楼梦中大量活灵活现的人物对话都为狭义和广义的语用分析提供了沃土。) (2).

In *DRM* the multitude of characters, the complexity of their relationships, the distinctness of their personalities, the colourfulness of their language and a variety of contexts have all proved contributory to a wealth of resources for the present study. For the sake of coherence, the present study takes as its main and first-hand source of euphemisms the first eighty chapters (allegedly composed by Cao Xueqin) of *A Dream of Red Mansions* in a Chinese-English format, published by the Foreign Language Press and Hunan People's Publishing House (1999). The Chinese version of the novel is the Youzheng large-type edition carrying a preface by Qi Liaosheng for the first eighty chapters. The English version is provided by Yang Xianyi and Gladys Yang (the Yangs). Although it is a problem that the English version does not remain an absolute counterpart to the Chinese version (and it does not have to be, though), it does not influence the final result of the study.

The study encompasses euphemisms in the character utterances throughout the first eighty chapters. Records are carefully kept with regard to the interlocutors' information as contextual variables for the pragmatic analysis. Generally, the euphemisms are gathered, processed, analyzed and discussed in line with Spencer-Oatey's theoretical framework of rapport management.

Euphemisms can be classified into conventional and situational ones. Conventional euphemisms are usually standard expressions well tested by time and remain relatively stable. The collection and processing of the conventional euphemisms basically rely on *A Dictionary of Chinese Euphemisms* (《汉语委婉语词典》) compiled by Zhang Gonggui (1996). The dictionary is acclaimed as the first dictionary of Chinese euphemisms, which provides origins, explanations and usages for over 3,000 Chinese euphemisms ranging from ancient to modern ones. Situational euphemisms have not yet been socially conventionalized as they are context-dependent. That means situational euphemisms are more semantically, syntactically, rhetorically and pragmatically dependent. In this sense, the task of judging and collecting of situational euphemisms is thorny and challenging.

Some secondary written examples are also referred to and collected from various sources such as publications, authoritative periodicals and PhD dissertations. They are culled and adopted in the analysis. For the convenience of reading and comprehension, sample euphemisms in the character utterances of the novel are provided in two languages: Chinese and English. They are presented first in Chinese as they are in the Chinese version of the novel and then in English. All the translations from Chinese to English are excerpted from the Yangs.

1.7   Organization of the Book

This Book falls into seven chapters. Chapter One makes a general introduction, explaining the background of conducting this research, setting up purposes and designing questions for the study. Significance of the study, research methods, collection of euphemisms and general organization of the whole book are also presented. Chapter Two revisits notions and principles related to the present study. Definitions and origin of euphemism are retrospected. At the same time, previous approaches to the study of euphemism and the euphemisms in *A Dream of Red Mansions* are reviewed so that the necessity of the present study is clarified. Chapter Three expounds the theoretical framework for the present study: Helen Spencer-Oatey's theory of rapport management. Chapter Four delineates and categorizes the collection of euphemisms from the novel. Chapter Five carries out a demonstration analysis of the euphemisms in the character utterances of *DRM* within the theoretical framework of Spencer-Oatey's rapport management. As a variable power is taken as a major factor influencing the characters' option and use of euphemisms. Chapter Six conducts discussions on the relationship between euphemisms in *DRM* and the theory of rapport management mainly for the purpose of verifying the controlling force and explanatory power of the theory. In addition, related theories and principles are comparatively and contrastively examined in reference to Spencer-Oatey's theory of rapport management and euphemisms. They are Grice's CP and CI, Leech's PP, Brown and Levinson's face theory as well as Gu Yueguo's PP. Based on the overlaps, similarities and differences found in the comparative and contrastive analysis, some conclusions are drawn. Chapter Seven highlights major findings, presents implications, reveals limitations and offers friendly suggestions for related studies that may further the present research.

Chapter Two

Literature Review

‧❯❯ 2.1   Introduction

This book is intended to investigate euphemisms in the character utterances of *DRM* for the purpose of detecting how variables may affect the characters' communicative strategies, namely, their option for euphemisms as against direct and plainspoken expressions. Literature review in this chapter is subdivided into four parts. Part One revisits the related notions and theories; Part Two unfolds an overview of euphemism with regard to its definitions and origin. Part Three retrospects studies of euphemism and research approaches adopted so far to euphemism both at home and abroad; Part Four delineates related research on the euphemisms in *DRM* and rationalizes the necessity of the present study.

‧❯❯ 2.2   Fundamentals Revisited

As euphemism is an indirect form of language and has much to do with face and facework, the discussion in this part is divided into two sections: review of indirectness, Grice's CP and CI as well as Leech's PP; retrospect of face, facework, Brown and Levinson's face theory, and Gu Yueguo's PP.

2.2.1 Indirectness, Grice's CP & CI and Leech's PP

Indirectness

Indirectness is a universal phenomenon that is believed to occur in all natural languages. Indirectness means the quality or state of being indirect, deviousness, or deviation from an upright or straightforward course. This language phenomenon is discussed by Thomas within the scope of pragmatics. Here Thomas proposes four prerequisites with which indirectness can be put under discussion, four factors that govern the use of indirectness and four reasons why indirectness is preferred.

According to Thomas (1995: 119-122), four prerequisites must be kept in mind as far as indirectness is concerned:

We shall be concerned with intentional indirectness.

Indirectness is costly and risky.

We assume (unless we have evidence to the contrary) that the speakers are behaving in a rational manner and, given the universality of indirectness, that they obtain some social or communicative advantage through employing indirectness.

For the purpose of this argument, we shall ignore the possibility that X cannot be expressed (According to Thomas' principle of expressibility, "anything that can be meant can be said." In other words, "human beings can find a way of putting into words anything they need to say.")

Dascal (1983) rightly observes that "indirect expression is costly and risky" (159). Thomas (1995) elaborates on the costliness and riskiness of indirectness, saying,

It is "costly" in the sense that an indirect utterance takes longer for the speaker to produce and longer for the hearer to process (a fact that has frequently been confirmed in psycholinguistic experiments). It is "risky" in the sense that the hearer may not understand what the speaker is getting at (120).

Thomas (1995) furthers her idea of indirectness into axes governing indirectness. She proposes that these axes are "'universal' in that they capture the types of consideration likely to govern pragmatic choices in any language, but the way they are applied varies considerably from culture to culture" (124).

When people opt for indirectness in preference to directness, a number of factors must be at work. "Individuals and cultures vary widely in how, when and why they use an indirect speech act in preference to a direct one. Nevertheless, there are a number of factors which appear to govern indirectness in the same circumstances" (He Zhaoxiong, 2003: 349). Here Thomas (1995) proposes four factors that govern the varying extents to which indirectness can be appropriately manipulated (124):

The relative power of the speaker over the hearer

The social distance between the speaker and the hearer

The degree to which X is rated an imposition in culture Y

Relative rights and obligations between the speaker and the hearer

Likewise, Thomas reveals the reasons that may help explain the pervasive use of indirectness (ibid.):

The desire to make one's language more/less interesting

To increase the force of one's message

Competing goals

Politeness/regard for "face"

Here Thomas lends emphasis to politeness/regard for face, which is deemed more important than the rest of the three reasons.

Indirectness is characteristic of euphemism, or rather, euphemism is a typical form of indirect language in contrast with plainspoken and straightforward language. That's why Wu Liquan (2002) maintains that any manner of speaking that leans towards indirectness may be taken as a euphemism. It is noteworthy that the above four prerequisites, four factors and four reasons proposed by Thomas significantly throw light on the pragmatic study of euphemism.

Grice's CP

Grice (1975, 1989) rightly observes that communication is generally under the control of a set of norms that readily find their root in human rationality. To be more exact, "What he was actually doing was suggesting that in conversational interaction people work on the assumption that a certain set of rules is in operation, unless they receive indications to the contrary" (Thomas, 1995: 62). Grice alerts to the fact that people comply with certain principles in communication, which he develops into a set of regulations that govern the generation and interpretation of conversational implicature as a result of non-observance of these maxims.

Human talk exchanges, in general, are taken as a result of "cooperative effort, and each participant recognizes in them, to some extent, a common purpose or set of purposes, or at least a mutually accepted direction" (He Zhaoxiong, 1995: 370). In "Logic and conversation" Grice (1989) introduces the Cooperative Principle (CP) and four conversational maxims. By CP Grice means,

> a rough general principle which participants will be expected (ceteris paribus) to observe, namely: Make your conversational contribution such as is required, at the stage at which it occurs, by the accepted purpose or direction of the talk exchange in which you are engaged (26).

This principle, in Levinson's (1983) words, "is essentially a theory about how people use language" "to further cooperative ends" (101). Grice identifies four maxims as guidelines for the efficient cooperative use of language, which jointly express a general cooperative principle. These maxims are Quantity, Quality, Relation and Manner. They are stipulated detailedly in the following (Grice, 1975: 45):

Quantity: Make your contribution as informative as is required (for the current purpose of exchange).

Do not make your contribution more informative than is required.

Quality: Do not say what you believe to be false.

Do not say that for which you lack adequate evidence.

Relation: Be relevant.

Manner: Avoid obscurity of expression.

Avoid ambiguity.

Be brief.

Be orderly.

Obviously, these conversational maxims serve to specify what interlocutors must do in order that the talk exchange can be fulfilled in a maximally efficient, rational and cooperative way. That is, while participants provide adequate information, they should speak sincerely, relevantly and clearly.

However, "Grice's main concern was the role of these maxims in the explanation of the way speakers may communicate more than what they actually say" (Blakemore, 1992: 26) because "the ability to attribute intentions to each other" is "one of the most important abilities underlying human interaction" (ibid.). This non-observance of CP generates what is termed as conversational implicature (CI).

CI

"To imply is to hint, suggest, or convey some meaning indirectly by means of language" (Thomas, 1995: 57). An implicature is generated intentionally by the speaker for the hearer to infer. Grice notices that interactants frequently do not adhere to the CP and flouting any of the maxims may give rise to what he terms as "implicature".

Grice makes a list of different kinds of non-observance of maxims. Yet what interests him most is the situation where "the speaker blatantly fails to observe a maxim, not with any intention of deceiving or misleading, but because the speaker wishes to prompt the hearer to look for a meaning which is different from, or in addition to, the expressed meaning" (ibid. 64). This very additional meaning is referred to, by Grice, as "conversational implicature" (CI). Besides, the process by which conversational implicature is generated is "flouting a maxim". "A flout occurs when a speaker blatantly fails to observe a maxim at the level of what is said, with the deliberate intention of generating an implicature" (Thomas, 1995: 64).

By conversational implicature, Grice means that the matter of understanding utterances goes far beyond simply knowing the literal meanings of a string of words uttered. "It also involves drawing inferences on the basis of non-linguistic information and the assumption that the speaker has aimed to meet certain general standards of communication" (Blakemore, 1992: 57). Stressing the importance of the hearer's comprehension, Blakemore further points out "the recovery of an implicature hinges on the hearer's understanding of what the speaker has said" (ibid. 59).

It turns out that Grice's conversational implicature is embraced and acclaimed as one of the most important ideas and significant theories in the development of pragmatics. In Levinson's (1983) words, "The principles that generate implicatures have a very general explanatory power: a few basic principles provide explanations for a large array of apparently unrelated facts" (100). In praise of the paramount significance of the notion of conversational implicature Thomas (1995) also notes,

> Jane Austin made the distinction between what speaker says and what they mean. Grice's theory is an attempt at explaining how a hearer gets what from what is said to what is meant, from the level of expressed meaning to the level of implied meaning (56).

A flout of the CP frequently results from language indirectness, which in turn, gives rise to the CI. In that sense, the CI may also be verbally realized by indirectness, which generally manifests itself in the form of euphemism.

Leech's PP

Leech (1980, 1983) believes that interlocutors sometimes infringe one or more maxims of the CP for the sake of politeness, which is usually realized in an indirect or roundabout way. He argues that when the CP fails to sufficiently explain indirectness in a conversation the PP may be put in operation. So he is convinced that politeness and its related notion of "tact" are of paramount importance in interpreting "why people are often so indirect in conveying what they mean" and in "rescuing the Cooperative Principle from serious trouble" (Leech, 1983: 80) in the sense that politeness can satisfactorily account for exceptions to and deviations from the CP.

Leech develops politeness into the Politeness Principle and its six maxims are translated into Tact, Generosity, Approbation, Modesty, Agreement and Sympathy. To be specific, the PP can be stated as follows: Other things being equal, minimize the expression of beliefs that are unfavorable to the hearer and at the same time (but less important) maximize the expression of beliefs which are favorable to the hearer. In other words, the core of the PP is to minimize the expression of impolite beliefs and maximize the expression of polite beliefs. The maxims are (ibid.132):

Tact Maxim (in impositives and commissives)

a. Minimize the cost to other   [b. Maximize the benefit to other]

Generosity Maxim (in impositives and commissives)

a. Minimize benefit to self   [b. Maximize cost to self]

Approbation Maxim (in expressives and assertives)

a. Minimize dispraise of other   [b. Maximize praise of other]

Modesty Maxim (in expressives and assertives)

a. Minimize praise of self   [b. Maximize dispraise of self]

Agreement Maxim (in assertives)

a. Minimize disagreement between self and other

[b. Maximize agreement between self and other]

Sympathy Maxim (in assertives)

a. Minimize antipathy between self and other

[b. Maximize sympathy between self and other]

It is evident that while focus in Brown and Levinson's model is on the speaker, the one in Leech's model is on the hearer.

Leech emphasizes the imbalanced importance within each pair of twinned maxims—Maxims (I) & (II), Maxims (III) & (IV) and sub-maxims. It is found that Maxims (I) and (III) take into account other's benefits and losses whereas Maxims (II) and (IV) concern self's benefits and losses. Besides, there is no apparent relation between Maxims (V) and (VI). "Of the twinned maxims (I)-(VI), (I) appears to be a more powerful constraint on conversational behaviour than (II), and (III) than (IV)" (ibid. 133). In other words, Leech's tact maxim appears to be a more powerful constraint on conversational behaviour than generosity maxim, and approbation maxim more important than modesty maxim. In this sense, Leech's PP is largely other-directed. In his own words, "This, if true, reflects a more general law that politeness is focused more strongly on other than on self" (ibid.). In addition, within each pair of sub-maxims, sub-maxim (b) seems to be more important than sub-maxim (a). This again manifests "the more general law that negative politeness (avoidance of discord) is a more weighty consideration than positive politeness (seeking concord)" (ibid.). Likewise, politeness is more oriented towards the addressee rather than a third party (ibid.).

At the same time, Leech points out the potential danger of rigid observance of the maxims by saying,

> These maxims are observed "up to a certain point", rather than as absolute rules. It is particularly important to remember this with the weaker submaxims, those in square brackets, such as "Maximize dispraise of self." A person who continually seeks opportunities for self-denigration quickly becomes tedious, and more importantly, will be judged insincere. In this way the CP (Maxim of Quality) restrains us form being too modest, just as in other circumstances it restrains us from being too tactful (ibid. 133).

It is found that Leech's Tact Maxim, Approbation Maxim, Modesty Maxim and Sympathy Maxim have a lot to do with language indirectness and can all be verbally realized by euphemisms.

2.2.2 Face, Facework, Brown & Levinson's Face Theory and Gu's PP

This section reviews the notions of face and facework. Then it focuses on Brown and Levinson's face theory and Gu Yueguo's politeness principle.

Face

In daily interaction, people tend to make use of communicative messages to preserve each other's image or identity. Diachronic study shows that "face" has its origin in Chinese culture. In Thomas' (1995) words,

> The term "face" in the sense of "reputation" or "good name" seems to have been first used in English in 1876 as a translation of the Chinese term "diulian" (丢脸) in the phrase "Arrangements by which China has lost face". Since then it has been used widely in the phrases such as "losing face" (168).

It is true that "face" is assumed vulnerable and held dear in Chinese culture. As Hu (1944) rightly notices, "face" connotes two meanings in Chinese context: *mianzi* and *lian*. Here *mianzi* refers to one's social prestige. To be more exact, *mianzi* "is a reputation achieved through getting on in life, through success and ostentation" (45). This is evinced in a typical example, "他很有面子" (literally meaning: He has a lot of face). On the other hand, *lian* indicates one's basic moral worth and good quality. An example is a popular curse "不要脸" (shameless), addressing a person's base or immoral act or behaviour in contradiction with the commonly accepted moral values or behaviours. So the double-faced "face" has two opposing but correlated aspects: *mianzi* that is social and *lian* that is personal.

In Goffman's (1972) pioneering work on social interaction and facework (1959, 1971, 1972) he takes "face" as "the positive social value a person effectively claims for himself by the line others assume he has taken during a particular contact" (5).

"Face" has long gained much attention in interpersonal relations. Generally speaking, "face" is posited positive by nature, for it is "an image of self delineated in terms of approved social attributes—albeit an image that others may share, as when a person makes a good showing for his profession or religion by making a good showing for himself" (Goffman, 1967: 5). Obviously it is everyone's positively-valued social identity. This notion of "face" has been accepted by quite a few scholars and allowed for more elaboration. Much of ensuing research finds its immediate intellectual root in Goffman's notion of face (Hu, 1944; Ho, 1976; Brown and Levinson, 1978/1987; Thomas, 1995; Spencer-Oatey, 2007).

Facework

Goffman (1972) defines facework as "the actions taken by a person to make whatever he is doing consistent with face" (5). Taking "face" as largely a notion of situated identities, Tracy and Coupland (1990) refer to facework as a set of "communicative strategies that are the enactment, support, or challenge of those situated identities" (210). So facework is the management of identity, or rather, it is a way people protect their face, prevent a loss of face or regain a face once lost or tarnished. In reality, "face" and facework are two inseparable and interdependent notions in terms of one's situated identities and communicative strategies for the purpose of managing such identities.

It is seen that euphemisms can be used as a linguistic means of facework in place of dispreferred expressions so that possible loss of face can be avoided either on the part of the speaker him/herself or other or, the third party.

Brown and Levinson's Face Theory

More often than not Brown and Levinson's (1987) theory of linguistic politeness is identified as the "face-saving" theory of politeness owing to the fact that it is built upon Goffman's (1967) notions of face. In other words, central to Brown and Levinson's theory of politeness is Goffman's concept of "face" .

Brown and Levinson (1987) assume that every individual of a society has (and knows each other to have) "face", which, in their words, is "the public self-image that every member wants to claim for himself" (61). In their point of view, "face" is something that is "emotionally invested, and that can be lost, maintained, or enhanced, and must be constantly attended to in interaction" (ibid.). Face is classified into two types: positive and negative. Positive face is the individual's desire that his/her wants be appreciated and approved of in social interaction, whereas negative face is the desire for freedom of action and freedom from imposition. In this sense, politeness strategies are intended to maintain or enhance the addressee's positive face (positive politeness) and avoid transgression of the addressee's freedom of action and freedom from imposition (negative face).

In their theory a Model Person (MP) is posited as one who is supposed to have the ability to rationalize from the communicative goals to the optimal means of achieving those goals. The MP must estimate the potential danger of threatening other participants' (and hence his/her own) face and choose the appropriate strategies in order to minimize any face threats that might be involved in carrying out the goal-directed activity. Noticing a crucial role that the MP assumes in the theory and comparing Brown and Levinson's model with that of Leech, Watts (2003) concludes,

> The MP in Brown and Levinson's model refers to the "speaker", and the only reason the addressee is brought into the picture is in order that the MP can assess which is the most appropriate politeness strategy to use in the circumstances. No mention is made of the ways in which the addressee may react to the politeness strategy produced. Focus in Brown and Levinson's model is thus on the speaker, whereas in Leech's model it is on the hearer (85).

The following figure is Brown and Levinson's (1987) model of strategies available to the speaker as to how face wants can be attended to.

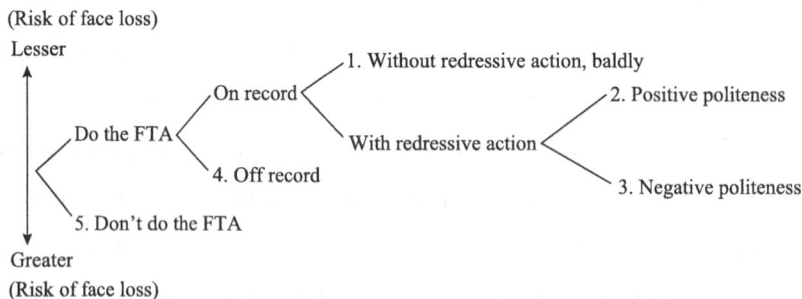

Figure 1　Strategies to attend to face wants (Brown & Levinson, 1987: 60)

In Figure 1, the scale on the left indicates the degree to which the strategies are face-threatening to the addressee. The scale ranges from the best case (Strategy 5 "Don't do the FTA") to the worst (Strategy 1 "Do the FTA and go on record as doing so baldly and without any redressive action", i.e. without atoning for the FTA in any way). To go on record baldly and do the FTA without taking any redressive action entails the greatest amount of face-threat and can only be used as a strategy if there is minimal risk of threatening the addressee's face. To avoid doing an FTA is obviously least face-threatening of the strategies. In order of the degree of face-threat, Strategy 1 is more likely to involve face-threat to the addressee than Strategies 2 and 3. Strategy 4 is next on the scale followed by the least face-threatening action. Strategy 5 is by no means face-threatening.

Over the past decades, Brown and Levinson's theory of politeness has laid an important basis for a wide range of studies and has had a substantial impact in the field of conversational analysis or discourse analysis.

Gu Yueguo's PP

Goffman's notion of face and facework is self-directed, so is Brown and Levinson's theory of politeness. Neither of them could claim universality in explicability or applicability especially in face of the Chinese culture characterized with collectivism.

Gu Yueguo is a pioneer in an attempt to systematically investigate politeness in Chinese culture. Gu Yueguo (1990) maintains "the Chinese concept of politeness is to some extent moralized, which makes it more appropriate to analyze politeness in terms of maxims" (243). Having his study closely based on the origin of the notion of Chinese politeness and critically adopting Leech's maxims of politeness with some reservations, Gu Yueguo postulates politeness principle in Chinese culture that is translated into a number of maxims distinct from those of Leech's PP yet virtually characteristic of the Chinese setting.

Gu Yueguo's politeness principle is "a sanctioned belief that an individual's social behavior ought to live up to the expectations of respectfulness, modesty, attitudinal warmth and refinement" (ibid. 245). That means his study sees to four essential elements that are deep-rooted and well-established in the Chinese culture,

notions underlying the Chinese conception of politeness: respectfulness, modesty, attitudinal warmth, and refinement. "Respectfulness" is self's positive appreciation or admiration of other concerning the latter's face, social status, and so on. "Modesty" can be seen as another way of saying "self-denigration". Attitudinal warmth is self's demonstration of kindness, consideration, and hospitality to other. Finally, "refinement" refers to self's behaviour to other which meets certain standards (ibid.).

The above-mentioned notions are developed into the politeness principle and its maxims (In his 1985 MA thesis, Gu Yueguo formulated seven politeness maxims, four of which were emphatically addressed in his 1990 paper, namely, the Self-denigration maxim, the Address-term maxim, the Tact maxim and the Generosity maxim). It followed that in 1992, Gu Yueguo developed them into five maxims (11-14):

The Self-denigration maxim

a. Denigrate self   b. Elevate other

The Address-term maxim

Address your interlocutor with an appropriate address term.

The Refinement maxim

Use refined language, including the use of euphemisms and indirectness, and avoid foul language.

The Agreement maxim

Maximize agreement and harmony between interlocutors, and minimize disagreement between them.

The Virtues-words-deeds Maxim

Minimize cost and maximize benefit to other at the motivational level, and maximize benefit received and minimize cost to self at the conversational level.

With Gu Yueguo's (1990) maxims, politeness can be both instrumental and normative, for "Interactants can use politeness to further their goals (e.g. redress FATs), but at the same time are constrained by it" (257). Gu Yueguo's contribution to the study of Chinese politeness is much acclaimed by such renowned scholars as He Zhaoxiong. Commenting on Gu Yueguo's strength of a delineation of Chinese politeness in his 1995 paper, He Zhaoxiong remarks, "it has integrated certain features universally recognized in the conception of politeness in carious cultures and certain features so much emphasized in the Chinese culture as to be almost uniquely Chinese" (6). According to He Zhaoxiong,

> The first notion "respectfulness" is largely identical with the need to maintain the hearer's positive face; the fourth notion "refinement" represents the normative character of politeness, which, though universal, has not been mentioned in any important theory concerning politeness raised by western scholars so far; the second notion "modesty", though varying in the importance attached to it in different cultures, is to a large extent universal; but to interpret modesty as self-denigration is uniquely Chinese; the third notion "attitudinal warmth" bears a strong Chinese trait for, according to Brown and Levinson, demonstrating kindness, consideration and hospitality, the speaker runs the risk of infringing on the hearer's personal freedom, thus threatening his negative face (ibid.).

2.3   Euphemism

This part provides an overview of euphemism in terms of its definitions and origin. The definitions are comparatively and contrastively delineated in detail to verify a more comprehensive one especially in terms of pragmatics. Then what follows is a brief review of the origin of euphemism both etymologically and historically.

2.3.1 Definitions

The word "euphemism" derives from the Greek "eu", meaning "good" and "pheme", meaning "speech" or "saying", which in all literally means "to speak good words" or, "to speak with good words or in a pleasant manner" (Neaman & Silver, 1983: 1). In the early 1580s, George Blunt, a British writer, created the term "euphemism" and introduced it into the English language. A simple yet panoramic picture of euphemism may unfold by virtue of the following definitions.

George Blunt defined euphemism as "a good or favourable interpretation of a bad word" (qtd. Neaman & Silver, 1983: 4), which now seems rather simplistic. Ever since then, euphemism has been defined from different perspectives with the progress of people's understanding and application of language.

Primarily taken as a figure of speech, euphemism is "rhetorical trope: a pleasant replacement for an objectionable word that has pejorative connotations." (*Routledge Dictionary of Language and Linguistics*)

For a time, the study of the formational devices of euphemism was quite limited, which was reflected in its definitions: "Use of pleasant, mild or indirect words or phrases in place of more accurate or direct ones" (*Oxford Advanced Learner's English-Chinese Dictionary*, 4th ed.); "Word, etc. used in place of one avoided as e.g. offensive, indecent or alarming" (*Oxford Concise Dictionary of Linguistics*). These two definitions restrict the construction of euphemism to lexical and phrasal levels. However, euphemism may also occur at linguistic levels other than words and phrases. In *Aspects of Language*, Bolinger and Sears (1981) note that "euphemism is not restricted to the lexicon, there are grammatical ways of toning down without actually changing the content of the message" (149). They further point out that whereas both "He has been known to take a bribe now and then" and "He is known to have taken a bribe now and then" report the same single event, the first sentence sounds milder and more euphemistic owing to the suggestion of less immediacy with the help of tense. Bolinger and Sears' insightful remark pins on the fact that euphemism can occur at all linguistic levels and thereby has significantly inspired the study of the formational devices of euphemism into a larger scope. This also concords with the definition given by Chen Wangdao (2002). Referring to euphemism as "婉转辞", Chen defines it as "that which is implicit and indirect rendered from what is explicitly sad or distasteful in speech" (109).

Being aware that euphemism is not simply a concern of rhetoric, Li Junhua (2004) attempts to approach the definition of euphemism in relation to pragmatics, semantics, ways of expression and scope of euphemism in hopes of providing precise connotation and definite denotation (162-165). However, he is not able to come up with a clear definition.

In fact euphemism has been defined in terms of pragmatics once such pragmatic factors as interlocutor and face are taken into account. "A euphemism is used as an alternative to a dispreferred expression, in order to avoid possible loss of face: either one's own face or, through giving offence, that of the audience, or of some third party" (Allan & Burridge, 1991: 18). An even more recent and comprehensive definition reads, "Euphemism is the non-direct expressions or utterances for the things which bring information organizer and interpreter pains such as reverence, fear, shame, discomfort, etc. and which is formed by using phonetic, semantic and grammatical methods" (Shao Junhang, 2007: ix). In the present researcher's humble opinion, the definition proposed by Shao Junhang is so far the most advanced owing to its inclusive coverage of all the context-related factors that euphemism involves: the context in its broad sense and narrow sense including topics and talking parties, the target (that which brings pains to information organizer and interpreter), formational devices (phonetic, semantic and grammatical), the accompanying character (non-direct expressions or utterances) and the motivation (avoiding pains on the part of information organizer and interpreter).

2.3.2 Origin of Euphemism

Euphemism is first and foremost a product of ancient taboo. The co-existence of the two has made them inherently inseparable from each other. They are, to some extent, as Adler vividly describes, "the two sides of the same coin. Without taboo there is no euphemism" (Adler, 1978: 66). The word "taboo" has its origin in Polynesian, meaning either "sacred" or "accursed". Generally speaking, those within the sphere of taboo are either holy and sacred things that are to be worshipped or held in awe or, filthy or evil things that are expected to be avoided or discarded. So the psychology of adoration or dread is the basis of taboo.

With the passing of time, taboo has become a normative matter. Tracing the origin and development of taboo, Allan and Burridge (2006) rightly observe,

> Taboos arise out of social constraints on the individual's behaviour where it can cause discomfort, harm or injury. People are at metaphysical risk when dealing with sacred persons, objects and places; they are at physical risk from powerful earthly persons, dangerous creatures and disease. A person's soul or bodily effluvia may put him/her at metaphysical, moral or physical risk, and may contaminate others; a social act may breach constraints on polite behaviour. Infractions of taboos can lead to illness or death, as well as to the lesser penalties of corporal punishment, incarceration, social ostracism or mere disapproval. Even an unintended contravention of taboo risks condemnation and censure; generally, people can and do avoid behaviour unless they intend to violate a taboo (1).

Reflected in thinking, taboo manifests itself by virtue of language. Specific language concerning the supernatural is also deified and has developed into word Fetishism. People are inclined to shun taboos with mild substitutes to imply those things which they are reluctant to mention or voice directly. That which is tabooed is euphemized. So such mild substitutes or indirect terms are the earliest euphemisms. Neaman and Silver (1983) also note, "When unpleasant elements of response attach themselves strongly to the word used to describe them, we tend to substitute another word free of these associations. In this way, euphemisms are formed" (9). Nowadays everything that is tabooed readily finds one or more euphemistic expressions in language.

·❯❯ 2.4   Studies of Euphemism in Retrospect

The task of this part is to retrospect studies on euphemism and approaches already adopted so far to euphemism both at home and abroad.

2.4.1   Studies of Euphemism Abroad

As Euphemism is traditionally taken as a figure of speech, the study of English euphemism in the West is primarily restricted to the domain of rhetoric. The research afterwards is devoted to the formation and classification of euphemism.

Dictionaries and Monographs

Based on the historical and cultural background of American society, American linguist Menken (1936) discusses quite a number of euphemistic words in American English in *The American Language* and traces their origins. In their publication of *Aspects of Language*, Bolinger and Sears

(1981) wisely observe that "euphemism is not restricted to the lexicon, there are grammatical ways of toning down without actually changing the content of the message" (149). This illuminating idea necessitates expansion of the study of the formational devices of euphemism into all linguistic levels.

The past three decades has been a time of remarkable productiveness in dictionaries and monographs on English euphemisms. British linguist Hugh Rawson's (1981) *Dictionary of Euphemisms and Other Doubletalk* turns out to be a large collection of euphemisms and doubletalk that ranges from the Victorian period to the twentieth century. In prefacing the dictionary Rawson not only introduces the study of the history and development of euphemism but also discusses the features, definition, classification and scope of euphemism. Neaman and Carole's (1983) *Kind Words—A Thesaurus of Euphemisms*, a book with more than four thousand entries, is mainly devoted to euphemisms in terms of body parts, bathrooms and other blush-inducing subjects. Enright's (1985) *Fair of Speech—the Uses of Euphemism*, a collection of works of sixteen eminent experts in the field of euphemism, is concerned with not only history and development of euphemisms but also their meaning and usage.

In Allan and Burridge's 1991 publication *Euphemism and Dysphemism*, euphemisms and dysphemisms are discussed from a variety of aspects: linguistic, physical, psychological, religious, social, political and even military. John Ayto's (1993) *Euphemism*, arguing that today is virtually a "euphemistic society", covers a wide range of euphemisms from the twentieth century back to earlier centuries with detailed explanation of meaning and illustration of usage. Anne Bertram's (1998) *NTC's Dictionary of Euphemism* updatedly collects a wide variety of more than two thousand euphemisms with example sentences showing how they are commonly used in everyday life.

Following their 1991 work, the collaboration of Allan and Burridge

(2006) yields a new academic product entitled *Forbidden Words: Taboo and the Censoring of Language.* "It is a book about taboo and the way in which people censor the language that they speak and write" (1). Very interestingly, euphemism in the book is termed as "sweet talking". The book is also eye-catchy in that the authors attempt to differentiate orthophemism, euphemism and dysphemism on a X-phemisms bar and examine this union set (in Figure 2).

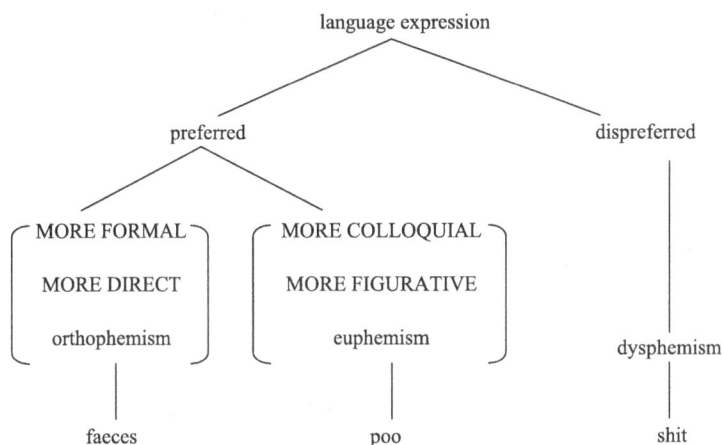

Figure 2   Distinguishing X-phemisms (Allan & Burridge, 2006: 34)

The figure of X-phemisms presents a distinct picture of the differences as far as orthophemism, euphemism and dysphemism are concerned. In addition, a set of examples are provided: for starkly the same thing *faeces* is an orthophemism, *poo* is a euphemism and *shit* a dysphemism. They provide more sets of examples (in Table 1):

Table 1   Contrasting X-phemisms (Allan & Burridge, 2006: 32)

Orthophemism	Euphemism	Dysphemism
faeces	*poo*	*shit*
toilet	*loo*	*shithouse*
menstruate	*have a period*	*bleed*
my vagina	*my bits*	*my cunt*
Jesus	*Lord*	*Christ?* [blasphemy]

Holder's (2007) *Oxford Dictionary of Euphemisms* entertains around five thousand British and American euphemisms with an extensive coverage of all aspects of life. What is new is that examples from famous writers such as Charles Dickens are also offered.

Warren's Formational Model of New Euphemisms

Apart from the numerous publications on euphemisms, there have been concerns about the formation of novel euphemisms. In her 1992 paper, Warren presents a formational model of new euphemisms in English (in Figure 3).

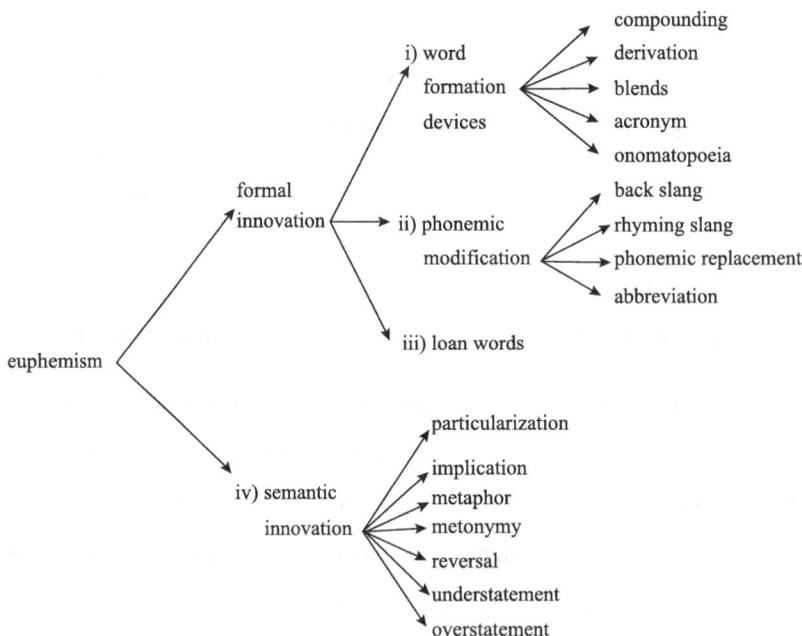

Figure 3   Classification of the main devices for constructing euphemisms

(Warren, 1992: 133)

According to Warren's model, there are four ways of forming new euphemisms. In addition, subcategories are provided in detail to cope with the construction of a large array of euphemisms.

In this model, "innovation" is salient owing to the primary goal of delineating the creation of new euphemisms. In effect, the model complies with the idea that "'novel contextual meanings', i.e. new meanings for words in a particular context, are constantly created in language" (Ham, 2005: 230).

Studies of Euphemisms in Literary Works

Apart from dictionary compilation, analyses of euphemisms in literary works are also noteworthy. Eric Partridge (1968), an etymologist and lexicographer, is ambitious and courageous enough to have conducted a challengingly comprehensive study of slang and innuendo in Shakespeare's plays and accomplished a book shockingly entitled *Shakespeare's Bawdy*. It is estimated that Shakespeare, a great expert of language, unprecedentedly made use of forty-five synonyms for "penis", sixty-eight for "vagina" and two hundred and seventy-five for "copulation". Many items in the big glossary of bawdry are in effect found euphemistic. For example, "riggish" in *Cleopatra* means "lascivious" and "hardening of one's brows" in *The Winter's Tale* means "being cuckolded".

In the vein of Warren's formational model of new euphemisms, Linfoot-Ham (2005) adopts a diachronic study in investigating the sex euphemisms in three British novels that span one hundred and eighty years: Jane Austen's *Emma*, D. H. Lawrence's *Lady Chatterly's Lover* and Fiona Walker's *Well Groomed*. Ham brings her study to the conclusion that "personal linguistic choices are actually products of societal mores and pressures. How people use euphemism to talk about sex is a direct reflection of these social concerns" (227). At the same time, she points out the deficiencies of the model and supplies two more new categories of euphemisms that may be put under Warren's umbrella model: naming and deletion.

Still what is noticeable is that some theories and principles have also been applied to the study of euphemism. The CP is of course a pragmatic strategy for successful communication, yet CI makes it possible for a speaker to convey his/her truly intended meaning beyond what is literally expressed.

It happens that euphemism is a communicative strategy that has resulted from people's flouting one or more of the four maxims.

Miscellaneous

Leech (1983) believes that "If we want to explain why many speakers prefer to use euphemistic words or phrases to substitute for those unpleasant ones in their interpersonal communication or to express their meanings in a roundabout way, the reason is for politeness." (46) Politeness is displaying awareness of another person's public self-image or awareness of others' expectations that their public self-image will be respected. "Being cooperative is being polite (mostly)" (Allan, 1986: 10). Very frequently flouting one or more of the maxims of the CP is also out of the consideration of being polite. Cooperativeness is a way of showing politeness, a practice that is commonly upheld and observed in interpersonal communication for the sake of saving face on the part of either the speaker or other.

Furthermore, euphemisms have also been investigated in terms of fuzzy theory, relevance theory (Sperber & Wilson, 1986), conceptual integration theory (Fauconnier & Turner, 1994) and adaptation theory (Verschueren, 2000).

2.4.2 Studies of Euphemism at Home

The study of euphemism at home dates back to the study of taboo because of the close relationship between taboo and euphemism. Ancient Chinese scholars studied euphemism mainly from two perspectives: evasion of taboo and avoidance of vulgarity. Qian Daxin, a scholar in the Qing Dynasty, conducted a relatively systematic study on the practice of evasion of taboos.

In modern times like their overseas counterparts Chinese scholars have produced a number of dictionaries and monographs on euphemisms and the following ones are well worth mentioning.

Dictionaries and Monographs

In his *A Dictionary of English Euphemisms* (《英语委婉语词典》)

Liu Chunbao (1993) presents a panoramic picture of over 8,000 English euphemisms, from which learners enjoy an opportunity to take a glimpse of those English-speaking countries in respect of their social mentalities, cultures and customs. What follows is *A Dictionary of Chinese Euphemisms* (《汉语委婉语词典》) compiled by Zhang Gonggui (1996). It is a pace-setting dictionary of Chinese euphemisms with an extensive coverage of origins, explanations and usages of over 3,000 euphemisms ranging from ancient to modern ones. *A Dictionary of Chinese Self-depreciatory Terms, Honorifics and Euphemisms* (《谦词敬词婉词词典》) compiled by Hong Chengyu (2004) is a collection of 3,000 self-depreciatory terms, honorifics and euphemisms from ancient Chinese works. However, the dictionary contains a limited scope of euphemisms that are classified into twelve categories. In *An Application Dictionary of Euphemisms* (《委婉语应用辞典》) Wang Yajun (2011) offers a large collection of about 5,100 euphemisms in twelve categories. The euphemisms are mostly Chinese with a small number of those from the West.

Wu Liquan (2008) makes unprecedentedly a comprehensive study of euphemism in *A Rhetorical Study of Euphemism* (《委婉修辞研究》). He proceeds with clarification of a number of definitions and then approaches euphemism in respect of its expressive forms (typical, atypical), scope of linguistic levels (text, chapter, sentence and word), depth differences (deep and surface), fundamental motivations (subjective and objective), psychological mechanism (distance) as well as political and cultural factors (political system, "*Li*", and law; national mentality; literary tradition). Li Junhua's (2010) *On Chinese Euphemism* (《汉语委婉语研究》) is viewed as a landmark contribution to the study of euphemism for his systematic research on Chinese euphemism in terms of definition, standards of categorization, features, social mentalities, formational principles, pragmatic principles, social functions, historical evolvement, cultural implications, cognitive interpretations and aesthetic implications. What is noteworthy is that he has done laboriously a case study of euphemisms for death, elaborating on such relevant aspects as categorization, cultural concepts and cultural mentalities.

Apart from the dictionaries and monographs, euphemisms have mainly been investigated from such perspectives as rhetoric, semantics, sociolinguistics, pragmatics and cognitive linguistics.

Rhetorical Approach

Many modern scholars have been studying euphemism from the perspective of rhetoric for a relatively long period of time. Chen Wangdao, a pioneer and founder of the study of modern Chinese rhetoric, is acclaimed as one of the earliest scholars who have contrived to define euphemism. He studies euphemism as a rhetorical device in his 1932 publication, *The Origin of Rhetoric* (《修辞学发凡》), which is hailed as a cornerstone of modern Chinese rhetoric for founding a systematic and complete system of rhetoric. Its contribution to this field of research lies in the expansion of the study of euphemism from the traditionally restricted lexical level to syntactical and even discoursal levels.

Wu Liquan (1994, 1995, 1997a, 1997b, 1998), an expert in the field of Chinese rhetoric, studies euphemism mainly in terms of rhetoric. He discusses the psychological mechanism of euphemism (1998: 11-12) by pointing out that euphemism gives rise to "distance" between sender and receiver, and the "distance" thus created is the root of euphemistic beauty. He also examines the scope of the rhetorical devices of euphemism (1994: 65-68), euphemizing devices in written literary works (1995: 70-74), ways of expression and expressive effects of euphemism (1997b: 94-97). And in his 1997 paper *On the Formation and Deoelopment of Euphemism: a Historical and Cultural Perspective* (《论委婉修辞生成与发展的历史文化缘由》), Wu (1997a: 56-60), taking euphemism as a figure of speech, delineates the pervasiveness of euphemism in ancient China. At the same time, he attributes its longevity and sustained popularity to the long-standing constraint of political environment, namely, feudalism and Confucianism; the reservedness of the Han nationality; and the long advocacy of impilcative beauty in Chinese literature.

Nevertheless, the traditional categorization of euphemism as a sheer rhetorical device has met disagreement. Wu Tieping (1989) argues,

> It is a logically inappropriate categorization in traditional rhetoric to place euphemism on a par with metonymy in that the two are figures at different levels. Euphemism is oriented towards the purpose of speech (with the referent implied) whereas metonymy the way of formation. So the two are not conflicting (⋯⋯传统修辞学把委婉格同借代格并列，从逻辑上说是不妥当的，因为这是不同层面上的格。委婉是从说话的目的（不说明言语指称对象）着眼的，借代是从修辞方法着眼的，二者并不矛盾。) (19).

In addition, Li Guonan (1989) believes that euphemism should be identified more as a communicative effect than a rhetorical device.

Semantic Approach

The semantic approach so far adopted mainly manifests itself in the application of the fuzzy theory. Although fuzzy linguistics got off to a late start in China, its development has been the fastest and its influences the most far-reaching among many branches of linguistics. Fuzzy linguistic research started in China in the late 1970s. The publication of Wu Tieping's (1979) article *A Preliminary Research on Fuzzy Language* (《模糊语言初探》), which was highly regarded by academia as the earliest essay in China dealing with fuzziness of language in terms of the fuzzy theory, marked the birth of fuzzy linguistics in China. In the following 20 years, Wu published more than thirty-six research papers on fuzzy linguistics, playing an essential role in pushing forward the study of fuzzy linguistics in China.

Wu Tieping (1989) also takes the lead in applying the fuzzy theory to the analysis of euphemism with his representative paper *On the Explanatory Power of the Fuzzy Theory: from the Perspective of the Mechanism of Euphemism* (《从委婉语的机制看模糊理论的解释能力》). Against the background that Chomsky has never made any effort to explain the mechanism of euphemism by virtue of his own theory and the situation that the study of euphemism then was confined to mere examples, Wu attempts to explain the mechanism of euphemism with the help of the fuzzy theory and concludes that vagueness contributes to the creation of euphemisms. Wu maintains that the fuzzy theory is central to the classification of the formation of euphemisms. According to him, there are four ways in operation: the substitution of a word with a vague meaning for one with a precise meaning (e.g. "老了" for "死"); the substitution of a word with a vaguer meaning for one with a less vague meaning within the same word set (e.g. "年纪大了" or "上了年纪" for "老了"); the substitution of a word with a vague meaning for one from a different word set (e.g. "发福" or "富态" for "胖"); the substitution of a word with a precise meaning for one also with a precise meaning (e.g. "胸" or "胸脯" for "乳房") (16-18). Following his examples, Wang Yongzhong (2001) discusses five communicative effects of euphemisms in light of the fuzzy theory: avoidance of taboo words, politeness, withholding information, persuasion and self-protection. He is convinced that the realization of the five functions of euphemism consists in the application of the fuzzy language (27-30).

Sociolinguistic Approach

Since euphemism is also viewed as a social phenomenon, the sociolinguistic approach, taking social factors into consideration, has been introduced to the study of euphemism in terms of the socio-cultural influences on the development of euphemism as well as its socio-cultural functions.

In the 1970s through 1980s China witnessed the introduction of

Western theories in terms of sociolinguistics. The special social functions of euphemism immediately became a concern of those scholars in the field of sociolinguistics. In his book *Sociolinguistics* (《社会语言学》), Chen Yuan (1983) accords a whole chapter to taboos and euphemisms, discussing the historical, social and psychological background of euphemism with profound examples in an elaborate and exhaustive way. Moreover, the composition and usage of euphemisms are well exemplified. With the rise and development of social psychology and culturology, attempts have been made at the analysis of the causes why euphemism came into being, mainly from the cultural and social psychological perspectives. Wu Liquan (1987) conducts a constructive discussion in his paper *A Tentative Study of the Historical and Cultural Background of Euphemism as a Figure of Speech* (《试论汉语委婉辞格的历史文化背景》). In his 1999 article *Euphemism: Linguistic Mapping of Community* (《委婉语——社会文化域的语言映射》), Peng Wenzhao argues that euphemism is born socially, psychologically and culturally marked and has shown a strong communicative power. At the same time, he summarizes the social properties and functional characteristics of euphemism. He further points out, "Euphemisms are first and foremost a language phenomenon. Words and sentences themselves do not claim to be euphemisms. Only when they are put in use can they become euphemisms" (委婉语首先体现为一种言语现象，词和句子本身并不是委婉语，只是在语言的运用中才使它们成为委婉语。) (66).

Ye Kun and Zhang Lan (2010) approach euphemism from the sociolinguistic perspective and explore its social significance embedded in social mentality, socio-cultural context, social development as well as hybridization of language and culture (257-259). Ren Chi and Yu Hao (2013), stressing the importance of its sociolinguistic aspect, holds the view that "euphemism is deeply rooted in social culture. It is impossible to have a profound understanding of language without referring to social culture" (45).

What's more, in their article Li Landong and Xing Wenying (2014) analyze English euphemism in terms of the rules and principles of its generative mechanism and functions (146-148).

Pragmatic Approach

The introduction and development of pragmatics have also triggered a pragmatic approach to the study of euphemism among some researchers (Shu Dingfang, 1989; Shu Dingfang & Xu Jinyuan, 1995; Xu Haiming, 1996; Liang Hongmei, 2000; Tian Jiusheng, 2001; Shao Junhang, 2002).

In his 1989 article *Euphemism in Contemporary Chinese* (《现代汉语中的委婉语》Shu Dingfang pioneeringly embarks on the description and analysis of modern Chinese euphemism in terms of its formational device and scope. And again in the same year, a second article *A New Exploration of Euphemism* (《委婉语新探》) carries Shu Dingfang's (1989) idea that apart from the Cooperative Principle and the Politeness Principle governing the building of new euphemisms, there is one more principle at work in interpersonal communication, namely, the defensive principle. In Shu's opinion, interpersonal communication is more of a self-oriented matter. The interlocutor attempts to protect self's interest and dignity by using "good" words to describe self or self-related people or things. The defensive principle complements the PP yet at the same time governs the PP to some extent. Whenever clashes arise between the defensive principle and the PP, it is always the PP that falls under the control of the defensive principle. In addition, Shu proposes indirect speech act as a formational device of euphemism. Re-examination should be conducted concerning the previously mentioned division of euphemism by Hugh Rawson: positive euphemism and negative euphemism. Shu maintains that the indirect speech act and the grammatical device should both be categorized into the domain of negative euphemism. He suggests that the formational devices of euphemism other than semantic and grammatical ones should be grouped under a new heading, namely, neutral euphemism. Come under this heading are also phonetic distortion, abbreviation, apocopation (dropping or omission of a letter or syllable from the end of a word), initialing, backformation and loan words (28-34). Then with some reservations, Shao Junhang (2006: 39-43) accepts Shu Dingfang's opinion of the formational principles of euphemism by arguing that there are only two principles governing euphemism: appropriateness principle and defensive principle in its broad sense. Other principles are by no means pragmatic principles. They merely indicate the functions of euphemism or intentions of the speaker.

Xu Haiming (1996: 21-24, 47) addresses euphemisms for strategic use in light of context, Grice's CP and other related theories. His discussion focuses on the option and interpretation of euphemisms in communication and argues for the importance of social and cultural context in which euphemisms are put into operation. Xu Haiming maintains that a high frequency of the strategic use of euphemism means its effectiveness in communication. In addition, follow-up principles guiding the strategic use of euphemisms are put forward. Liang Hongmei (2000: 30-34) points out that the use of euphemisms is a result of flouting the Cooperative Principle but observing the Politeness Principle, indirect speech acts and face theory. Tian Jiusheng (2001:18-21) proposes that considering the fact that euphemisms in one context may not be all the same in another and that they change with the lapse of time, euphemisms should be redefined from the pragmatic perspective. Besides, he is convinced that there are two principles governing the use of euphemism: appropriateness principle and self-defensive principle.

In the past twenty-odd years, quite a number of books, papers and essays on euphemism in both English and Chinese languages have come out. Scholars have investigated euphemism in terms of its ways and effects of expression (Wu Liquan, 1997), its principles and formational devices (Shu Dingfang, 1995), and its categorization (Li Guonan, 1989; Shu Dingfang,

1995). Their studies have enriched the research proper and broadened people's vision of euphemism.

There is no denying that some of the principles and theories in the field of pragmatics, such as Grice's CP and CI, Leech's PP as well as Brown and Levinson's face theory have proved to have a strong explanatory power over this language phenomenon. It is also believed that the defensive principle proposed by Shu Dingfang assists with the CP and the PP.

In addition to the above-mentioned publications, a number of MA theses and PhD dissertations have studied euphemism pragmatically in the case of either flouting the CP or observing the PP, or both. What's more, quite a few articles address euphemism in light of Brown and Levinson's face theory.

Cognitive Approach

Drawing upon Ludwig Wittgenstein's theory of family resemblance, Liu Yuelian's (2010) research is devoted to the categorization of both euphemism and taboo as well as the generation of euphemism (10-13). Following the idea that euphemism is conceptualized metaphor Wang Dongmei (2010) conducts a tentative interpretation of the cognitive motivation of euphemism (132-136). Holding a different view Huang Yaying (2014) takes a metonymy approach to the generation of euphemism (52-54). In their article Wang Guodong, Gan Shi'an and Zhou Chunyan (2011) discuss the impact of a cognitive context view on the cognition paradigm of English euphemism (164-166).

Miscellaneous

The past couple of years has witnessed a new approach to euphemism. In her PhD dissertation Liu Qian (2013) tentatively applies a philosophy-of-mind approach to the study of euphemistic expressions, focusing on their generative process and features by means of discussing language subjects' conscious activities. Wang Qiuxiang and Lang Jia (2015) adopt the same approach to the generative mechanism of euphemism, believing that the philosophy-of-mind approach can powerfully reveal and interpret the thinking process and cognitive process of humans, which bring both traditional and stylistic euphemisms into being (88-91).

Conclusively, great progress has been made in the studies of euphemism mainly from five perspectives: rhetoric (Chen Wangdao, 1976; Wu Liquan, 1994, 1995, 1997a, 1997b, 1998; etc.), semantics (Neaman & Silver, 1983, 1990, 1991; Wu Tieping, 1989; Liu Chunbao, 1994; Wang Yongzhong, 2001; etc.), sociolinguistics (Chen Yuan, 1983; Wu Liquan, 1987; Peng Wenzhao, 1999; Ye Kun & Zhang Lan, 2010; Ren Chi & Yu Hao, 2013; Li Landong & Xing Wenying, 2014; etc.), pragmatics (Shu Dingfang, 1989; Xu Haiming, 1996; Shao Junhang, 2002, 2007; etc.) and cognitive linguistics (Liu Yuelian, 2010; Wang Dongmei, 2010; Wang Guodong, Gan Shi'an & Zhou Chunyan, 2011; Huang Yaying, 2014; etc.)

2.5   Studies of Euphemisms in *DRM*

As a masterpiece of Chinese vernacular literature and magnificent encyclopedic book, *A Dream of Red Mansions* is generally acknowledged as a pinnacle of classical novels. The first eighty chapters of the novel were allegedly composed by Cao Xueqin in the mid-18th century during the Qing Dynasty.

The novel teems with a multitude of characters. According to Feng Qiyong's 2008 paper *A Few Issues in the Research of A Dream of Red Mansions* (《红楼论要——解读〈红楼梦〉的几个问题》) there are seven hundred and seventy-four named characters, of whom nearly thirty are deemed main characters (28). The remarkableness of the novel lies not only in its politic handling of a huge cast of characters but also in its acute and detailed delineation of social hierarchy and family life characteristic of the 18th-century Chinese aristocracy. The intricate social network and officialdom, intriguing social and cultural norms, entwined family relationships as well as the distinctive personality and characteristic language of all the characters boast rich resources for studies from various perspectives.

Research shows that rhetorically euphemisms in *DRM* have been approached in the following ways: analysis of euphemisms in the chapter titles of *DRM*, investigation of euphemisms regarding particular subject matters such as death, disease, sex as well as excreta and secretion in the novel. Efforts have also been made at the rhetorical art of the novel. For example, *The Rhetorical Art of A Dream of Red Mansions* (《〈红楼梦〉的修辞艺术》) edited by Lin Xingren (1984) is taken as the first academic publication on the rhetorical art of the novel. The book is devoted to the description of all the rhetorical devices and features as well as analysis of their thematic contribution to the novel. Euphemisms such as "那件东西", "老了人口", "见喜" are dealt with in detail. In his monograph *A Dream of Red Mansions and Chinese Culture*《红楼梦与中国文化论稿》), Hu Wenbin (2005) accords a chapter to the subject matter of the Chinese taboo system reflected in the novel. Hu discusses state taboos, family taboos and taboos concerning everyday life, which all find themselves readily substituted with euphemisms. For example, an Emperor's name is a state taboo, which is euphemized as "上" and "当今". Lin Daiyu's mother's name "敏" is a family taboo, which is phonologically replaced by "密" and orthographically remains roughly the character "敏" but with one or two strokes missing. Hu also illustrates "死" as a taboo concerning everyday life. Related euphemisms are "去世", "先", "没了", "回去", "伸腿去了" and so on. By examining taboos in *DRM*, Hu comes to conclude,

> Taboo language and taboo system delineated in the novel are both an art of language and a politically and culturally special phenomenon. They are no longer what were held conventionally by the primitives. With several thousand years of development the taboo custom has evolved into a shell of *Li*, a servant to *Li*, and an instrument to perfect and strengthen *Li* (小说中所描写的避讳语言和避讳制度，既是一种语言艺术，又是一种政治的和文化的特殊

现象，它早已不是原始初民们所奉行的那种约定俗成的避讳。经过封
建制度的数千年发展，避讳风俗逐渐演化为"礼"的一种外壳，成为
"礼"的仆从，成为完善和健全"礼"治的工具。) (ibid. 361).

In addition, Wang Guofeng (2011) approaches the close relationship between *DRM* and "*Li*" (礼) from the perspective of sociolinguistics and explores the rigid rites and politeness features in the feudal society.

Euphemisms in *DRM* have always been a major concern in the field of translation. So there have been great efforts devoted to the study of the translation of euphemisms in *DRM*, especially as far as David Hawke's version and that of the Yangs are comparatively studied. In his 2006 work *On the Translation of Hong Lou Meng* (《红译艺坛——〈红楼梦〉翻译艺术研究》), Feng Qinghua, a renowned specialist in translation, conducts a comprehensive analysis of the two English versions emphatically with regard to the art of translation. For example, he makes a comparative study of the strengths and weaknesses between the two versions in terms of the translation of particular subject matters such as death and funeral affairs ("回去", "后事", "寿木", etc.), disease ("见喜", "欠安", "不爽快", etc.), excreta and secretion ("解手", "小恭", "庚信", etc.), and sex ("春兴", "爬灰", "首尾", etc.).

Co-authors Ren Xiankai and Ke Xinli (2011), and Liu Jinbao (2013) take a strong interest in the translation of euphemisms for death. Ren and Ke devote much attention to the translation strategies (73-85) whereas Liu focuses more on the cultural differences behind the Chinese and English languages (75-79, 82).

Based on the English translation of "*Panci*" (fated predictions) in *DRM* Zhang Rui'e and Dong Jie's article (2012: 35-41) takes a combined approach of both macroscopically a multi-dimensional view and microscopically a binary analysis in investigating the juxtaposition and transformation of binary translation elements. They come to the conclusion that such an approach can help strike balance between intuitive perception and theoretical rigidity in the process of translation (35-41).

What is noteworthy is that attention has also been paid to the pragmatic element of the novel. For example, in her 1997 book, Sun Ailing argues for the applicability of Austin's speech act theory and Grice's CP to Chinese novels. Her study mainly puts the Jias in *DRM* and their speech acts under investigation. Lan Chun (2006) conducts a pragmatic approach to *DRM*. In each chapter of her book, she introduces a pragmatic theory, such as deixis, CP, CI or speech act. The book is entertaining in that each theory is plainly couched and illustrated with interesting examples from the character utterances of the novel. Apart from that, a combined rhetorical, translational and pragmatic investigation of the euphemisms in the novel has a place in Chen Kefang's (2010) work. She devotes a whole chapter to the relationship between politeness and the construction and use of euphemism. According to her, euphemism is a unity of contradictions between politeness and cooperativeness. Chen proceeds to examine the translation of ten one-character euphemisms for "death" in *DRM* by virtue of the two English versions. Furthermore, with the politeness approach she analyzes the different translations of such euphemisms in the two versions. Then she comes to the conclusion that a study of euphemism helps overcome cross-cultural ignorance, culture shock and socio-pragmatic breakdown.

Literature review evidences an inadequacy of a systematic investigation on euphemisms in the character utterances of the novel. What's more, such attempt has never been made in light of Helen Spencer-Oatey's theory of rapport management. Now the present research is intended to be a tentative study of the euphemisms in the character utterances of *DRM* within the theoretical framework of Helen Spencer-Oatey's rapport management. The research is designed to investigate the controlling force and explanatory power of Helen Spencer-Oatey's theory of rapport management over the characters' option and use of euphemisms in *DRM*.

2.6 Summary

This chapter has revisited the notions and theories in terms of indirectness, face and the Politeness Principle, euphemism with regard to its definitions and origin as well as related studies and approaches both at home and abroad. Besides, research done so far on the euphemisms in *DRM* is presented. Literature review adequately demonstrates that great achievements have been made in the study of euphemisms at both national and international levels. Based on the previous research, the present book is going to undertake a pragmatic analysis of euphemisms in the character utterances of *DRM* within a new theoretical framework: Helen Spencer-Oatey's theory of rapport management.

Chapter Three

Theoretical Framework: Rapport Management

3.1 Introduction

"Face" is intuitively significant and plays a crucial role in human interactions, for it is concerned with people's sense of worth, dignity and identity, and is associated with issues such as respect, honor, status, reputation and competence (Ting-Toomey & Kurogi, 1998). Consequently, face is generally perceived as one's positive values in the society. In Lim's words, "people do not claim face for what they think are negative" (Lim, 1994: 210).

Brown and Levinson's conceptualization of face meets challenges and questions from scholars all over the world, especially as far as the Oriental culture is concerned. Chang and Holt (1994) maintain that their concept is more rational than relational. According to Ting-Toomey (1988), owing to the fact that Brown and Levinson's idea of face is rooted in an individualistic culture their model is applicable or confined only to such a culture. Based on close observation of the matter of face in the Japanese culture, Matsumoto (1988) is convinced that in Brown and Levinson's conception of face individual freedom is overemphasized yet the social aspect of face overlooked. By truthfully examining the Chinese context, Gu Yueguo (1998) also denies its applicability to the Chinese culture and maintains it is not that concerns about autonomy, imposition and so on do not exist in Eastern cultures, but rather that they are not regarded as face concerns (qtd. Spencer-Oatey, 2007: 13).

At the same time, another drawback is questioned in Brown and Levinson's model: neglect of social identity. Matsumoto (1988), Ide (1989) and Mao (1994) all acknowledge the paramount significance of social identity as a concept especially in Oriental culture.

Taking all these arguments into consideration, a modified framework is put forth by Helen Spencer-Oatey for the conceptualization of face and rapport. She maintains "Brown and Levinson's (1987) conceptualization of positive face has been underspecified, and that the concerns they identify as negative face issues are not necessarily face concerns at all" (Spencer-Oatey, 2007: 13). Consequently, her theory of rapport management is identified as the management of harmony or disharmony in interactions with two key concerns that are highlighted: the management of face and the management of sociality rights.

▶ 3.2 Components of Rapport Management

Being keenly aware of the fact that face is not only universal but also culture-specific, Spencer-Oatey holds that face is "a universal phenomenon: everyone has the same fundamental face concerns. However, culture can affect the relative sensitivity of different aspects of people's face, as well as which strategies are most appropriate for managing face" (ibid. 12).

Buttressed by the politeness theory, Spencer-Oatey's theory of rapport management draws particular attention to the notion of face and focuses on the function of language in its management of social relations. Spencer-Oatey proposes the term "rapport management" in preference to "face management" owing to the fact that "'face' seems to focus on concerns for self, whereas rapport management suggests more of a balance between self and other" (ibid. 12). In that sense, importance is attached to balance between self and other rather than unilaterally self-directed or other-directed imbalance.

In view of the above consideration, the concern of rapport management is extended to not only the management of face and rights but also the way in which language is used to manage rapport. In opposition to Brown and Levinson's conceptualization of positive face and negative face, Spencer-Oatey proposes two components of rapport management. According to her, rapport management, which is indeed the management of harmony-disharmony among people, involves the management of face and sociality rights. To be more exact, face management involves the management of face needs whereas the management of sociality rights concerns the management of social expectancies, which are referred to, by Spencer-Oatey, as "fundamental personal/social entitlements that individuals effectively claim for themselves in their interactions with others" (ibid. 14). That is to say, face is generally concerned with personal/social value, dignity, honor, reputation and competence that all contribute to people's sense of worth, personal/social expectancies and so on. In contrary to face, sociality rights "are concerned with personal/social expectancies, and reflect people's concerns over fairness, consideration, social inclusion/exclusion and so on" (ibid. 14).

3.2.1　Quality Face and Identity Face

In the theory of rapport management, face is identified into two aspects that appear opposing but in effect correlated. In essence quality face is personal yet identity face social.

Quality Face

By quality face, Spencer-Oatey means "We have a fundamental desire for people to evaluate us positively in terms of our personal qualities, e.g. our competence, abilities, appearance, etc." (ibid. 14). She further points out that quality face is concerned with the value that people effectively claim for themselves with regard to such qualities as are typically personal and help establish or maintain their sense of personal self-esteem.

Identity Face

By identity face, Spencer-Oatey means "We have a fundamental desire for people to acknowledge and uphold our social identities or roles, e.g. as group leader, valued customer, close friend" (ibid.14). She also emphasizes that identity face is closely associated with the value that people effectively claim for themselves with regard to their roles in the society or within a group, which can be deemed recognition of their value in the eyes of the public and help establish or maintain their sense of public worth.

3.2.2　Equity Rights and Association Rights

Likewise, sociality rights are also classified into two opposing yet correlated aspects: equity rights and association rights. While equity rights are personal association rights social.

Equity Rights

By equity rights, Spencer-Oatey means "We have a fundamental belief that we are entitled to personal consideration from others, so that we are treated fairly: that we are not unduly imposed upon, that we are not unfairly ordered about, and that we are not taken advantage of or exploited" (ibid. 14). Spencer-Oatey insists that two components of this equity entitlements merit attention: "the notion of *cost-benefit* (the extent to which we are exploited or disadvantaged, and the belief that costs and benefits should be kept roughly in balance through the principle of reciprocity), and the related issue of *autonomy-imposition* (the extent to which people control us or impose on us)" (ibid. 14).

Association Rights

By association rights, Spencer-Oatey means "We have a fundamental belief that we are entitled to an association with others that is in keeping with the type of relationship that we have with them" (ibid. 14). That is to say, such association rights are interactional on the one hand and affective on the other. Involvement with others and share of concerns, feelings or even interests are the core of association rights.

It is self-evident that the management of face and sociality rights has both a personal component (quality face and equity rights respectively) and a social component (identity face and association rights respectively). Therefore, this framework in general is distinct from Brown and Levinson's (1987) face theory mainly in two ways. On the one hand, Brown and Levinson's model remains personal or individualistic whereas Spencer-Oatey's theory of rapport management is inclusive of the social or relational properties of face. On the other hand, her theory "draws a distinction between face needs (where one's sense of personal/social *value* is at stake), and sociality rights (where one's sense of personal/social entitlements is at stake)" (ibid. 15). Apparently Brown and Levinson's (1987) identification of "negative face" is not deemed a face want in Spencer-Oatey's rapport but coincides with what she terms as sociality rights. This is diametrically shown in Table 2.

Table 2   Components of rapport management (Spencer-Oatey, 2007: 15)

	face management (personal/social value)	sociality rights management (personal/social entitlements)
personal/independent perspective	quality face (cf. Brown and Levinson's positive face)	equity rights (cf. Brown and Levinson's negative face)
social/interdependent perspective	identity face	association rights

Taking culture specificity into consideration, Spencer-Oatey points out,

different cultures may place different emphases on these various components of rapport management. Firstly, there may be differing sensitivities to the varying components, so that more rapport management work is necessary for certain aspects than for others. Secondly, there may be different ways of addressing or orienting towards these different sensitivities; some cultures may prefer one type of strategy to mitigate a potential threat to rapport, whereas others may prefer another type of strategy (ibid. 15-16).

It is noteworthy that while Spencer-Oatey intends her formulation of rapport management to be universal, she keeps alert to the fact that culture remains specific. In that sense, stress may be put on different components of rapport management so that communicative strategies can be adopted correspondingly.

·❯❯ 3.3 Rapport-Threatening Behavior: Managing Face and Sociality Rights

In Brown and Levinson's politeness model (1987), there is the notion of face-threatening acts, which, in communication, may intrinsically threaten the interlocutors' face needs. These illocutionary acts are generally referred to as face-threatening acts (FTAs).

Spencer-Oatey does not fail to elaborate on her belief that rapport between people can be threatened in two main ways in terms of the two primary components of rapport: "through face-threatening behavior" and "through rights-threatening behavior" (Spencer-Oatey 2007: 16). According to her, threat to one's rights means infringement of his/her sense of personal/

social entitlements. For example, if he/she is forced to do something but feels that nobody else is entitled to expect him/her to do that, his/her equity rights are threatened. Similarly, he/she may be spoken to in a way that is so much personal that he/she may think his/her (dis)association rights are threatened. In this case, he/she may feel embarrassed or offended but it does not mean to him/her a loss of face. In cases where he/she feels personally devaluated in one way or another it is a loss of face. In Spencer-Oatey's opinion, criticism or opposition is typically face-threatening because it is inclined to belittle or even humiliate an individual, as a result of which his/her sense of self-esteem or public-worth is harmed.

Spencer-Oatey goes on to specify the role of speech act in the management of rapport. Generally speaking, orders and requests are rapport-threatening, for they can affect one's "autonomy, freedom of choice, and freedom from imposition" (ibid. 17). In consequence, they tend to threaten an individual's "sense of equity rights (one's entitlements to considerate treatment)" (ibid. 17). Compliments, in contrary to criticism or opposition, are typically face-enhancing in that they are likely to strengthen an individual's quality face or identity face or, both. In Spencer-Oatey's words, "Personal compliments typically enhance people's quality face. They can also boost identity face, if they are perceived as enhancing the complimentee's position or role within a group" (ibid. 18).

However, it remains a fact that the effects of the same speech act may vary a great deal when it is perceived differently by different people on different occasions. In this case, orders or requests may turn out to be face-enhancing or rapport-enhancing rather than supposedly face-threatening or rapport-threatening. In addition, compliments may not necessarily be face-enhancing. Instead, they can also prove to be face-threatening, or rather, rapport-threatening. In that sense effective management of rapport seems rather a complicated and thorny issue to cope with, for "rapport threat and rapport enhancement are subjective evaluations, which depend not simply on the content of the message, but on people's interpretations and reactions to who says what under what circumstances" (ibid. 19).

3.4   Rapport-Management Strategy Domains

It is certainly an unwelcome experience for people to lose face in interpersonal communication. In view of this human mentality Brown and Levinson (1987) are convinced that it is "in every participant's best interest to maintain each other's face" (61). Referring to the paramount role that language assumes in facilitating the management of rapport, Spencer-Oatey (2002) observes,

> Every language, therefore, provides a very wide range of linguistic options that can be used for managing face and sociality rights, and hence for managing rapport. Naturally, the exact range of options, and their social significance, varies from language to language. However, every level of language can play a role in each of the rapport management domains (20).

Rapport management strategies generally operate in the following five domains that are all interrelated and react on rapport management. In other words, these domains can affect strategies that are applied to the creation and maintenance of harmonious relations. They are, according to Spencer-Oatey, illocutionary domain, discourse domain, participation domain, stylistic domain and non-verbal domain (ibid. 19-20), of which illocutionary domain and stylistic domain relate to the present study.

Illocutionary domain is the domain to which Brown and Levinson (1987) address themselves. It is a domain on which a great deal of work on politeness and hence rapport management has focused for the reason that

"It concerns the rapport-threatening/enhancing implications of performing speech acts such as apologies, requests, compliments, and so on" (Spencer-Oatey, 2002: 19). Within this domain, three features, namely, "the selection of speech act components, the degree of directness/indirectness, and the type and amount of upgraders/downgraders" (ibid. 21) are found at work in the wording of speech acts.

Stylistic domain, on the other hand, "concerns the stylistic aspects of an interchange, such as choice of tone (for example, serious or joking), choice of genre-appropriate terms of address or use of honorifics" (ibid. 20).

Both the illocutionary domain and the stylistic domain are supposed to contribute to the management of rapport as far as the present study is concerned. Adequate attention must be paid to the two domains and appropriate handling of the two seems most necessary in order for harmonious interactions to be created or maintained in a desirable way.

3.5   Factors Influencing Strategy Use

Strategies that can be applied to rapport management are governed by such factors as rapport orientation, contextual variables and pragmatic conventions, which will be discussed in the following.

3.5.1   Rapport Orientation

Rapport orientation is a crucial factor that influences people's strategy use. Rapport generally entails consideration of two orientations in communication with regard to self and other: "support of one's own face needs and sociality rights, and support of the other person's" (ibid. 29). Brown and Levinson (1987: 61) also rightly observe that in practice any individual taking part in an interaction manages to maintain each other's face with keen awareness that face is intrinsically vulnerable and held dear by all. So revenge for a loss of face is certainly uncomfortable to both sides. In this case, Ting-Toomey and Cocroft (1994: 323) wisely suggest that a third orientation be taken into account, namely, mutual support.

Spencer-Oatey specifies rapport orientation into four types: rapport-enhancement orientation, rapport-maintenance orientation, rapport-neglect orientation and rapport-challenge orientation.

Rapport-enhancement orientation is "a desire to strengthen or enhance harmonious relations between the interlocutors" (Spencer-Oatey, 2007: 29). In this sense, rapport-enhancement orientation assumes a positive role and is generally characterized with "giving face" in interactions.

Rapport-maintenance orientation is "a desire to maintain or protect harmonious relations between the interlocutors" (ibid. 29). In other words, rapport-maintenance orientation, characterized with preservation of the current quality of relations, still plays a positive role. It necessitates "the choice of appropriate terms of address, honorifics, social indexing markers, and other relevant aspects of register" (ibid. 30). As rapport-maintenance orientation is also concerned with appropriate handling of such face-threatening acts as orders, criticisms, complaints, disagreements and threats, appropriate rapport-management strategies must be taken into consideration and brought into full play in order for the negative impact to be reduced to a minimum.

Rapport-neglect orientation refers to "a lack of concern or interest in the quality of relations between the interlocutors (perhaps because of a focus on self)" (ibid. 29). Such orientation is negatively characterized with little concern or apathy as a result of full occupation with an emergency or an important task, or intentional neglect of current relations or, more concern of one's own face needs than that of a balanced rapport.

Rapport-challenge orientation is "a desire to challenge or impair harmonious relations between the interlocutors" (ibid. 30). Such orientation is negatively characterized with deliberate challenge or impairment of the quality and state of current relations. Intentional offence by means of making people lose face is deemed a common practice.

3.5.2 Contextual Variables

A second set of factors in Spence-Oatey's rapport that determine people's choice of rapport management strategies are a number of contextual variables. The contextual variables encompass four important elements: "participant relations, message content, rights and obligations, and communicative activity" (ibid. 31).

Participants and Their Relations

Participant relations have already proved central to the use of rapport-management strategies in that numerous classic studies have helped "establish *power* and *distance* as key variables relating to participant relations" and "a large number of empirical studies have proved considerable evidence for an association between language use and the variables *power* and *distance*" (ibid. 32).

What is power? It is defined by Brown and Gilman as "a relationship between at least two persons and it is nonreciprocal in the sense that both cannot have power in the same area of behaviour" (Brown & Gilman, 1960/1972: 255). This variable is labeled with a variety of terms: "power, social power, status, dominance, authority" (Spencer-Oatey, 2007: 32), which all indicate unequal role relations in the domains of sociolinguistics and pragmatics. So in essence power is nonreciprocal and unequal in terms of role relations. Teacher-student or employer-employee relations, for instance, are a typical type of nonreciprocal unequal role relations.

Like power, the variable distance is also identified and labeled variously as "distance, social distance, solidarity, closeness, familiarity, relational intimacy" (ibid. 33). Again Brown and Gilman define this variable as "a set of relations which are symmetrical" (Brown & Gilman, 1960/1972: 258). According to them, "likemindedness or similar behavior dispositions" can matter a great deal in contributing to solidarity apart from the supposed frequency of contact or length of acquaintance.

Message Content: Cost–Benefit Considerations

Message content plays an important role in people's choice and use of rapport-management strategies. Messages can have either costs or benefits associated with them. Costs or benefits may intuitively be thought of as financial in the first place, but they can also be costs or benefits in many other ways. To be more exact, costs may manifest themselves in terms of "time, effort, imposition, inconvenience, risk, and so on" (Spencer-Oatey, 2007: 35) whereas benefits in terms of time, effort, convenience, and the like.

For example, as far as costs are concerned, asking a friend to help look after the kids can certainly be costly for the friend in terms of time, effort, imposition, inconvenience and risk. However, offering to help look after the kids can be costly for the offerer in terms of time, effort, inconvenience and risk. Conversely, with regard to benefits, asking a friend to help look after the kids can certainly be beneficial to the asker him/herself in terms of time, effort and convenience yet offering to help look after the kids can be beneficial to the friend in terms of time, effort and convenience. In addition, it is commonly accepted that "some messages are more 'costly' than others" (ibid. 35). Asking a friend to help look after a kid is supposedly more costly than asking him/her to help look after a pet. "And so normally this difference in the 'costs' associated with the requests would result in different wording" (ibid. 36). Occasionally a message is also inclined to be interpreted as costly or beneficial, making cost-benefit anticipation even more difficult and complicated. For instance, in many cases the offer "Have some ice-cream!" may be interpreted as beneficial if the guest really loves ice-cream and wants to have some at the moment. However, the offer might be perceived as costly if the guest dislikes ice-cream or has a stomachache.

As messages are interpreted differently by different people on different occasions, any type of message may result in "a sense of indebtedness" (ibid. 36) and the disequilibrium thus created calls for "book balancing" (ibid. 36) so that equilibrium can verbally be restored especially in the illocutionary and the stylistic domains.

Social/Interactional Roles

A third set of factors that may influence people's choice and use of rapport-management strategies are social/interactional roles because they are perceived as closely associated with assessments of rights and obligations. The following incident related by Thomas (1995) exemplifies the importance of rights and obligations:

> [...] two elderly women [were] travelling on a country bus service. On country routes the driver stops only when requested to do so. The first woman wanted to get off at a scheduled stopping place, and as the bus approached it she simply called out: "Next stop, driver!" Her companion wanted to get off where there was no official stop, and asked the driver, "Do you think you could possibly let me out just beyond the traffic lights, please?" (131)

The request of the first lady and that of the second lady can be taken as two events. Both of them want to get off at a certain place. It is self-evident that "the parameters of power, social distance and size of imposition" (Spencer-Oatey, 2007: 37) remain exactly the same. "The role relations are the same, and in terms of driving difficulty, it costs the driver no more effort to stop beyond the traffic lights than at the bus stop" (ibid. 37). The first lady wants the driver to stop at a scheduled stopping place and she has the right to do so. The second lady desires to get off at an unscheduled stopping place beyond the traffic lights yet it seems that she is not so much entitled to do so as the first lady is. This difference is closely associated with the passengers' rights and the driver's obligations. In the first event, the driver is undeniably obligated to stop as he is told. However, in the second event, the driver is not supposed to be under such an obligation.

Social/interactional roles are operative in not only determining power and distance but also specifying rights and obligations of the role members in social interactions. Spencer-Oatey rightly puts,

> When people interact with each other, they often take up clearly defined social roles, such as teacher-student, employer-employee, friend-friend, sales assistant-customer, chairperson-committee member. These sole relationships not only partially determine the power and distance of the relationship, but also help specify the rights and obligations of each role member. People have the right to expect certain things of the other member and an obligation to carry out certain other things (ibid. 37).

However, Spencer-Oatey also warns against limits to the scope of rights and obligations within each pair of relations, saying both "the nature of the role relationship" and "the specific content of the message" (ibid. 37) contribute to the choice and use of rapport management strategies.

Communicative Activity

Communicative activity is a fourth major factor that influences the choice and use of rapport management strategies. Different communicative activities are characterized with different communicative genres. In other words, communicative activities are genre-specific in that they have their own "historically and culturally specific, prepatterned and complex solutions to recurrent communicative problems" (Günthner & Knoblauch, 1995: 8). In general genre-specific communicative activities are found in all of the previously mentioned five domains of rapport management. They are culturally constrained and significantly practical to how interactions are verbally constructed and interpreted.

A job interview allows a candidate to be moderately more boastful than absolutely modest. In contrary, a winner at an awarding ceremony is expected to appear modest and sing the praises of whomever his/her achievements may concern. Spencer-Oatey keenly observes that "obtaining an appropriate balance between modesty and boasting is a recurrent communicative problem, but what counts as appropriate can vary from one communicative activity to another" (Spencer-Oatey, 2007: 37).

3.5.3 Pragmatic Conventions

Pragmatic conventions are a fifth set of factors that play a key role in people's choice and use of rapport management strategies. Both Leech (1983) and Thomas (1983) have drawn a distinction between sociopragmatics and pragmalinguistics, which are believed to affect the management of rapport.

Sociopragmatic Conventions

"Self-centered pursuit and gratification of face needs and sociality rights" (Spencer-Oatey, 2007: 39) are individually intuitive to human beings. It is found that there are rules or principles socially helping minimize the unpleasantness or clashes that may result from such personal pursuit or gratification. For example, being fully aware of this very fact Leech stipulates a number of maxims and sub-maxims of PP.

According to Spencer-Oatey, such maxims can be taken as "sociocultural conventions governing the pursuit of social goals. The conventions would be rapport-focused, in that they would relate to rapport-management concerns of face (quality face and identity face) and of sociality rights (equity rights and association rights)" (ibid. 40). For instance, Spencer-Oatey associates her components of rapport management with Leech's maxims of PP, saying "Leech's (1987) approbation and modesty maxims could be seen as addressing quality face concerns; and his tact and generosity maxims could be seen as addressing concerns over equity rights" (ibid. 40).

Pragmalinguistic Conventions

Apart from sociopragmatic conventions, pragmalinguistic conventions also affect the management of rapport in that they contribute to the conveyance of a given pragmatic meaning in a given context. "All the conventions are context-specific; in other words, for a given pragmatic message the conventions of strategy use are affected by the contextual factors" (ibid. 41). Spencer-Oatey illustrates the idea with greetings to an acquaintance in both Chinese and English contexts:

> For example, in British English, it is common (especially among older people) to greet an acquaintance with a remark about the weather such as "Hello, a bit colder today, isn't it?' in order to show pleasant friendliness. Yet in Chinese, it is more common (especially among older people) to ask about meal in such a context and say, for example, "Hello, have you had lunch?" The functions of the two remarks are virtually identical in the respective languages, but in English the latter remark would probably be interpreted as a preliminary to an invitation. In other words, the two languages have different pragmalinguistic conventions for conveying a friendly greeting to an acquaintance (ibid. 40-41).

This example manifests the fact that the two different cultures may have different pragmalinguistic conventions for the very same event like greeting a friend.

3.6   Rapport Management Outcomes

Rapport-management outcomes are opposite but correlated to rapport-management orientations. Spencer-Oatey holds that they are "similar in type to rapport-management orientations. In other words, the degree of rapport between interlocutors can be enhanced, maintained or reduced" (ibid. 41). Stressing the usefulness and applicability of Goffman's (1963) concept of "negatively eventful" behaviour, Spencer-Oatey observes,

> Some types of behaviour (routine expression of thanks) may pass unperceived as an event when they are performed, but give rise to negative relational outcomes when they are not. Conversely, other types of behaviour (e.g. appropriate degree of unsolicited help given to a stranger) may pass unperceived as an event when they are not performed, but give rise to positive relational outcomes when they are (ibid. 41).

Based on the above exposition, the present research attempts to translate Spencer-Oatey's theoretical framework of rapport management into the following figure. The figure is supposed to be cyclic: components of rapport—factors influencing strategy use—rapport strategy domains—components of rapport. It runs with components of rapport and ends with components of rapport (see Figure 4).

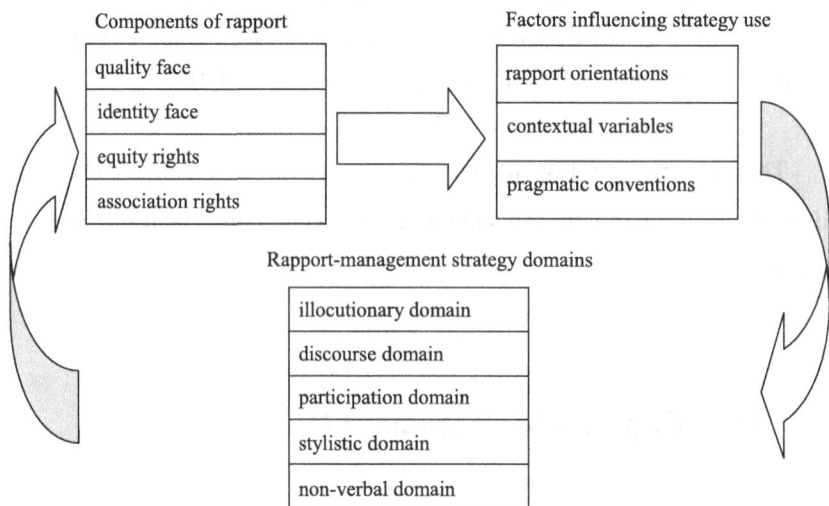

Components of rapport

quality face
identity face
equity rights
association rights

Factors influencing strategy use

rapport orientations
contextual variables
pragmatic conventions

Rapport-management strategy domains

illocutionary domain
discourse domain
participation domain
stylistic domain
non-verbal domain

Figure 4   Spencer-Oatey's framework of rapport management

The figure reveals that in order to manage rapport interlocutors must take into account three types of factors that may have an impact on rapport. Such factors determine the strategy domains that in turn contribute to rapport management.

⟩ 3.7 Summary

This chapter has expounded the core components of Spencer-Oatey's theory of rapport: face (quality face and identity face) and rights (equity rights and association rights). Quality face and equity rights are personal whereas identity face and association rights social. As far as the present study is concerned, rapport management is supposed to operate in the illocutionary domain and the discourse domain. At the same time, as the influencing factors of strategy use assume important roles they should be taken seriously. In practice, people need to employ strategies such as degree of directness/ indirectness in order for communication to be successfully completed with face and rights appropriately managed. The indirect expressions such as euphemisms are supposed to be able to help avoid abruptness and rudeness so that harmony can be achieved.

Chapter Four

Description and Categorization of Euphemisms in *DRM*

4.1 Introduction

Euphemism was originally restricted to taboo but its studies have ranged over a wide field. As for the taxonomy of euphemisms, Enright (1985: 3) finds that English euphemisms encompass almost all spheres of human life: from the largely private realms of sex, bowel movements, menstruation, money, sickness and natural death to the public affairs that are political, military, commercial and social. Zhang Gonggui (1996: 3) has collected about 3,000 ancient and modern Chinese euphemisms and classified them into thirteen categories, in one of which even the names of some animals and plants have claimed euphemistic terms.

The classification of euphemisms varies a great deal by different criteria. In general, they can be classified into two big categories: conventional and situational euphemisms on the one hand and positive and negative euphemisms on the other.

Conventional euphemisms are regarded as standard expressions that have undergone a great length of time. The connotations of conventional euphemisms are well accepted in common practice, so they are relatively stable. Situational euphemisms function temporarily because they have not yet been socially conventionalized as euphemisms. They are largely context-dependent and determined by specific communicative situations and topics.

The division of positive and negative euphemisms is proposed by Hugh Rawson (1981). Positive euphemisms "inflate and magnify the word meaning, making the euphemized seem altogether grander and more important than they really are" (1). They are used to show politeness, avoid hurting other people and meet the psychological needs of both sides. Such euphemisms include occupational titles, personal honorifics and institutional names. Negative euphemisms are old-fashioned, for they only relate to tabooed topics such as birth, age, illness and death, genitals, sex, and physiological reaction. They are characterized with deflation and diminishment. Negative euphemisms are defensive in nature in that they offset or eradicate the power of tabooed terms that people do not prefer to deal with directly.

A wide variety of euphemisms abound in the character utterances of *DRM*. Generally speaking, the two big categories of euphemisms in the novel are found overlapping to some extent. That is, while a conventional euphemism is either positive or negative a negative euphemism might also be conventional or situational. Therefore, the euphemisms thus collected from the novel are classified into conventional euphemisms and situational euphemisms.

4.2 Conventional Euphemisms

In the present study, conventional euphemisms in *DRM* are subcategorized roughly in accordance with Zhang Gonggui's (1996) classification of Chinese euphemisms. Conventional euphemisms are largely an inventory of negative euphemisms with a limited number of positive ones.

Negative euphemisms are traditionally substitutes for taboos. In general, they are related to devil and disaster, death and funeral affairs, disease and ill health, sex, excreta and secretion, pregnancy and birth, ageing, love and affection, marriage and concubinage, jealousy, address terms (self-effacing terms) for interpersonal relations, servants and housemaids, names regarded as taboos, moral standing and disposition, and Buddhist practice and practitioner. Positive euphemisms, however, only relate to such address terms for interpersonal relations as honorifics. The various types of conventional euphemisms in *DRM* are exemplified as follows.

4.2.1　Devil and Disaster

"撞客" and "红脸的" are euphemisms indicating devil.

> Example 1:
> 马道婆道："这个容易，只是替他多作些因果善事也就罢了。再那经上还说，西方有位大光明普照菩萨，专管照耀阴暗邪祟，若有善男子、善女子虔心供奉者，可以永佑儿孙康宁安静，再无惊恐邪祟撞客之灾。"(*DRM*, Chap. 25: 688)
>
> [Priestess Ma saying] "Of course there is. Just do more good deeds on his behalf. The sutras tell us of a great Bodhisattva in the west whose glory illuminates all around and whose special charge it is to bring to light the evil spirits in dark places. If faithful believers worship him devoutly, their descendants are assured of peace and health and no evil spirits can get possession of them." (*DRM*, Chap. 25: 689)

Obviously, as a euphemism "撞客" refers to the evil spirits, which are believed to be horrible and hence unmentionable.

In the novel, "走水" is a euphemistic expression for "走火" (catch fire). In traditional Chinese philosophy, all the natural phenomena are generally categorized into "五行" (Five Elements/Five Phases): metal, wood, water, fire and earth. The five elements are supposed to interact with one another. Water is believed to be able to check fire. In old times, "火" (fire) was thought of as a manifestation of punishment of man exerted by the supernatural. In that sense, fire was held in awe and subsequently tabooed. "水", its antonym, was largely preferred owing to the belief that water was powerful enough to quench fire.

Example 2:

丫鬟回说：“南院马棚里走了水，不相干，已经救下去了。”(*DRM*, Chap. 39: 1094)

A maid explained that a fire had broken out in the stables in the south court, but there was no danger as it was now under control. (*DRM*, Chap. 39: 1095)

According to the above explanation, fire is disastrous and tabooed. Therefore, "走水" is used as a euphemism for "catch fire".

4.2.2 Death and Funeral Affairs

There is a number of euphemisms denoting death. They are used to refer to the death of people with regard to social status, religion, age, and the like: "终", "违", "亡", "殂", "薨", "夭"; "辞世", "度脱", "仙逝", "回去", "没了", "捐馆", "圆寂", "归西", "殡天"; "入黄泉", "大梦归", "归地府"; "下世光景", "呜呼哀哉", "上五台山", "寿终正寝", "身亡命陨"; "已出苦海", "脱去皮囊，自了去也"; "伸腿去了", "闭了这眼，断了这口气", etc. Euphemisms such as "度脱", "圆寂", "归西" and "上五台山" are religion-laden whereas some other euphemisms are tied to social hierarchy. *On Li*《礼记·曲礼》stipulates, "天子死曰崩，诸侯死曰薨，大夫死曰卒，士曰不禄，庶人曰死". In such cases, "崩", "薨", "卒" and "不禄" are all euphemisms denoting death of persons of various social ranks.

Example 3:

"她师父极精演先天神数，于去冬圆寂了。" (*DRM*, Chap. 18: 468)

"Her tutor was an excellent diviner, but she passed away last winter."

(*DRM*, Chap. 18: 469)

"圆寂" refers typically to the death of a Buddhist monk or nun.

Example 4:

正玩笑不绝，忽见东府中几个人慌慌张张跑来说："老爷仙逝了。"
众人听了，唬了一大跳，忙都说："好好的并无疾病，怎么就没了？"
家下人说："老爷天天修炼，定是功行圆满，升仙去了。"(*DRM*, Chap.
63: 1884)

[…] they were scuffling in fun when some servants form the Eastern
Mansion came rushing up frantically. "The old master's ascended to
Heaven!" they announced.

Everybody was consternated.

"He wasn't even ill, how could he pass way so suddenly?" they
exclaimed.

The servants explained, "His Lordship took elixirs every day; now he
must have achieved his aim and become an immortal." (*DRM*, Chap. 63:
1885)

In referring to the old master's death, three euphemisms are used: "仙
逝", "没了" and "升仙". "没了" is a common euphemism. Yet "仙逝"
and "升仙" are more formal and have a lot to do with Taoism, which is the
religious belief of Jia Jing (the old master).

There are also euphemisms related to funeral affairs: "丧事", "白事",
"红白大礼" and "丁忧". Euphemisms that denote coffin are: "寿木", "板",
"灵", "慈柩", "灵柩" and "仙輀". Tomb-related euphemisms are: "丘",
"穴", "家", "阴宅", "北郊", "地宫" and "寝庙".

Example 5:

贾珍看父亲不管，亦发态意奢华。看板时，几副杉木板皆不中意。
可巧薛蟠来吊，因见贾珍寻好板，便说："我们木店里有一副板，叫
作什么樯木，出在潢海铁网山上……"(*DRM*, Chap. 13: 338)

His father's indifference gave Jia Zhen a free hand to indulge his extravagance. He decided that the cedar-boards he had seen would not do for the coffin and was searching for something better when Xue Pan called to offer condolences.

"In our timber-yard is some qiang wood from the Iron-Net Mountain across the sea […]" (*DRM*, Chap. 13: 339)

Here "板" euphemistically denotes coffin.

Example 6:

于是贾赦、贾珍一齐上来请回舆，水溶 [北静王] 道："逝者已登仙界，非碌碌你我尘寰中之人也。小王虽上叨虚邀郡袭，岂可越仙轜进也？" (*DRM*, Chap. 15: 378)

Then Jia She and Jia Zhen stepped forward and begged the prince to return, but he demurred: "The deceased has become an immortal and left our dusty world. Although by the favour of the Son of Heaven I have succeeded to this title, how can I precede the carriage of an immortal?" (*DRM*, Chap. 15: 379)

Here " 仙轜 " is also a euphemism referring to a carriage for carrying a coffin at a funeral.

4.2.3 Disease and Ill Health

Euphemisms about disease and ill health are: "见喜", "出花", "血山崩", "采薪之忧" and "欠安".

Example 7:

谁知凤姐之女大姐儿病了，正乱着请大夫来诊脉。大夫便说："替夫人奶奶们道喜，姐儿发热是见喜了，并非别病。" (*DRM*, Chap. 21: 582)

"I am happy to inform Her Ladyship and Madam Lien that the little girl's fever is simply due to smallpox." (*DRM*, Chap. 21: 583)

"见喜" euphemistically means "to have smallpox". Wang Xifeng's elder daughter has smallpox, but the name of the disease is not to be directly mentioned. Rather, "见喜" is commonly accepted and used for the sake of good luck. Therefore, "见喜" is a negative euphemism.

Example 8:

贾芸笑道："总是我没福，偏偏又遇着叔叔欠安。叔叔如今可大安了？"(*DRM*, Chap. 26: 718)

"That was my misfortune," replied Jia Yun with a smile. "And then you fell ill, uncle. Have you recovered completely?" (*DRM*, Chap. 26: 719)

"欠安" means not feeling well.

4.2.4　Sex

Euphemisms related to sex are: "风月"，"云雨"，"春兴"，"人事"，"圆房"，"求欢"，"偷期"，"偷情爬灰"，"上手"，"入港"，"偷试"，"缝络"，"爬灰"，"赏花玩柳"，"拈花惹草"，"眠花卧柳"，"问柳评花"，"赏花玩柳"，"沾风惹草"，"眠花宿柳"，"问柳评花"，"招风惹草"，"追欢买笑"，"流荡优伶"，"偷鸡戏狗"，"偷鸡摸狗"，"男风"，"龙阳之兴" and "嫉衰妒枕". While "烟花巷" is a brothel, "风尘"，"流荡女子" or "粉头" refers to a prostitute.

Example 9:

焦大越发连贾珍都说出来，乱嚷乱叫说："我要往祠堂里哭太爷去。那里承望到如今，生下这些畜生来！每日家偷狗戏鸡，爬灰的爬灰，养小叔子的养小叔子，我什么不知道？咱们'胳膊折了往袖子里藏'！"(*DRM*, Chap. 7: 214)

Then he let loose a flood of abuse in which even Jia Zhen was included.

"Let me go to the Ancestral Temple to weep for my old master," he fumed. "Little did he expect to beget such degenerates, a handful of rutting dogs and bitches in heat, day in and day out scratching in the ashes and carrying on with younger brothers-in-law. Don't think you can fool me. I only tried to hide the broken arm in your sleeve..." (*DRM*, Chap. 7: 215)

"偷狗戏鸡" is a euphemism indicating adultery between a married man and a married woman, which is unknown to his wife or her husband. "爬灰" euphemistically refers to adultery between a man and his daughter-in-law. "养小叔子" means adultery between a woman and her younger brother-in-law.

4.2.5   Excreta and Secretion

Euphemisms related to excreta are "小恭", "小解", "解手", "更衣", "方便" and "净桶". Euphemisms for secretion of women are "月信", "庚信", "下红" and "行经".

> Example 10:
> 那先生笑说道："大奶奶这个症候，可是那众位耽搁了。要在初次行经的日期，就用药治起来，不但断无今日之患，而且此时已痊愈了。"(*DRM*, Chap. 10: 282, 284)
> "Those gentlemen have delayed your lady's recovery," said the doctor. "If she had taken the right medicine when she first missed her menses, she'd have been quite well by now." (*DRM*, Chap. 10: 283, 285)

"行经" is a euphemism for menses.

4.2.6   Pregnancy and Birth

Related euphemisms for pregnancy and birth are "喜", "喜脉", "落草", "膝下荒凉", "支庶不盛", "子孙有限", "不大生养" and "子嗣艰难".

> Example 11:
> 邢夫人接着说道："别是喜罢？"(*DRM*, Chap. 10: 290)
> "Can she be pregnant?" asked Lady Xing. (*DRM*, Chap. 10: 291)

"喜" is a commonly accepted expression that euphemistically means pregnancy.

Example 12:

袭人道："连一家子也不知来历，上头还有现成的眼儿，听得说，落草时是从他口里掏出来的。等我拿来你看便知。"(*DRM*, Chap. 3: 90)

Xiren told her [Daiyu], "Not a soul in the whole family knows where it comes from. It was found in his mouth, we hear, when he was born, with a hole for a cord already made in it. Let me fetch it here to show you." (*DRM*, Chap. 3: 91)

"落草" euphemistically refers to one's birth.

4.2.7 Ageing

Euphemisms indicating ageing are: "有了春秋", "上年纪", "有年纪" and "暮年人".

Example 13:

贾政便使人上来对王夫人说："姨太太已有了春秋，外甥年轻，不知庶务，在外住着，恐又要生事……"(*DRM*, Chap. 4: 114)

Then Jia Zheng sent a message to his wife saying, "My sister-in-law has seen many springs and autumns, and my nephew is young and inexperienced. He may get into some scrapes if they live outside…" (*DRM*, Chap. 4: 115)

"有了春秋" means getting on years.

4.2.8 Love and Affection

Euphemisms of this type are: "儿女私情", "女怨男痴", "缠绵", "私传表记", "表赠私物", "风情月债" and "私情密意".

Example 14:

那仙姑笑道："吾居离恨天之上，灌愁海之中，乃放春山遣香洞太虚幻境警幻仙姑是也：司人间之风情月债，掌尘世之女怨男痴……"

(*DRM*, Chap. 5: 130)

"My home is above the Sphere of Parting Sorrow in the Sea of Brimming Grief", she answered with a smile. "I am the Goddess of Disenchantment from the Grotto of Emanating Fragrance on the Mountain of Expanding Spring in the Illusory Land of Great Void. I preside over romances and unrequited love on earth, the grief of women and the passion of men in the mundane world [...]" (*DRM*, Chap. 5: 131)

Here "风情月债" and "女怨男痴" euphemistically refer to the love and affection especially between young men and young women.

4.2.9　Marriage and Concubinage

Euphemisms for marriage are: "大喜", "出阁", "出门", "圆房", "终身大事" and "男女大事". And there is a great variety of euphemisms for concubinage: "二房", "姨娘", "妾", "偏房", "通房丫头", "旁边人", "跟前人", "房里人", "屋里人", "收", "收房", "收在房里", "收在屋里", "收在屋内" and "放在屋里".

> Example 15:
> "……从小儿大妹妹顽笑着，就有杀伐决断，如今出了阁，又在那府里办事，越发历练老成了……" (*DRM*, Chap. 13: 346)
> "[...] Ever since she was a child at play Cousin Xifeng has known her own mind, and by managing the other house since her marriage she's gained experience [...]" (*DRM*, Chap. 13: 347)

This is uttered by Jia Zhen when he pleads with Wang Xifeng to help handle Qin Keqing's funeral affairs. Now he's commending Xifeng for her prominent capabilities. Here "出了阁" means "get married".

> Example 16:
> 金桂笑道："这话好不通。你爱谁，就把谁收在房里，省得别人

看着不雅。我可要什么呢？"(*DRM*, Chap. 80: 2442)

"What senseless talk!" she retorted. "If you've taken a fancy to someone, say so outright, and we can make her your concubine to avoid any hint of scandal. Why should I care?" (*DRM*, Chap. 80: 2443)

Xue Pan, a frivolous guy, takes a fancy to Baochan, his wife's maid. Here "收在房里" means to marry the maid and take her as his concubine.

4.2.10　Women's Jealousy in Love

Euphemisms related to women's jealousy in love are: "醋", "泼醋", "吃醋", "揽酸", "醋罐", "醋坛", "醋瓮", "吃醋拈酸", "醋汁子老婆" and "争风吃醋".

Example 17:

迎春方哭哭啼啼的在王夫人房中诉委曲，说孙绍祖"一味好色，好赌酗酒，家中所有的媳妇、丫头将及淫遍。略劝过两三次，便骂我是'醋汁子老婆拧出来的'。又说老爷曾收着他五千银子，不该使了他的……"(*DRM*, Chap. 80: 2462)

"Sun Shaozu cares for nothing but women, gambling and drinking," she [Yingchun] sobbed. "He's had affairs with practically all our maids and young servants' wives. When I remonstrated mildly two or three times, he cursed me for being jealous, saying I must have been steeped in vinegar. He also says he put five thousand taels in father's safe-keeping and he shouldn't have spent it […]" (*DRM*, Chap. 80: 2463)

Here "醋汁子老婆" refers to a woman who is jealous of her rival in love.

4.2.11　Address Terms for Interpersonal Relations

There are mainly two types of euphemisms for interpersonal relations in the novel. Honorifics are a type of commonly used euphemisms: "老爷",

"太太", "先父", "令亲大人", "大爷", "先生", "西宾", "尊兄", "世兄", "老兄", "老先生", "尊夫人" and "尊府". These terms are intended to show respect for others and satisfy their need for self-esteem or even vanity. The other type includes self-denigrating terms or self-effacing terms such as "寒族", "在下", "敝友", "贱荆", "贱内", "小女", "晚生", "晚晚生", "弟" and "小弟". "先" is a term of respect for the deceased. A typical example is "这是你先珠大哥的媳妇珠大嫂" (This is the wife of your late cousin Zhu).

Example 18:

贾蓉道: "先生实在高明, 如今恨相见之晚。就请先生看一看脉息, 可治不可治, 以便使家父母放心。" (*DRM*, Chap. 10: 280)

"I see you are an authority," replied Jia Rong. "I am only sorry we did not meet earlier. Do examine her and let us know if she can be cured, to spare my father further anxiety." (*DRM*, Chap. 10: 281)

Jia Rong, showing his due respect for Doctor Zhang for his superior medical knowledge or expertise, addresses him as "先生".

Example 19:

如海道: "天缘凑巧, 因贱荆去世, 都中家岳母念及小女无人依傍教育, 前已遣了男女船只来接, 因小女未曾大痊, 故未及行……" (*DRM*, Chap. 3: 58)

"What a lucky coincidence!" exclaimed Ruhai. "Since my wife's death my mother-in-law in the capital has been worried because my daughter has no one to bring her up. She has sent two boats with male and female attendants to fetch the child, but I delayed her departure while she was unwell [...]" (*DRM*, Chap. 3: 59)

Two self-depreciatory euphemisms are used here: "贱荆" and "小女". "贱荆" refers to Lin Ruhai's late wife, Jia Min whereas "小女" refers to his daughter, Lin Daiyu.

4.2.12 Servants and Housemaids

Euphemisms referring to servants and housemaids are: "家人", "家里人", "家下人", "家下众人" and "底下姑娘们". Their children are called "家生", "家生子", "家生子儿", "家生女儿" and "小子".

Example 20:

饭毕，因天黑了，尤氏说："先派两个小子送了这秦相公家去。"(*DRM*, Chap. 7: 210)

After dinner, because it was dark, Madam You suggested that they send two men-servants to see Qin Zhong home... (*DRM*, Chap. 7: 211)

Madam You refers to the men-servants as "小子".

4.2.13 Personal Names Regarded as Taboos

In one of Mencius' dialogues is an exposition of the long-held tradition of name taboo in ancient China: "An individual's given name, rather than his/her family name, is to be tabooed. The family name is common whereas the given name is unique." (讳名不讳姓，姓所同也，名所独也。) One's given name, especially the one of an emperor or a senior is not to be directly mentioned. Such practice was prevalent in old times and is still fairly popular in modern times. A typical example is found in the novel.

Example 21:

雨村拍案笑道："怪道这女学生读至凡书中有"敏"字，皆念作"密"字，每每如是，写字遇着"敏"字，又减一二笔，我心中就有些疑惑。今听你说的，是为此无疑矣。怪道我这女学生言语举止另是一样，不与近日女子相同，度其母必不凡，方得其女，今知为荣府之孙，又不足罕矣，可伤上月竟亡故了。"(*DRM*, Chap. 2: 52)

Yucun pounded the table with a laugh. "No wonder my pupil always pronounces min as mi and writes it with one or two strokes missing. That puzzled me, but now you've explained the reason. Now no wonder she talks and behaves so differently from the general run of young ladies nowadays. I suspected she must have had an unusual mother. If she's a grand-daughter of the Rong family that explains it. What a pity that her mother died last month." (*DRM*, Chap. 2: 53)

Lin Daiyu's mother's name is "贾敏". The given name "敏" is not to be mentioned directly. Whenever she has to pronounce "敏" or write the character "敏", she will pronounce it as "密" or write it with one or two strokes missing. This is a practice out of sheer respect for her late mother.

4.2.14   Moral Standing and Disposition

Euphemisms describing one's low moral standing and unpleasant disposition are: "不好听", "不干净", "性子不好", "不妥" and so on.

> Example 22:
> [王熙凤] 无人处只和尤二姐说："妹妹的名声很不好听，连老太太、太太们都知道了，说妹妹在家做女孩儿就不干净，又和姐夫有些首尾……" (*DRM*, Chap. 69: 2074)
>
> When the two of them were alone she told Second Sister, "You have such a bad name, sister, even the old lady and the mistresses have heard about it. They say that while still a girl you were unchaste and intimate with your brother-in-law." (*DRM*, Chap. 69: 2075)

Both "名声很不好听" and "不干净" euphemistically refer to Second Sister's frivolity.

4.2.15   Buddhist Practice and Buddhist Practitioner

The traditional Chinese idea of family-orientedness holds it a shame to the whole family for its member to become a monk or nun. This gives rise to a number of euphemisms: "入空门", "独卧青灯古佛旁", "绞头发的念头",

"这几根烦恼鬓毛剃去", "斩情归水月", "出家人" and "槛外人".

Example 23:

话未说完, 把个贾政气的面如金纸, 大喝: "快拿宝玉来!" 一面说一面便往里边书房去, 喝令: "今日再有人劝我, 我把这冠带家私一应交与他与宝玉过去! 我免不得做个罪人, 把这几根烦恼鬓毛剃去, 寻个干净去处自了, 也免得上辱先人下生逆子之罪。" (*DRM*, Chap. 33: 912)

"Fetch Baoyu! Quick!" he roared.

He strode to his study fuming, "If anybody tries to stop me this time, I'll make over to him my official insignia and property and let him serve Baoyu! How can I escape blame? I'll shave off these remaining hairs to a monastery, there to atone for disgracing my ancestors by begetting such a monster." (*DRM*, Chap. 33: 913)

"把这几根烦恼鬓毛剃去" means to have the hair shaven off and become a monk.

4.3   Situational Euphemisms

In contrast to conventional euphemisms, situational euphemisms are not yet conventionalized as set expressions. They are context-dependent and conversely work for the context.

4.3.1 Euphemisms with Semantic Fuzziness

Words that are abstract, fuzzy and general in meaning are characterized with vagueness, which produces indeterminacy and ambiguity. With such properties, a euphemistic effect may be achieved because such words can blur or obscure the undesirable meanings of those tabooed words.

Typical examples are "事", "东西" and "原故". In Li Guonan's (2001) words, "那件事", "那个问题" and "那东西" are words of a high degree of vagueness. In the novel, "事", for example, is in frequent collocation with other words for a certain degree of specificity: "人事", "房帷事" and "男女之事", which all implicitly indicate sexual intercourse.

Besides, both "东西" and "原故" refer, in a roundabout way, to something that is tabooed or unwanted.

Example 24:
"……老太太的事出来,一应都是全了的,不过零星杂项使费……"
(*DRM*, Chap. 55: 1604)
"[…] As for the old lady's funeral, all the preparations have already been made […]" (*DRM*, Chap. 55: 1605)

Wang Xifeng is talking to Ping'er about household expenses. She first mentions the forthcoming marriages of Baoyu, Daiyu, Yingchun and Jiahuan, which will not cost too much. Then when she speaks of "老太太的事", it is easily understood as the funeral preplanned for the Lady Dowager.

Example 25:
尤氏道:"我也暗暗的叫人预备了。就是那件东西不得好木头,且慢慢的办着呢。"(*DRM*, Chap. 11: 306)
"I've had them secretly prepared. But I can't get any good wood for you know what, so I've let that go for the time being." (*DRM*, Chap. 11: 307)

Tabooed and unspeakable is death as well as anything related to it. The interpretation of "那件东西" is context-dependent. Wang Xifeng and Madam You are talking about preparations that have to be made considering the rapidly worsening health of Qin Keqing. "那件东西", according to the context, refers to the "coffin" for Qin Keqing's funeral should anything unwanted happen very soon.

Example 26:

袭人亦含羞笑问道："你梦见什么故事了？是那里流出来的那些脏东西？"宝玉道："一言难尽。"(*DRM*, Chap. 6: 164)

With an embarrassed smile, she asked, "What did you dream about to dirty yourself like that?"

"It's a long story," answered Baoyu. (*DRM*, Chap. 6: 165)

"那些脏东西", according to the context, is sperm.

4.3.2 Euphemisms with Syntactical Devices

According to Bolinger and Sears (1981), "Euphemism is not restricted to the lexicon. There are grammatical ways of toning something down without actually changing the content of the message" (149). That means syntactical devices are also a way of mitigating the force of message and creating euphemistic flavor. The process of mitigation, in Fraser's (1978) words, is "the intentional softening or easing of the force of the message— a modulation of the basic message intended by the speaker" (22). And such mitigation can be realized both internally and externally.

Negation

In the novel there are such negative expressions as "不好", "不牢", "不快", "不宁", "不大好", "不爽快" and "不自在". These are all context-dependent and have much to do with health problems. A negative expression sounds milder than the sheer opposite/antonym of what follows "不".

Example 27:

凤姐儿说："蓉哥儿，你且站住。你媳妇今日到底是怎么着？"贾蓉皱皱眉说道："不好么！婶子回来，瞧瞧去，就知道了。"于是贾蓉出去了。(*DRM*, Chap. 11: 292)

"Just a minute, Master Rong," interposed Xifeng. "Tell me, how is your wife today?"

"Not well at all." The young man's face clouded. "Do go and see for yourself, aunt, on your way home." He left without saying any more. (*DRM*, Chap. 11: 293)

Wang Xifeng is inquiring about Qin Keqing's health. "不好" actually means "bad". According to the context, it refers to Qin Keqing's extremely terrible state of health. But "不好" sounds milder than "坏" or "糟糕".

Hedges

The term hedge was coined by George Lakoff as a linguistic device to create semantic indistinctness. In his article *Hedges: A Study in Meaning Criteria and the Logic of Fuzzy Concepts* (1972) Lakoff defines hedges as "words whose job is to make things fuzzier or less fuzzy" (459). A hedge can occur as an approximator or a shield. As an approximator, it serves to diminish the truth value of an utterance.

In the novel, "不大" contextually means "not at all" in effect. But the speaker usually denies this absoluteness of negation. So "不大" euphemistically means "not quite" or "not exactly" for the purpose of toning down the extremity. For example, "不大认得" euphemistically means "not know quite well" and "不大走动" means "not call on each other frequently".

> Example 28:
> 凤姐忙说:"周姐姐,快搀起来! 别拜罢,请坐。我年轻,不大认得,可也不知是什么辈数, 不敢称呼。" (*DRM*, Chap. 6: 180)
> "Help her up, Sister Zhou, she mustn't curtsey to me. Ask her to be seated. I'm too young to remember what our relationship is, so I don't know what to call her." (*DRM*, Chap. 6: 181)

According to the context, Wang Xifeng has never met Granny Liu before. In fact, she does not know her at all. But Wang Xifeng tactfully and euphemistically diminishes the truth value by saying "不大认得", meaning "not know quite well". The tone is softened and the speaker-listener relations are thus shortened to a certain extent.

"未免" is also a euphemistic expression that helps mitigate the tone of complaint or criticism.

Example 29:

周瑞家的听了道："咳，我的姥姥，告诉不得你呢。这位凤姑娘年纪虽小，行事却比世人都大。如今出挑的美人一样的模样儿，少说些有一万个心眼子。再要赌口齿，十个会说话的男人也说他不过。回来你见了就信了。就只一件，待下人未免太严些个。"(*DRM*, Chap. 6: 174, 176)

"You don't know the half of it, my dear granny. Young as she is, she handles things much better than anyone else. She's growing up a beauty too. Clever isn't the word for her! As for talking, ten eloquent men are no match for her. You'll see for yourself by and by. If she has a fault, it's that she's rather hard on those below her." (*DRM*, Chap. 6: 175, 177)

This is Mrs. Zhou's comment on Wang Xifeng. According to her, Wang Xifeng is beautiful, clever, eloquent and sophisticated on the one hand, but on the other hand, she is inclined to treat the servants harshly. Since it is a complaint that Mrs. Zhou is not entitled to make straightforwardly, "未免" is deviously used to soften the tone of complaint and a euphemistic effect is achieved.

In addition, "未必" can be used euphemistically to mean "not likely".

Example 30:

秦氏拉着凤姐儿的手，强笑道："……公婆跟前未得孝顺一天，就是婶娘这样疼我，我就有十分孝顺的心，如今也不能够了。我自想着，未必熬的过年去呢。"(*DRM*, Chap. 11: 294, 296)

Holding Xifeng's hand, Keqing forced a smile.

"[...] and I haven't been able to be a good daughter-in-law. I want so much to show how I appreciate your goodness, aunt, but it's no longer in my power now. I doubt I shall last the year out." (*DRM*, Chap. 11: 295, 297)

Qin Keqing is pining away and she is quite aware that her poor health will not spare her much time. Given the present condition, she is not likely to last the year out. Yet she uses "未必" to soften the tone.

When the act referred to by the speaker is compulsory, "少不得" can be used to euphemistically tone down the imposition (Lu Xingji & Gao Mingluan, 1985: 430).

Example 31:

凤姐听说，笑着忙跪下，将尤氏那边所编之话，一五一十细细的说了一遍，"少不得老祖宗发慈心，允许他进来，住一年以后再圆房。"(*DRM*, Chap. 69: 2066)

Smiling, Xifeng promptly knelt down to relate in detail the story she had made up in Madam You's room. "Do take pity on her, Old Ancestress," she pleaded. "Let her move in now, and after a year they can be formally married." (*DRM*, Chap. 69: 2067)

"少不得" helps soften the tone of request or compulsion.

Example 32:

贾瑞只要暂息此事，又悄悄的劝金荣说："俗话说的好，'杀人不过头点地。'你既惹出事来，少不得下点儿气儿，磕个头就完事了。"(*DRM*, Chap. 9: 268)

Jia Rui, anxious to smooth things over, urged Jin Rong softly, "Remember the proverb 'A murderer can only lose his head.' Since you began this, you must humble yourself a little. Once you've kowtowed, that will be the end of it." (*DRM*, Chap. 9: 269)

Here Jia Rui advises Jin Rong to be sensible enough to make an apology with the act of kowtow although this might not readily be acceptable to Jin Rong.

"未必不" is double negation euphemistically referring to possibility.

Example 33:

贾琏道："真不真，他那官儿也未必保得长。将来有事，只怕未必不连累咱们，宁可疏远着他好。"(*DRM*, Chap. 72: 2182)

"Whether it's true or not, he's not likely to keep his present post for long," replied Jia Lian. "If he gets into trouble, I'm afraid we'll be involved. It would be better to keep clear of him." (*DRM*, Chap. 72: 2183)

Jia Lian is worried that they are likely to get involved should anything unwanted happen to Jia Yucun. So "未必不" refers to possibility.

"且", "暂且" and "还" can also help soften the tone and achieve a euphemistic effect.

Example 34:
贾母道："你看他是怎么样?"凤姐儿说："暂且无妨，精神还好呢。"(*DRM*, Chap. 11: 306)

[The Lady Dowager] "How did she seem?"

[Wang Xifeng] "For the present there's nothing to fear. She's in good spirits." (*DRM*, Chap. 11: 307)

"暂且" means "for the time being" or "temporarily". "还" means "still". Wang Xifeng is not prepared to worry the Lady Dowager at the moment and a delay of report seems the best policy. So she uses "暂且" and "还" to mitigate the seriousness of Qin Keqing's illness.

Unlike an apporximator, a shield does not have anything to do with the truth value of an utterance, but with the speaker. That is, it reveals the speaker's wishfulness, uncertainty or ambivalence. The following are examples of shields that are adopted to create a euphemistic effect.

As mild ways of expression "只怕" and "恐" are shields meaning "be afraid".

Example 35:
贾珍笑问："价值几何?"薛蟠笑道："拿一千两银子来，只怕也没处买去。什么价不价，赏他们几两工钱就是了。"(*DRM*, Chap. 13: 338)

Jia Zhen, his face radiant, inquired the price.

"You couldn't buy this for a thousand taels," replied Xue Pan with a smile. "Don't worry about the price. All you need pay for is having it made up." (*DRM*, Chap. 13: 339)

"只怕" here indicates in a roundabout way the fact that such timber is not available anywhere else.

Face Markers

"望", "祈" and "请" are face markers that help soften the force of imposition or compulsion.

Example 36:

黛玉笑回道："舅母爱恤赐饭，原不应辞，只是还要过去拜见二舅舅，恐领了赐去不恭，异日再领，未为不可。望舅母容谅。"(*DRM*, Chap. 3: 72, 74)

"Thank you very much, aunt, you're too kind," said Daiyu. "Really I shouldn't decline. But it might look rude if I delayed in calling on my second uncle. Please excuse me and let me stay another time." (*DRM*, Chap. 3: 73, 75)

In this example, "望" helps mitigate the imposing force of the request.

Rhetorical Questions

"岂不" is usually used to help give mild suggestions, advice or invitation.

Example 37:

宝钗便道："还像适才坐着，大家说说笑笑，岂不斯文些儿。"(*DRM*, Chap. 22: 620)

"Why not sit down as you were before," said Baochai, "and chat with us in more civilized way?" (*DRM*, Chap. 22: 621)

Baochai is making a suggestion that Baoyu keep quiet. To make her advice sound mild and acceptable, she uses "岂不".

Example 38:

宝玉道："好容易会着，晚上同散岂不好？"湘莲道："你那令姨表兄还是那样，再坐着未免生事，不如我回避了倒好。"(*DRM*, Chap. 47: 1336)

"It's so rarely we have a chance to meet, can't you stay until the party breaks up this evening?"

"That honourable maternal cousin of yours is up to his old tricks again. If I stay, there may be trouble. I'd better keep out of his way." (*DRM*, Chap. 47: 1337)

In this example, Baoyu asks Liu Xianglian to stay for the party.

Particles

Particles like "罢" are usually placed at the end of a sentence to help modulate the imposing force of a message.

Example 39:

凤姐乃道："这是二十两银子，暂且给这孩子做件冬衣罢。若不拿着，就真是怪我了。这钱雇车坐罢。改日无事，只管来逛逛，方是亲戚们的意思。天也晚了，也不虚留你们了，到家里该问好的问个好儿罢。"（*DRM*, Chap.6: 186)

"Here's twenty taels to make the child some winter clothes. If you refuse it, I shall think you're offended. With the cash you can hire a cart. When you've time, drop in again as relatives should. It's growing late, I won't keep you for no purpose. Give my compliments to everyone at home to whom I should be remembered." (*DRM*, Chap.6: 187, 189)

"做件冬衣"，"雇车坐" and "问个好儿" are all imperatives that sound imposing even though they are well-intended. When the particle "罢" is put at the end of such imperatives , the tone is softened and a euphemistic effect is achieved.

Question Words

Question words are used in statements to indicate something unwanted or tabooed. "怎样" and "怎么样" are typical examples that euphemistically refer to poor health or death.

Example 40:

秦氏说道："好不好，春天就知道了。如今现过了冬至，又没怎样，或者好的了也未可知。"（*DRM*, Chap. 11: 306)

"Whether I'll ever recover or not we'll know when spring comes," said Keqing. "Maybe I shall, for the winter solstice has passed and I'm no worse." (*DRM*, Chap. 11: 307)

"没怎么样" implicitly means nothing worse has happened.

4.4   Summary

In this chapter euphemisms are classified into two main categories: conventional and situational. Then each category is subdivided with adequate examples that are selected inclusively from the character utterances in *DRM*. In general, conventional euphemisms in the collection are varied. The subcategories are found in extensive reference to devil and disaster, death and funeral affairs, disease and ill health, sex, excreta and secretion, pregnancy and birth, ageing, love and affection, marriage and concubinage, jealousy, address terms for interpersonal relations, servants and housemaids, personal names regarded as taboos, low moral standing and unpleasant disposition as well as Buddhist practice and practitioner. As is mentioned earlier, situational euphemisms are largely context-dependent, so the judgment of situational euphemisms has proved to be a tough job. This chapter has faithfully and objectively summarized and demonstrated two major ways that contribute to the construction of situational euphemisms: semantic fuzziness and syntactical devices. It is notewhothy that euphemized sentences are heavily context-dependent. They are not discussed in this chapter, but examples will be provided in the forthcoming chapter.

In Chapter Five demonstration analysis is going to be conducted. In the process of the analysis a variety of euphemisms that have been collected from the character utterances of *DRM* will be put under discussion within the theoretical framework of Spencer-Oatey's rapport management.

Chapter Five

Demonstration Analysis of Euphemisms in *DRM*

5.1 Introduction

It seems ubiquitous that every language is in possession of an array of linguistic options and devices in aid of the management of interpersonal relations. This is generally found in the illocutionary domain. According to Helen Spencer-Oatey (2007), the selection of speech act components, the degree of directness/indirectness, and the type and amount of upgraders/ downgraders all operate in the wording of speech acts. For instance, significant effects on interpersonal relationships can be achieved at all linguistic levels: "the choice of intonation and tone of voice, choice of lexis, choice of morphology and syntax, choice of terms of address and honorifics" (21).

It can be seen that in the categorization and description of euphemisms in Chapter Four euphemisms in *DRM* largely concern the wording of speech acts. To be more exact, they have resulted from choice of indirectness, choice of lexis, choice of morphology and choice of terms of address and honorifics.

According to Spencer-Oatey's theory of rapport management, there are three types of factors that influence strategy use. The first factor, namely, rapport orientation, is targeted at enhancement, maintenance, neglect or even challenge of rapport. The second set of factors relates to contextual variables. They are participation relations, message content, social/interactional roles, and communicative activity. A third set of factors has reference to pragmatic conventions.

Considering the major functions of euphemism and the remarkable characteristics of *DRM*, that is, the strict and rigid social hierarchy, complicated network of officialdom and intricate family relationship, Chapter Five aims to give prominence to one of the participation relations: power. In other words, the demonstration analysis will focus on the strategic use of euphemisms in the character utterances in terms of the effect of power relations. Meanwhile, all the other related factors such as rapport orientation, message content, social/interactional role and community activity will be included and discussed.

·❯ 5.2   Power

According to Spencer-Oatey (2007), power has a number of different labels: "social power, status, dominance, authority" (32). In essence, power means unequal relationship. Social psychologists French and Raven (1959) have identified five forms of power. They are coercive power (control over negative outcomes), reward power (control over positive outcomes), legitimate power (right to prescribe), referent power (power of example to be followed) and expert power (special knowledge or expertise control).

DRM boasts a cast of characters of every description that build up the hierarchical framework of power relations. There are about thirty main characters and quite a number of minor ones. The novel charts in detail two branches of the Jia clan. They are the Rongguo House and the Ningguo House, which adjacently stand in grandeur and splendor in the capital. Jia Yan and Jia Yuan, ancestors of the two houses, win the royal favour and are made Dukes respectively. This makes it possible for the two families to live in ease and comfort with substantial riches and power for quite a lengthy period of time. Jia Jing is grandson of Duke of Ningguo and has two children: Jia Zhen and Xichun. Qin Keqing, Jia Zhen's daughter-in-law, allegedly has affairs with him and dies young and childless. The Lady Dowager is wedded to Jia Daishan, son of Duke of Rongguo, and gives birth to three children: Jia She, Jia Zheng and Jia Min. It seems that the Rongguo House is a growing family. Jia Baoyu, son of Jia Zheng and Lady Wang, heir to the house, is one of the protagonists of the novel. He is much frowned on by his father but excessively doted on by his grandmother, the Lady Dowager. Lin Daiyu is granddaughter of the Lady Dowager. Xue Baochai is Baoyu's cousin on his mother's side. Jia Yuanchun, granddaughter of the Lady Dowager and Baoyu's elder sister, is made Imperial Consort. Wang Xifeng, Lady Wang's niece, is also Baoyu's cousin-in-law. She is arguably sophisticated, crafty but capable of managing the house. Jia Tanchun and Jia Huan are daughter and son of Concubine Zhao, who is inferior to Lady Wang and thus much despised by her. Such characters and all others are entwined in a network of power relations of various types.

The chief characters and their relationships in the Jia Family are presented in the following table.

Table 3   Chief characters in the novel and their relationships (Source: Preface, *DRM*)

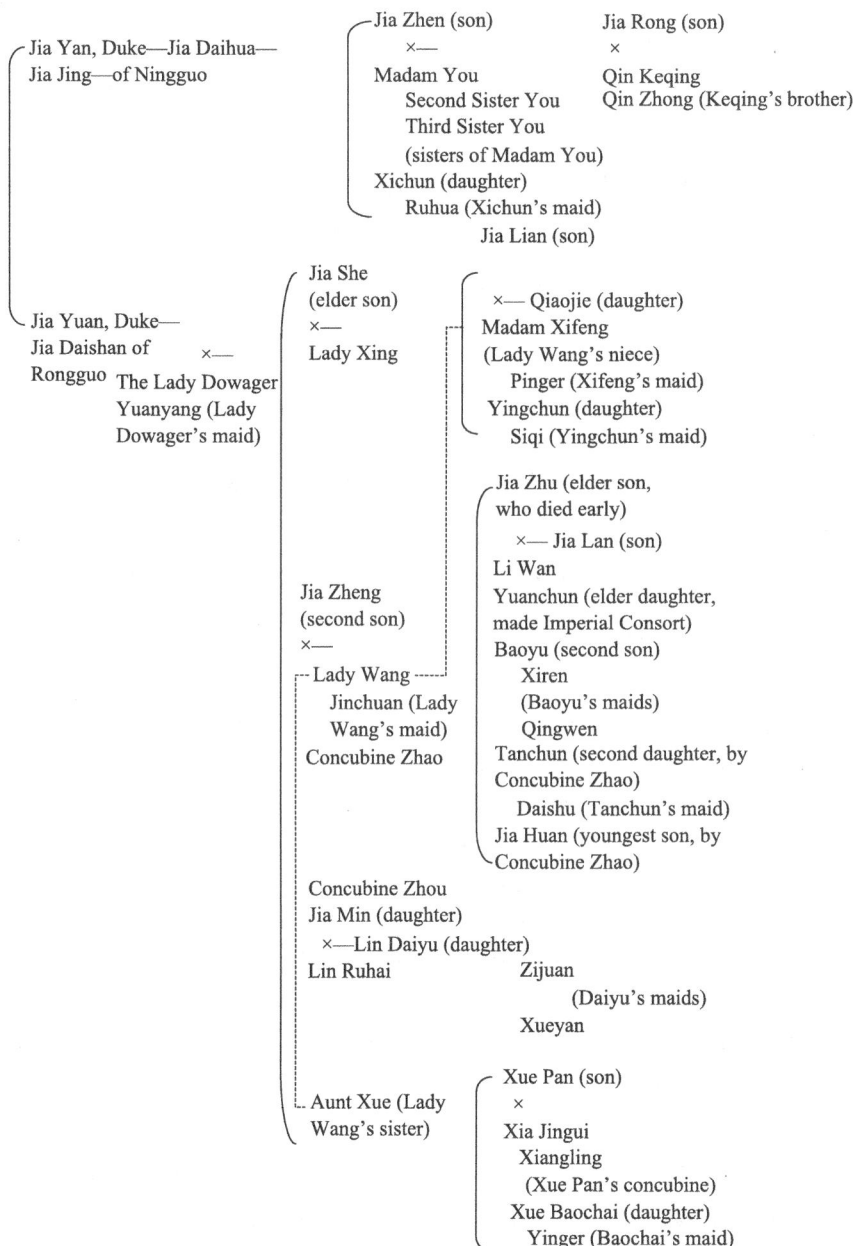

Jia Yan, Duke—Jia Daihua—
Jia Jing—of Ningguo

Jia Zhen (son)
×—
Madam You
   Second Sister You
   Third Sister You
   (sisters of Madam You)
Xichun (daughter)
   Ruhua (Xichun's maid)
    Jia Lian (son)

Jia Rong (son)
×
Qin Keqing
Qin Zhong (Keqing's brother)

Jia Yuan, Duke—
Jia Daishan of   ×—
Rongguo   The Lady Dowager
   Yuanyang (Lady
   Dowager's maid)

Jia She
(elder son)
×—
Lady Xing

×— Qiaojie (daughter)
Madam Xifeng
(Lady Wang's niece)
   Pinger (Xifeng's maid)
Yingchun (daughter)
   Siqi (Yingchun's maid)

Jia Zheng
(second son)
×—
Lady Wang
   Jinchuan (Lady
   Wang's maid)
Concubine Zhao

Jia Zhu (elder son,
   who died early)
   ×— Jia Lan (son)
Li Wan
Yuanchun (elder daughter,
made Imperial Consort)
Baoyu (second son)
   Xiren
   (Baoyu's maids)
   Qingwen
Tanchun (second daughter, by
Concubine Zhao)
   Daishu (Tanchun's maid)
Jia Huan (youngest son, by
Concubine Zhao)

Concubine Zhou
Jia Min (daughter)
  ×—Lin Daiyu (daughter)
Lin Ruhai

Zijuan
   (Daiyu's maids)
Xueyan

Aunt Xue (Lady
Wang's sister)

Xue Pan (son)
×
Xia Jingui
Xiangling
   (Xue Pan's concubine)
Xue Baochai (daughter)
   Yinger (Baochai's maid)

Some preliminary remarks are deemed most necessary with regard to the parties that are involved in a talk exchange. They are, according to Xu Shenghuan

(1992), "self, other, and the third party" (自身一方、对方、第三方) (1). As far as politeness is concerned, this tripartite framework is translated into "self's appropriate speech, respect for other and consideration of the third party" (注意自身、尊重对方、考虑第三方) (ibid. 1).

Xu Shenghuan believes that the third party deserves much notice. By the third party, Xu means "the one/those the communicative content concerns; the one/those present when communication is going on" (交际内容涉及到的人；交际时在场的人) (ibid. 3). This coincides with Spencer-Oatey's (2007) consideration of rapport in communication when she says "rapport management suggests more of a balance between self and other" (12). And in effect Spencer-Oatey's "other" refers to a combined idea of other and the third party.

As to the problem of what can be done and how to handle the third party, Xu Shenghuan (1992) proposes,

> Adequate attention should be paid to the third party present in the communication. Do not say anything that harms his/her identity or status. If necessary, say whatever suits his/her identity or status. Again adequate attention should be paid to the third party the communication concerns. Do not say anything that harms his/her identity or status. If necessary, say whatever suits his/her identity or status (充分注意到交际时在场的第三方，不说影响他们的身份地位的话，如果有需要，可以说适合于他们身份地位的话；充分注意到话语中提及的第三方，不说影响他们身份地位的话，如果有需要，可以说适合于他们身份地位的话。) (4).

Based on this trinity, Xu Shenghuan proposes a politeness principle that is made up of two components: "promoting relations among all the parties" (促进各方关系) (ibid. 4) and "applying politeness strategies" (运用礼貌策略) (ibid. 4). To be more exact, the promotion of relationships can be translated into self's appropriate speech, respect for other and consideration of the third party. And politeness strategies can be applied in two ways: positive (using modest, respectful or courteous speech) and negative (using moderate and neutral speech).

It must be pointed out that the third party is involved in a number of examples that have been collected from *DRM* for the sake of the present study. In such cases, Xu Shenghuan's consideration and Spencer-Oatey's idea of the third party will be taken into account in the demonstration analysis.

In the following examples, discussions are focused on the strategic use of euphemisms with regard to the influence of a number of power relations. The investigation is targeted at taking the relative power as a variable that influences the strategic use of euphemisms. The power relation types under study are mainly social power relations and familial power relations.

5.3   Social Power Relations

Social power relations in the present study include the relative power relations between the royal members and officials/subjects as well as those between social unequals.

5.3.1   The Absolute Royal Power

This section is meant to discuss the use of euphemisms as far as the absoluteness of royal power is concerned. Two examples are presented in which Yuanchun, the Imperial Consort is a central figure undeniably with a dominant power.

Imperial Consort-Official (Jia Yuanchun-Jia Zheng)

Jia Yuanchun is promoted to be Secretary of the Phoenix Palace with the title Worthy and Virtuous Consort. Now her Imperial Visitation to her parents' house is royally granted. The following are utterances with which Jia Zheng greets Yuanchun, his daughter, at the Grand View Garden.

Example 41:

贾政向元妃含泪启道："臣草芥寒门，鸠群鸦属之中，岂意得征凤鸾之瑞。今贵人上锡天恩，下昭祖德，此皆山川日月之精华，祖宗之远德，钟于一人，幸及政夫妇。且今上体天地生生之大德，垂古今未有之旷恩，虽肝脑涂地，岂能报效万一！惟朝乾夕惕，忠于厥职。伏愿圣君万岁千秋，乃天下苍生之福也。贵妃切勿以政夫妇残年为念。更祈自加珍爱惟勤慎肃恭以待上，庶不负上眷顾隆恩也。"(DRM, Chap. 18: 482, 484)

With tears too he replied, "Your subject, poor and obscure, little dreamed that our flock of common pigeons and crows would ever be blessed with a phoenix. Thanks to the Imperial favour and the virtue of our ancestors, your Noble Highness embodies the finest essence of nature and the accumulated merit of our forbears—such fortune has attended my wife and myself.

"His Majesty, who manifests the great virtue of all creation, has shown us such extraordinary and hitherto unknown favour that even if we dashed out our brains we could not repay one-thousandth part of our debt of gratitude. All I can do is to exert myself day and night, loyally carry out my official duties, and pray that our sovereign may live ten thousand years as desired by all under heaven.

"Your Noble Highness must not grieve your precious heart in concern for your ageing parents. We beg you to take better care of your own health. Be cautious, circumspect, diligent and respectful. Honour the Emperor and serve him well, so as to prove yourself not ungrateful for His Majesty's bountiful goodness and great kindness." (DRM, Chap. 18: 483, 485)

This is part of the conversation between Jia Zheng and Jia Yunachun, the Imperial Consort, who has recently won the favour of the Emperor and got promoted. In fact two pairs of relations are involved: Imperial Consort-official and father-daughter relations. But on this particular occasion the latter must give way to the former. That is, the Imperial Consort-official relational roles predominate the nature of the interaction. Therefore, Jia Zheng's utterances must be oriented towards rapport enhancement or at least rapport maintenance. All the influencing factors are shown in Table 4.

Table 4   Specification of all the influencing factors

Interactional roles	Imperial Consort-Official (Jia Yuanchun-Jia Zheng)
Rapport orientation	Jia Zheng's rapport enhancement/maintenance with Jia Yuanchun
Message content	Jia Zheng's encomia of the Imperial Consort; his unbounded gratitude to the Emperor; his utmost devotion to the Emperor; his exhortation to the Imperial Consort
Communicative activity	Greeting the Imperial Consort
Cost-benefit consideration	Making the utterances most beneficial to the Imperial Consort and least beneficial to the speaker himself

The absolute dominance of royal power determines that rapport-enhancement orientation or at least rapport-maintenance orientation must be held. As far as Jia Zheng is concerned, the message content is four-fold: singing the praises of the Imperial Consort, conveying his profound gratitude to the Emperor, showing his utmost devotion to the Emperor and expressing his exhortation to the Imperial Consort. The communicative activity is focused on greeting the Imperial Consort. When it comes to the cost-benefit consideration of the message content, Jia Zheng must make his remarks most beneficial to the Imperial Consort at the expense of the least benefit to himself. So appropriate wording of speech acts is of paramount importance. It is found that every word uttered by Jia Zheng is meticulously weighed and formally voiced. Despite the taking-for-granted closeness of father-daughter relationship, power precedes familial intimacy. Since monarch-official power relationship is put in the first place, Jia Zheng's utterances fully manifest his due respect for his daughter as

Imperial Consort and his own humbleness as an official.

Euphemisms like "臣", "草芥寒门", "鸠群鸦属", "贵人", "岂意得征凤鸾之瑞" and "虽肝脑涂地，岂能报效万一" are found in Jia Zheng's utterances. When he refers to himself as "臣" ("臣" and "君" are a pair of relation), his family as "草芥寒门", his family members as "鸠群鸦属", his wife and himself as "政夫妇" but his daughter as "贵人", he maintains the Imperial Consort's quality face and identity face (her public image as a consort) of inaccessible royal dignity. "岂意得征凤鸾之瑞" implies his pride in Yuanchun in terms of her quality face (her beauty, competence and virtue) and identity face of being an Imperial Consort much favoured by the Emperor and respected by all. "虽肝脑涂地，岂能报效万一" implicates the deep gratitude that he owes the Emperor. However, it is because of Yuanchun that he is lucky enough to win the Emperor's favour. So the utterance also means to maintain Yuanchun's quality face and identity face. Finally, to mitigate the imposing tone in his exhortation that sounds threatening to the Imperial Consort's equity right (in terms of her independent perspective), he uses "切勿以 …… 为念" and "更祈 ……".

In general, not a single face-threatening speech act is found in the lengthy strings of utterances. This might largely be attributable to the rigid social hierarchy and absolute monarchal power over everything including familial affection. In other words, familial intimacy must give way to the strict and inviolable social hierarchy. In this way, rapport between monarch and official is enhanced or at least maintained. "Giving face" to the hearer is typically significant to the management of this type of rapport. Consequently, this rapport-enhancement orientation or rapport-maintenance orientation has a desired orientation outcome. That is, the rapport outcome complies with the rapport orientation.

The management of the Imperial Consort's face and rights by means of euphemisms is thus shown in Table 5.

Table 5   Euphemisms used by Jia Zheng for the Imperial Consort's face and rights

Interactional roles		Face Management		Sociality Rights Management	
Imperial Consort-Official (Jia Yuanchun-Jia Zheng) Euphemisms		Quality face (personal/ independent perspective)	Identity face (social/ interdependent perspective)	Equity rights (personal/ independent perspective)	Association rights (social/ interdependent perspective)
Conventional euphemisms	Situational euphemisms				
臣			showing due respect for Jia Yuanchun in terms of her social role as the Imperial Consort		
草芥寒门		showing due respect for Jia Yuanchun in terms of her excellence and competence to be royally promoted	showing due respect for Jia Yuanchun in terms of her social role as the Imperial Consort (by denigrating self)		
鸠群鸦属		showing due respect for Jia Yuanchun in terms of her excellence and competence to be royally promoted	showing due respect for Jia Yuanchun in terms of her social role as the Imperial Consort (by denigrating self)		
贵人		showing due respect for Jia Yuanchun in terms of her excellence and competence to be royally promoted	showing due respect for Jia Yuanchun in terms of her social role as the Imperial Consort		
凤鸾之瑞		showing due respect for Jia Yuanchun in terms of her excellence and competence to be royally promoted	showing due respect for Jia Yuanchun in terms of her social role as the Imperial Consort		

Table 5   cont'd

Interactional roles		Face Management		Sociality Rights Management	
Imperial Consort-Official (Jia Yuanchun-Jia Zheng) Euphemisms		Quality face (personal/ independent perspective)	Identity face (social/ interdependent perspective)	Equity rights (personal/ independent perspective)	Association rights (social/ interdependent perspective)
Conventional euphemisms	Situational euphemisms				
贵妃		showing due respect for Jia Yuanchun in terms of her excellence and competence to be royally promoted	showing due respect for Jia Yuanchun in terms of her social role as the Imperial Consort		
上			showing due respect for the Emperor in terms of his social role		
	政夫妇		showing due respect for Jia Yuanchun in terms of her social role as the Imperial Consort (by humbling self)		
	虽肝脑涂地，岂能报效万一！	showing due respect for the Emperor in terms of His great virtue and benevolence	showing due respect for the Emperor in terms of his social role		
	切勿……为念			maintaining Jia Yuanchun's rights to freedom by mitigating the tone of imposition with "切勿……为念"	
	祈……			maintaining Jia Yuanchun's rights to freedom by mitigating the tone of imposition with "祈……"	

The following example shows how monarchal power precedes familial intimacy.

Imperial Consort–Subject (Jia Yuanchun-the Lady Dowager)

After Jia Zheng's withdrawal, the Imperial Consort inquires about Baoyu, her younger brother.

> Example 42:
>
> [贵妃] 因问："宝玉为何不进见?" 贾母乃启："无谕, 外男不敢擅入。" (*DRM*, Chap. 18: 484)
>
> Then she [the Imperial Consort] inquired why Baoyu had not come to greet her. The Lady Dowager explained that, unless specially summoned, as a young man without official rank he dared not presume. (*DRM*, Chap. 18: 485)

All the influencing factors are shown in the following table.

Table 6   Specification of all the influencing factors

Interactional roles	Imperial Consort-Subject (Jia Yuanchun-the Lady Dowager)
Rapport orientation	The Lady Dowager's rapport enhancement/maintenance with Jia Yuanchun
Message content	The reason for Baoyu's absence
Communicative activity	Answering the Imperial Consort's question
Cost-benefit consideration	Making the reply most beneficial to the Imperial Consort

Like Example 41, the nature of the Imperial Consort-subject relations predetermines the nature of the Lady Dowager's utterances to be a type of rapport-enhancement or rapport-maintenance orientation. The message content is about why Baoyu is not supposed to be present to greet the Imperial Consort. The communicative activity is for the Lady Dowager to answer the Imperial Consort's question in a most respectful way. As regards the cost-benefit consideration, the Lady Dowager must also make her reply most beneficial to the Imperial Consort. As far as the Lady Dowager, Yuanchun and Baoyu are concerned, Yuanchun's identity is three-fold: the Imperial

Consort, the Lady Dowager's granddaughter, and Baoyu's elder sister. Before Yuanchun enters the Palace, she's been under the care of the Lady Dowager. Needless to say, they are in very close grandmother-granddaughter relationship. As for Baoyu, her younger brother, she has been caring about him dearly. They are on intimate sister-brother terms. However, on this special occasion of Imperial Visitation, even the Lady Dowager is very scrupulous with etiquette and cautious with wording. Therefore, first consideration should be given to the Imperial Consort's social status as a royal member. Disregarding the sister-brother relations between Yuanchun and Baoyu, the Lady Dowager refers to Baoyu as "外男", which, in this particular context, is a euphemism that indicates a man other than a member of the royal house. Obviously, the Lady Dowager is trying to maintain Yuanchun's identity face as the Imperial Consort rather than her familial identity as Baoyu's elder sister. In other words, considering Yuanchun's social status as a royal member, Baoyu is not supposed to be her brother. In this case, the monarch-subject relations again overwhelm kinship and rapport-enhancement or rapport-maintenance orientation is thus achieved.

The management of the Imperial Consort's face by means of euphemism is thus shown in Table 7.

Table 7   Euphemism used by the Lady Dowager for the Imperial Consort's face

Interactional roles		Face Management		Sociality Rights Management	
the Imperial Consort-Subject (Jia Yuanchun-the Lady Dowager)		Quality face (personal/ independent perspective)	Identity face (social/ interdependent perspective)	Equity rights (personal/ independent perspective)	Association rights (social/ interdependent perspective)
Euphemism					
Conventional euphemism	Situational euphemism				
外男			showing due respect for Jia Yuanchun in terms of her social role as the Imperial Consort		

5.3.2 Social Unequals

Apart from the absolute dominance of royal power, the relationship between social unequals also takes effects on rapport orientation, interactional role, message content and rapport outcome.

Official–Attendant (Jia Yucun-Attendant)

Jia Yucun used to be the last of a line of scholars and officials. Being penniless, he had to stay with the monks in Gourd Temple, where he made a meagre living as a scrivener. Now he has taken up his post as prefect of Yingtian, where he chances upon an attendant, who happened to be one of those monks in Gourd Temple and knew him quite well.

> Example 43:
> ……至密室，侍从皆退去，只留门子服侍。这门子忙上来请安，笑问："老爷一向加官进禄，八九年来就忘了我了？"雨村道："却十分面善，只是一时想不起来。"那门子笑道："老爷真是贵人多忘事，把出身之地竟忘了，不记当年葫芦庙里之事了？"雨村听了，如雷震一惊，方想起往事。原来这门子本是葫芦庙内一个小沙弥，因被火之后，无处安身，欲投别庙去修行，又耐不得清凉景况，因想这件生意倒还轻省热闹，遂趁年纪蓄了发，充了门子。雨村那里辨得是他。便忙携手笑道："原来是故人。"(*DRM*, Chap. 4: 96)
>
> [...] Back in his private office he dismissed everyone but the attendant, who went down on one knee in salute, then said with a smile:
>
> "Your Honour has risen steadily in the official world. After eight or nine years, do you still remember me?"
>
> "Your face looks very familiar, but I can't place you."
>
> The attendant smiled. "High officials have short memories," he said. "So you've forgotten the spot you started from, Your Honour, and what happened in Gourd Temple?"
>
> At this disconcerting remark, the past came back to Yucun like the crash of a thunder-bolt. Now this attendant had been a novice in Gourd Temple. When the fire left him stranded he decided that work in

a yamen would be easier and, having had enough of monastic austerity, instead of going to another temple he had taken advantage of his youth to grow his hair again and get this post. No wonder Yucun had failed to recognize him.

Now, taking his hand, the prefect observed with a smile: "So we are old acquaintances." (*DRM*, Chap. 4: 97)

All the influencing factors are shown in the following table.

Table 8 Specification of all the influencing factors

Interactional roles	Official-Attendant (Jia Yucun-Attendant)
Rapport orientation	The attendant's rapport enhancement/maintenance with Jia Yucun
Message content	Their acquaintance in the old days; the attendant's flattery to Jia Yucun
Communicative activity	A chat between Jia Yucun and the attendant
Cost-benefit consideration	Making the message more beneficial to Jia Yucun; making the message somewhat beneficial to the attendant himself

Jia Yucun is now quite different from what he used to be. He has been working up from a pitiful penniless guy to prefect of Yingtian. Considering his current social status and relative power, the humble attendant means to enhance or maintain their rapport for possible promotion on his part in the future. For the attendant, his message content is mainly two-fold: their acquaintance in the old days and his flattery to Jia Yucun. The communicative activity is a chat between prefect of Yingtian (Jia Yucun) and his attendant.

Despite the fact that they used to be acquaintances the attendant now addresses Jia Yucun with an honorific "老爷" to maintain his identity face. To Jia Yucun flattery is deemed beneficial whereas the topic of the old days is certainly face-threatening. By euphemistically saying "老爷一向加官进禄" and "老爷真是贵人多忘事", the attendant means to maintain Jia Yucun's quality face in terms of his competence on the one hand and his identity face in terms of his social role on the other. Yet he does not fail to mildly complain about Jia Yucun's forgetfulness: "老爷一向加官进禄, 八九年来就忘了我了?" and "老爷真是贵人多忘事" serve to mitigate the tone of complaint.

Besides, "不记当年葫芦庙里之事了?" appears to be a rhetorical question, which implies that Jia Yucun surely remembers the very place (Gourd Temple) and the very people (the monks) he ever stayed and worked with there. "葫芦庙里之事" is now the background knowledge only shared by Jia Yucun and the attendant. To Jia Yucun, "葫芦庙" is an epitome of his past indecent life with hardly any ways and means for a living. In effect, mention of "葫芦庙" threatens Jia Yucun's equity rights because it is much too personal. It also threatens his quality face, in other words, his self-esteem in terms of his inability to make a living in the past. Meanwhile, his identity face is threatened in terms of his sense of public worth. Enough is enough. The attendant knows better than to hint more details in relation to "葫芦庙", for details seem more than unpleasant and face-threatening. The fuzzy word "事" in "葫芦庙里之事" serves euphemistically and inclusively to refer to Jia Yucun's past experience, a handle against him, but at the same time help tone down the threat. At this very moment Jia Yucun is at least not seemingly offended, for willingly or unwillingly he takes the attendant's hand with a smile and says, "So we are old acquaintances." (便忙携手笑道: "原来是故人。") There and then the rapport outcome complies with the rapport orientation. But later on, it turns out that Jia Yucun finds fault with the attendant and sends him into exile simply because the attendant seems to be quite in the know of his past life.

The management of Jia Yucun's face and rights by means of euphemisms is thus shown in Table 9.

Table 9　Euphemisms used by the attendant for Jia Yucun's face and rights

Interactional roles		Face Management		Sociality Rights Management	
Official-Attendant (JiaYucun-Attendant) Euphemisms		Quality face (personal/ independent perspective)	Identity face (social/ interdependent perspective)	Equity rights (personal/ independent perspective)	Association rights (social/ interdependent perspective)
Conventional euphemisms	Situational euphemisms				
老爷			showing due respect for Jia Yucun in terms of his social role as prefect of Yingtian		
	老爷一向加官进禄	showing due respect for Jia Yucun in terms of his competence and official advancement	showing due respect for Jia Yucun in terms of his social role as prefect of Yingtian		
	老爷真是贵人多忘事	threatening Jia Yucun's quality face in terms of his forgetfulness (poor memory)	mitigating the tone of complaint with "贵人", a term of respect for Jia Yucun regarding his social role		
	不记当年葫芦庙里之事了？	threatening Jia Yucun's quality face in terms of his incompetence to make ends meet in the past	threatening Jia Yucun's identity face in terms of his social inferiority in the past		maintaining Jia Yucun's rights to care and consideration from other people with "事", whose semantic fuzziness implicates his unmentionable past experience

Mistress–Doctor (Lady Wang & Wang Xifeng-Doctor)

Generally, a doctor claims authority and deserves respect because he/she has exclusive expertise in medicine. But the Jias, on the other hand, have the reward or coercive power over the doctor. Considering the relative power, the doctor is supposed to be cautious enough to use euphemisms when reporting Dajie's illness to Lady Wang and Wang Xifeng.

Example 44:

谁知凤姐之女大姐儿病了，正乱着请大夫来诊过脉。大夫便说："替夫人奶奶们道喜，姐儿发热是见喜了，并非别病。" (*DRM*, Chap. 21: 582)

"I am happy to inform Her Ladyship and Madam Lian that the little girl's fever is simply due to smallpox." (*DRM*, Chap. 21: 583)

All the influencing factors are shown in Table 10.

Table 10   Specification of all the influencing factors

Interactional roles	Mistress-Doctor (Lady Wang & Wang Xifeng-Doctor)
Rapport orientation	The doctor's rapport maintenance with the mistresses and Dajie
Message content	The result of a medical check on Dajie
Communicative activity	A report of the medical check
Cost-benefit consideration	Making the message most beneficial to Dajie, Lady Wang and Wang Xifeng

As is mentioned above, a doctor has the expert power (special knowledge or expertise control). However, the Jias are a wealthy and influential family, so they have the reward power (control over positive outcomes) and coercive power (control over negative outcomes). In such a case, the doctor means to maintain rapport with the Jias. The message content is about a medical check on Dajie and the communicative activity is reporting the result. Report of the illness with straightforward expressions is certainly not preferable, for it is supposed to sound costly to the patient or the hearer. As is discussed in Chapter Four, disease, like death, is verbally prohibited and substituted with euphemisms. "见喜" euphemistically means "to have smallpox". Wang Xifeng's daughter has smallpox, but this is not to be directly mentioned. Rather, "见喜" is commonly accepted as a negative euphemism that is used for the sake of good luck. It is meant to maintain Dajie's association rights in terms of her entitlements to appropriate considerations from other people.

And when making a medical report to Lady Wang and Wang Xifeng, the doctor uses "道喜", another euphemism meaning reporting the illness for the purpose of maintaining Lady Wang's and Wang Xifeng's association rights to concerns and sympathy rather than shock. At the same time, the doctor does not forget to address the two mistresses with honorifics "夫人" and "奶奶" to show his due respect and therefore maintain the two ladies' identity face. In this way, nobody feels offended or embarrassed so that the purpose of maintaining rapport is achieved.

The management of face and rights on the part of Dajie and the mistresses by means of euphemisms is thus shown in Table 11.

Table 11　Euphemisms used by the doctor for face and rights of mistresses and Dajie

Interactional roles		Face Management		Sociality Rights Management	
Mistress-Doctor (Lady Wang & Wang Xifeng-Doctor)		Quality face (personal/ independent perspective)	Identity face (social/ interdependent perspective)	Equity rights (personal/ independent perspective)	Association rights (social/ interdependent perspective)
Euphemisms					
Conventional euphemisms	Situational euphemisms				
夫人奶奶们			showing due respect for Lady Wang and Wang Xifeng in terms of their privileged family background		
道喜					maintaining the rights of Lady Wang and Wang Xifeng to concerns and sympathy from other people
见喜					maintaining Dajie's rights to concerns and sympathy from other people

5.4 Familial Power Relations

The family power relations in the novel are further divided into two types: relations between family members and master-servant relations.

5.4.1 Unequal Kinship

In this part, euphemisms in the character utterances are discussed with regard to several pairs of unequal relations between the family members.

Husband–Wife (Jia Zheng-Lady Wang)

The following example is intended to demonstrate how euphemisms have to be used in terms of unequal husband-wife relations, namely, manus (man's absolute authority over his wife).

> Example 45:
> 贾政还欲打时，早被王夫人抱住板子。贾政道："罢了，罢了！今日必定要气死我才罢！"
> 王夫人哭道："宝玉虽然该打，老爷也要自重。况且炎天暑日的，老太太身上也不大好，打死宝玉事小，倘或老太太一时不自在了，岂不事大！"贾政冷笑道："倒休说这话。我养了这不肖的孽障，已不孝；教训他一番，又有众人护持；不如趁今日一发勒死了，以绝将来之患！"
> (*DRM*, Chap. 33: 916)
> Before his father [Jia Zheng] could beat him [Baoyu] any further, Lady Wang seized the rod with both hands.
> "This is the end!" roared Jia Zheng. "You're determined to be the death of me today."
> "I know Baoyu deserves a beating," sobbed Lady Wang. "But you mustn't wear yourself out, sir. It's a sweltering day and the old lady isn't well. Killing Baoyu is a small matter, but should anything happen to the old lady that would be serious."
> "Spare me this talk." Jia Zheng gave a scornful laugh. "I've already proved an unfilial son by begetting this degenerate. When I discipline him all of you protect him. I'd better strangle him now to avoid further

trouble." (*DRM*, Chap. 33: 917)

All the influencing factors are shown in Table 12.

Table 12   Specification of all the influencing factors

Interactional roles	Husband-Wife (Jia Zheng-Lady Wang)
Rapport orientation	Lady Wang's rapport maintenance with Jia Zheng and the Lady Dowager
Message content	Jia Zheng's health, hot weather and the Lady Dowager's ailment
Communicative activity	Pleading with Jia Zheng to forgive Baoyu
Cost-benefit consideration	Making the message most beneficial to Jia Zheng and Baoyu

Lady Wang means to maintain the husband-wife rapport, for she is in no position to have such rapport neglected or challenged. The message content is about Jia Zheng's health, the hot weather and the Lady Dowager's ailment. The communicative activity is for Lady Wang to plead with Jia Zheng to forgive Baoyu. The interactional roles must be taken into account in this case: the husband-wife relations in the feudal society endow man with every right and deprives his wife of any right. Lady Wang is now put in a tight corner: as mother she wants to save Baoyu from his father's beating but as wife she cannot make any stark protest, for traditionally a woman is not entitled to any say in the family and supposed to be unconditionally submissive to her husband. Consequently, she has to make her message most beneficial to Jia Zheng so that there might be hope of forgiveness of their son. At this moment of emergency, she uses an honorific "老爷" to address her husband and euphemistically pleads with him to stop beating by saying "宝玉虽然该打, 老爷也要自重". In this way, she maintains Jia Zheng's identity face ("老爷" in terms of his group role in the family) and his association rights ("老爷也要自重" in terms of his entitlements to concerns from others). Apart from that, Lady Wang uses an honorific "老太太" and other euphemistic expressions "况且炎天暑日的, 老太太身上也不大好" and "倘或老太太一时不自在了,

岂不事大". In appearance Lady Wang shows her worries and cares about the Lady Dowager's health. That is, she's trying to maintain the Lady Dowager's association rights in terms of her entitlements to concerns from others. In effect, being quite aware that Jia Zheng is extremely filial to his mother, Lady Wang attempts to talk Jia Zheng out of beating Baoyu with such an excuse.

Table 13   Euphemisms used by Lady Wang for face and rights of

Jia Zheng and the Lady Dowager

Interactional roles		Face Management		Sociality Rights Management	
Husband-Wife (Jia Zheng-Lady Wang)		Quality face (personal/ independent perspective)	Identity face (social/ interdependent perspective)	Equity rights (personal/ independent perspective)	Association rights (social/ interdependent perspective)
Euphemisms					
Conventional euphemisms	Situational euphemisms				
老爷			showing due respect for Jia Zheng in terms of his role in the family		
自重	宝玉虽然该打，老爷也要自重。				maintaining Jia Zheng's rights to care and consideration from other people
老太太			showing du respect for the Lady Dowager in terms of her role in the family		
身上也不大好	况且炎天暑日的，老太太身上也不大好……				maintaining the Lady Dowager's rights to care and concerns from other people
不自在了	倘或老太太一时不自在了，岂不事大！				maintaining the Lady Dowager's rights to care and concerns from other people

The management of face and rights for the sake of both Jia Zheng and the Lady Dowager by means of euphemisms is shown in the table above. However, what follows is that Lady Wang's trick is immediately seen through by Jia Zheng. He cuts her short with a sneer and calls for a rope to strangle Baoyu. In this case, the rapport-management outcome fails to agree with the rapport-maintenance orientation. It is a typical example of a failure of the use of euphemisms owing to its futile attempt to achieve the communicative purpose of persuasion. Whatever the orientation or outcome, it is noteworthy that the prevalence of manus in old times abases a wife and compels her to use euphemisms when conversing with her husband. In short, euphemisms may not work yet they are still deemed preferable in such cases.

Mother–in–Law–Daughter–in–Law (the Lady Dowager-Lady Wang)

A typical example is an apology euphemistically made by the Lady Dowager to Lady Wang, her daughter-in-law. Jia She wants to take Yuanyang, the Lady Dowager's maid as his concubine. The news immediately plunges the old lady into a fit of rage. She blames Lady Wang, who happens to be one of those ladies present but does not venture a word in defence of her own innocence. Now the mother-in-law and daughter-in-law rapport is neglected or even challenged. Therefore, a certain degree of repair seems necessary. So after the Lady Dowager is made to see her own mistake, she decides to apologize to Lady Wang, but "in a most roundabout and complicated way" (Lan Chun & Zhao Yun, 2010: 82).

Example 46:
贾母笑道："可是我老糊涂了！姨太太别笑话我。你这个姐姐他极孝顺我，不像我那大太太一味怕老爷，婆婆跟前不过应景儿。可是委屈了他。"薛姨妈只答应"是"，又说："老太太偏心，多疼小儿子媳妇，也是有的。"贾母道："不偏心！"因又说道："宝玉，我错怪了你娘，你怎么也不提我，看着你娘受委屈？"宝玉笑道："我偏着娘说大爷大娘不成？通共一个不是，我娘在这里不认，却推谁去？我倒要认是我的不是，老太太又不信。"贾母笑道："这也有理。你快给你娘跪下，你说太太别委屈了，老太太有年纪了，看着宝玉罢。"宝玉听了，忙走过去，便跪下要说；王夫人忙笑着拉他起来，说："快起来，快起来，断乎使不得。终不成你替老太太给我赔不是不成？"宝玉听说，忙站起来。贾母又笑道："凤姐儿也不提我。"(*DRM*, Chap. 46: 1314, 1316)

At once the old lady chuckled, "I'm losing my wits with age," she exclaimed. "Don't laugh at me, Madam Xue. This elder sister of yours is a very good daughter-in-law, not like my elder son's wife who's so afraid of her husband she only makes a show of compliance to me. Yes, I was wrong to blame your sister."

Aunt Xue murmured agreement, then added, "I wonder if you're not, perhaps, rather partial to the wife for your younger son, madam?"

"No, I'm not partial," the old lady declared. She continued, "Baoyu, why didn't you point out my mistake and prevent me from blaming your mother so unfairly?"

"How could I stick up for my mother at the expense of my elder uncle and aunt?" he countered. "Anyway, someone's done wrong; and if mother here won't take the blame, who will? I could have said it was *my* fault but I'm sure you wouldn't have believed me."

"Yes, that's right," chuckled the Lady Dowager, "Now kneel to your mother and ask her not to feel hurt, but to forgive me for your sake on account of my old age."

Baoyu stepped forward and knelt to do as he was told, but his mother instantly stopped him.

"Get up," she cried with a smile. "This is absurd. How can you apologize for your grandmother?"

As Baoyu rose to his feet the old lady said, "And Xifeng didn't pull me up either." (*DRM*, Chap. 46: 1315, 1317)

All the influencing factors are shown in the following table.

Table 14   Specification of all the influencing factors

Interactional roles	Mother-in-law-Daughter-in-law (the Lady Dowager-Lady Wang)
Rapport orientation	The Lady Dowager's rapport maintenance with Lady Wang
Message content	The Lady Dowager's apology to Lady Wang
Communicative activity	Apologizing to Lady Wang in a devious way by talking to Aunt Xue, Baoyu and Wang Xifeng
Cost-benefit consideration	Making the message beneficial to Lady Wang and less threatening to the Lady Dowager herself

Both the message content and the communicative activity are for the Lady Dowager to apologize to Lady Wang, which is certainly threatening to the apology offerer (the Lady Dowager herself) and beneficial to the offended (Lady Wang). According to Spencer-Oatey (2007), "Apologies are typically post-event speech acts, in the sense that some kind of offence or violation of social norms has taken place. In other words, people's sociality rights have been infringed in some way" (18). And again in her words,

> [...] if someone commits an offence, a disequibrilium results, with a greater offence leading to a greater imbalance. In both cases, balance needs to be restored, and apologies and expressions of gratitude are typical verbal ways respectively of restoring the equilibrium (ibid. 36).

Apologies can be made in private or in public. If the apology is made in public, it may threaten the apologizer's identity face (sense of standing among others) (ibid. 18). However, in Spencer-Oatey's words, "if no apology is forthcoming, this can be rapport-threatening to the offended person. It can aggravate his/her sense of equity rights, because no (verbal) repair has been made for the infringement that occurred through the offence" (ibid. 18).

In fact, the Lady Dowager does not have to apologize to Lady Wang because as matriarch, she has an absolute power and say in the family, not to mention her relations with her daughter-in-law. If she has done wrong, nobody ventures any comment or criticism. But now several factors might contribute to her apology. First of all, in regard to her relationship with her two daughters-in-law, she is more in favor of Lady Wang than Lady Xing. Then among those present are Madam Xue (Lady Wang's younger sister) and Wang Xifeng (Lady Wang's niece), who are both kin to Lady Wang. Moreover, Baoyu, an apple in the eyes of the old lady, is son of Lady Wang. And a traditional saying goes, "A mother is prized because of her son." Finally, senior as she is, she wants to appear fair and generous.

Notice that the Lady Dowager does apologize but does not apologize to Lady Wang face to face. Instead, she speaks to all the people that are present other than Lady Wang: Madam Xue, Baoyu and Wang Xifeng. According to what is mentioned earlier, an apology made in public is itself threatening to the identity face of the offerer. If the Lady Dowager apologized to her daughter-in-law directly that would be more face-threatening to herself. Again in Spencer-Oatey's words, "Rapport-management norms seem to be 'number-sensitive', in that what we say and how we say it is often influenced by the number of people present, and whether they are all listening to what we say" (ibid. 35). Hence it is found that the old lady deviously manipulates the apology in a way that is minimally face-threatening to herself.

In her words with Madam Xue, the Lady Dowager uses "我老糊涂了", which more or less threatens her own quality face (sense of personal competence). Then she maintains Lady Wang's quality face by saying "你这个姐姐他极孝顺我" and apologizes again: "可是委屈了他," which is also meant to maintain Lady Wang's quality face (a woman's absolute submission to her mother-in-law without any means of self-defence, which was deemed one of the fine qualities of women in old times) as well as her association rights in terms of her entitlements to concerns from others.

After that, she pretends to blame Baoyu for not defending her mother:

"宝玉，我错怪了你娘，你怎么也不提我，看着你娘受委屈？" This again can be taken as an apology. "我错怪了你娘" threatens the Old Dowager's quality face (sense of personal competence) but maintains Lady Wang's association rights in terms of her entitlements to concerns from others. Furthermore, she instructs Baoyu to kneel an apology to his mother: "你快给你娘跪下，你说太太别委屈了，老太太有年纪了，看着宝玉罢。"

Then she pretends to scold Wang Xifeng by saying, "凤姐儿也不提我", which is also supposed to be threatening to her own quality face in terms of her personal competence (poor judgment) and identity face in terms of her authority in the family.

In the whole course of the conversation, the Lady Dowager makes use of quite a number of euphemisms mainly at the syntactical level in an attempt to protect her own face and rights and repair those of Lady Wang, her daughter-in-law. In their 2010 article, Lan Chun and Zhao Yun observe,

> This devious way of apologizing by the Lady Dowager is attributable to the extremely asymmetrical relationship between mother-in-law and daughter-in-law in feudal China. To her daughter-in-law, mother-in-law claims absolute authority and dignity. Hence, when an apology has to be made by mother-in-law to her daughter-in-law, it seems most embarrassing to both sides (贾母之所以采用这样迂回的道歉方式，是因为在封建社会的中国，婆婆和媳妇之间的关系是极不对称的，婆婆对媳妇有绝对的权力和威仪。因此，当婆婆不得已向媳妇道歉时，对双方来说都是一件十分尴尬的事情。) (82).

This apology is finally accepted by Lady Wang. That is, the rapport-maintenance outcome successfully complies with rapport-maintenance orientation. The management of Lady Wang's face and rights by means of euphemisms is thus shown in Table 15.

Table 15   Euphemisms used by the Lady Dowger for face and rights of Lady Wang

Interactional roles		Face Management		Sociality Rights Management	
Mother-in-law-Daughter-in-law (the Lady Dowager-Lady Wang)		Quality face (personal/independent perspective)	Identity face (social/interdependent perspective)	Equity rights (personal/independent perspective)	Association rights (social/interdependent perspective)
Euphemisms					
Conventional euphemisms	Situational euphemisms				
我老糊涂了！		threatening the Lady Dowager's own self-image in terms of her poor judgment; making her remarks most beneficial to Lady Wang in respect of her innocence			
	你这个姐姐他极孝顺我，	commending Lady Wang for being filial and obedient			
	可是委屈了他。	threatening the Lady Dowager's own self-image in terms of her poor judgment; making her remarks most beneficial to Lady Wang in respect of her innocence			maintaining Lady Wang's rights to care and consideration from other people
	宝玉，我错怪了你娘，你怎么也不提我，看着你娘受委屈？	threatening the Lady Dowager's own self-image in terms of her poor judgment; making her remarks most beneficial to Lady Wang in respect of her innocence	threatening the Lady Dowager's own role or credibility in the family		maintaining Lady Wang's rights to care and consideration from other people
	你快给你娘跪下，你说太太别委屈了，老太太有年纪了，看着宝玉罢。	threatening the Lady Dowager's own self-image in terms of her poor judgment; making her remarks most beneficial to Lady Wang in respect of her innocence			maintaining Lady Wang's rights to care and consideration from other people
	凤姐儿也不提我。	threatening the Lady Dowager's own self-image in terms of her poor judgment	threatening the Lady Dowager's own role or credibility in the family		

Father-in-Law-Daughter-in-Law (Jia Zhen-Qin Keqing)

The following is part of the conversation between Jia Zhen and his wife, Madam You. However, the third party is involved—Qin Keqing, their daughter-in-law. It turns out that the relational roles are mainly those of Jia Zhen and Qin Keqing. The father-in-law and daughter-in-law relations in old times are rather rigid and formal. This is verbally manifest in the use of euphemisms. Being worried about Qin Keqing's health Jia Zhen is speaking to Madam You.

Example 47:

"我正进来要告诉你：方才冯紫英来看我，他见我有些抑郁之色，问我是怎么了。我才告诉他说，媳妇忽然身子又好大的不爽快，因为不得个好太医，断不透是喜是病，又不知有妨碍无妨碍，所以我这两日心里着实着急。" (*DRM*, Chap. 10: 276)

"What I was going to tell you is that Feng Ziying called just now. He asked why I looked so worried. I told him I was upset because our daughter-in-law isn't well but we can't find a good doctor to tell whether she's ill or pregnant, and whether there's any danger or not." (*DRM*, Chap. 10: 277)

All the influencing factors are shown in the following table.

Table 16   Specification of all the influencing factors

Interactional roles	Father-in-law-Daughter-in-law (Jia Zhen-Qin Keqing)
Rapport orientation	Jia Zhen's rapport maintenance with Qin Keqing
Message content	Jia Zhen's anxiety about Qin Keqing's illness
Communicative activity	Jia Zhen's report of his talk with Feng Ziying
Cost-benefit consideration	Making the message most beneficial to Qin Keqing

What is told by Jia Zhen is apparently meant to maintain rapport with his wife, Madam You but, more importantly, with Qin Keqing, his daughter-in-law. In fact, the talk mainly involves the third party, Qin Keqing. So "other" here is inclusive of both Madam You and Qin Keqing. The message content is about Qin Keqing's illness. The communicative activity is for Jia Zhen to tell Madam You about his talk with Feng Ziying. When mentioning his daughter-in-law's poor health even in her absence, Jia Zhen is careful enough to use euphemisms such as "不爽快", "喜" and "有妨碍无妨碍" so that his words do not sound costly or threatening. On the one hand, this can be interpreted as intentional avoidance of taboos (illness and danger). On the other hand, despite the alleged affairs between Jia Zhen and Qin Keqing (it is believed that they have adultery), it can be taken as maintaining Qin Keqing's association rights in terms of her entitlements to concerns or considerations from other people. But if words of consideration sound much too personal, Qin Keqing's equity rights might be infringed on. In consequence, although deeply concerned about her, as father-in-law, Jia Zhen is not supposed to appear too verbally close or personal to his daughter-in-law, especially when he is having a conversing with his wife, Madam You. This intentional alienation creates distance which manifests itself in the use of euphemistic expressions. As a result, rapport is maintained to a great extent.

The management of Qin Keqing's rights by means of euphemisms is thus shown in Table 17.

Table 17   Euphemisms used by Jia Zhen for Qin Keqing's rights

Interactional roles		Face Management		Sociality Rights Management	
Father-in-law-Daughter-in-law (Jia Zhen-Qin Keqing)		Quality face (personal/ independent perspective)	Identity face (social/ interdependent perspective)	Equity rights (personal/ independent perspective)	Association rights (social/interdependent perspective)
Euphemisms					
Conventional euphemisms	Situational euphemisms				
	不爽快				maintaining Qin Keqing's rights to care and consideration from other people
喜					maintaining Qin Keqing's rights to care and consideration from other people
	妨碍				maintaining Qin Keqing's rights to care and consideration from other people

First Wife–Concubine (Lady Wang-Concubine Zhao)

The relations between a man's first wife and his concubine are also held unequal. The following example shows how Concubine Zhao makes efforts to flatter Lady Wang, Jia Zheng's first wife, by showering praises on Baochai, Lady Wang's niece.

Example 48:

赵姨娘因环哥得了东西，深为得意，不住的托在掌上摆弄。瞧看一回，想宝钗乃系王夫人之表侄女，特要在王夫人跟前卖好儿。自己蝎蝎螯螯的拿着那东西，走至王夫人房中，站在一旁说道："这是宝姑娘才刚给环哥的。他哥哥带来的，他年轻轻的人，想的周到，我还给了送东西的小丫头二百钱。听见姨太太也给太太送来了，不知是什么东西？你们瞧瞧，这一个门里头就是两份儿，能多少呢？怪不得老太太同太太都夸他疼他，果然招人爱。"说着，将抱的东西递过去与王夫人瞧。谁知王夫人头也没抬，手也没伸，只口内说了声："好，给环哥玩罢咧。"并无正眼看一看。 (*DRM*, Chap. 67: 2006)

Now when Concubine Zhao saw the presents sent to Huan, she seized on them gleefully, loud in her praise of Baochai.

As Concubine Zhao gloated over these presents for Huan, picking them up to play with and examine, it occurred to her that as Baochai was Lady Wang's niece this was a good opportunity to go and make up to her mistress. So she hurried over with the presents to Lady Wang's room.

Standing to one side there she said, "These are things Miss Baochai just gave Huan, things brought her by her brother. She's so young yet she thinks of everybody! I gave the maid who brought them two hundred cash. I heard that Aunt Xue sent you some gifts too, madam. I wonder what they are? So their family's sending us two lots of presents! How many things could they have got? Not wonder the old lady and you both praise Miss Baochai and make such a favourite of her. She's really most lovable."

While saying this she held out the things she had brought. But Lady Wang neither looked up nor reached out her hand.

"Good, let Huan play with them," was all she said, without so much as glancing at the toys. (*DRM*, Chap. 67: 2007)

All the influencing factors are shown in the following table.

Table 18   Specification of all the influencing factors

Interactional roles	First Wife-Concubine (Lady Wang-Concubine Zhao)
Rapport orientation	Concubine Zhao's rapport enhancement with Lady Wang, Xue Baochai and the Lady Dowager
Message content	Concubine Zhao's high praise of Baochai
Communicative activity	Conducting a chat with Lady Wang in praise of Baochai
Cost-benefit consideration	Making the message most beneficial to Baochai and Lady Wang; making the message somewhat beneficial to Concubine Zhao herself

The inferior status in the family leaves Concubine Zhao extremely sensitive to how she is treated by people around and she seizes every opportunity to please whoever is above her. The gifts that Baochai has sent Jia Huan fill Concubine Zhao with delight and thankfulness, for to her the gifts are meant to maintain their (Concubine Zhao and Jia Huan) association rights in terms of consideration from others and their identity face in terms of their sense of public worth in the big family. This offers her an opportunity to flatter Lady Wang by showing her gratitude to Baochai. Her purpose of conducting a chat with Lady Wang is to strengthen their rapport. The message content is to show her high opinion of Baochai, which is deemed by her most beneficial to Lady Wang. The communicative activity is for Concubine Zhao to conduct a chat with Lady Wang in praise of Baochai. The chat is meant to be most beneficial to Baochai.

With honorifics "老太太" and "太太", Concubine Zhao maintains the identity face of the Lady Dowager and Lady Wang. The comment "怪不得老太太同太太都夸他疼他" is a roundabout and euphemistic way of praising Baochai and showing Concubine Zhao's affection for Baochai in terms of her impartiality, generosity and popularity. It is meant to strengthen Baochai's quality face and identity face. At the same time, it is intended to strengthen Lady Wang's identity face owing to their aunt-niece kinship. In addition, with "这一个门里头就是两份儿，能多少呢?" Concubine Zhao attempts to maintain Baochai's quality face in terms of her generosity and, more importantly, her own identity face in terms of her family status as a concubine. The management of face by means of euphemisms for the sake of the Lady Dowager, Lady Wang, Baochai and Concubine Zhao herself is thus shown in Table 19.

Table 19   Euphemisms used by Concubine Zhao for Baochai's and Lady Wang's face

Interactional roles		Face Management		Sociality Rights Management	
First Wife-Concubine (Lady Wang-Concubine Zhao)		Quality face (personal/ independent perspective)	Identity face (social/interdependent perspective)	Equity rights (personal/ independent perspective)	Association rights (social/ interdependent perspective)
Euphemisms					
Conventional euphemisms	Situational euphemisms				
老太太			showing due respect for the Lady Dowager in terms of her role in the family		
太太			showing due respect for Lady Wang in terms of her role in the family		
怪不得老太太同太太都夸他疼他，	singing praises of Baochai for being considerate and kind		singing praises of Baochai for her popularity with the ladies in the family		
一个门里头就是两份儿，能多少呢?	singing praises of Baochai for her generosity		Making the remarks beneficial to Concubine Zhao herself in terms of her own family role; threatening Lady Wang's identity face in terms of her family role		

Everything seems fine until Concubine Zhao says "一个门里头就是两

份儿". With such remarks she is going out of her way to strengthen the quality face of Baochai for her generosity. Yet at the same time, she is trying to deviously maintain or even enhance her own identity face by placing her family status on a par with that of Lady Wang. In effect, what Concubine Zhao has just said (一个门里头就是两份儿) is a double-edged sword, for it strikes Lady Wang that her identity face is now threatened in point of her family role. This testifies to Lady Wang's displeasure—She is not prepared to pick the topic up. Nor is she ready to glance so much at those toys. As far as cost-benefit consideration is concerned, it is evident that by saying "一个门里头就是两份儿" Concubine Zhao is trying to make it sound beneficial to herself but costly to Lady Wang in terms of their family roles. In consequence, she spoils her previous efforts to enhance rapport with Lady Wang.

It is found that Concubine Zhao's rapport-enhancement orientation has only been partially achieved with her previous efforts. But with "一个门里头就是两份儿" she meets a cold reply from Lady Wang, which means that on this particular occasion Lady Wang's identity face matters and she is not to be challenged in terms of her family role as Jia Zheng's first wife.

5.4.2 Master–Servant Relations

The master-servant relations determine the authority and relative power of a master over his/her servant. The following examples demonstrate the use of euphemisms with regard to two pairs of master-servant relationship: the Lady Dowager and Lai Da; Lin Daiyu and Zijuan.

Mistress–Steward (the Lady Dowager-Lai Da)

Lai Da is a steward of the Jia Family. He has a higher status and relative power over many other servants. Nonetheless, he is quite aware that he must obey and respect those who are more powerful in the family.

Example 49:

贾母等合家人等心中皆惶惶不定，不住的使人飞马来往报信。有两个时辰工夫，忽见赖大等三四个管家喘吁吁跑进仪门报喜，又说"奉老爷命，速请老太太带领太太等进朝谢恩"等语。那时贾母正心神不定，在大堂廊下伫立，那邢夫人，王夫人，尤氏，李纨，凤姐，迎春姊妹以及薛姨妈等皆在一处，听如此信至，贾母便唤进赖大来细问端的。赖大禀道："小的们只在临敬门外伺候，里头的信息一概不能得知。后来还是夏太监出来道喜，说咱们家大小姐晋封为凤藻宫尚书，加封贤德妃。后来老爷出来亦如此吩咐小的。如今老爷又往东宫去了，速请老太太领着太太们去谢恩。"贾母等听了方心神安定，不免又都洋洋喜气盈腮。于是都按品大妆起来。(*DRM*, Chap. 16: 400)

The Lady Dowager sent one mounted messenger after another in search of news; but it was four hours before Lai Da and a few other stewards came panting through the inner gate, crying:

"Good news! His Lordship asks the old lady to go at once to the Palace with the other ladies to thank His Majesty."

The Lady Dowager had been waiting anxiously in the corridor outside the great hall with Lady Xing, Lady Wang, Madam You, Li Wan, Xifeng and the Jia girls, as well as Aunt Xue. On hearing this, they called Lai Da over and demanded more details.

"We had to wait in the outer court," Lai Da told them. "So we had no idea what was going on inside. But then Chief Eunuch Xia came out. He congratulated us on the promotion of our eldest young lady. She's to be Chief Secretary of the Phoenix Palace with the title of Worthy and Virtuous Consort. And then His Lordship came out and confirmed this. Now he has gone to the East Palace and he begs Your Ladyship and the other ladies to go at once to offer thanks."

They were all so relieved that their faces shone with delight as each dressed in the ceremonial robes appropriate to her rank. (*DRM*, Chap. 16: 401)

All the influencing factors are shown in the following table.

Table 20   Specification of all the influencing factors

Interactional roles	Mistress-Steward (the Lady Dowager-Lai Da)
Rapport orientation	Lai Da's rapport maintenance/enhancement with his masters and the ladies
Message content	A report of the royal promotion of Jia Yuanchun; a request of offering thanks to the Emperor
Communicative activity	Reporting news of Yuanchun's promotion and passing a message from Jia Zheng
Cost-benefit consideration	Making the message most beneficial to the Jias

On this occasion the rapport orientation is targeted at rapport maintenance or even enhancement. The message content is two-fold: a report of the royal promotion of Jia Yuanchun and a request that the ladies offer their thanks to the Emperor. The communicative activity is for Lai Da to report to the Lady Dowager what he has heard and seen and then pass a message from Jia Zheng that the ladies are supposed to offer thanks to the Emperor. The news of promotion is certainly beneficial to the Jias. However, the request of offering thanks to the Emperor threatens, to some extent, the ladies' sociality rights.

Lai Da is chief steward of the Jia Family. The relative power of those masters and ladies in the house determines his humbleness and submissiveness in performing his duties. He uses honorifics such as "老爷", "老太太" and "太太" to address the master and mistresses for the sake of maintaining their identity face. At the same time, in addressing himself and the like, he uses self-depreciatory terms "小的" once and "小的们" twice for the same purpose of maintaining the ladies' identity face. Even when he passes the message that all the ladies must hurry to the Palace and offer thanks to the Emperor, he uses "请" to soften the tone of request, which is otherwise meant to threaten the equity rights of those ladies. All these linguistic means result in an agreement between rapport-maintenance orientation and rapport-maintenance outcome.

The management of face and rights in relation to the masters and the ladies by means of euphemisms is thus shown in the table below.

Table 21   Euphemisms used by Lai Da for face and rights of his masters and the ladies

Interactional roles		Face Management		Sociality Rights Management	
Mistress-Steward (the Lady Dowager-Lai Da)		Quality face (personal/ independent perspective)	Identity face (social/interdependent perspective)	Equity rights (personal/ independent perspective)	Association rights (social/ interdependent perspective)
Euphemisms					
Conventional euphemisms	Situational euphemisms				
老爷			showing due respect for Jia Zheng in terms of his role in the family		
老太太			showing due respect for the Lady Dowager in terms of her role in the family		
太太			showing due respect for the ladies in terms of their roles in the family		
小的 小的们			showing due respect for the Lady Dowager in terms of her role in the family (by humbling self with such self-effacing terms), making the remarks threatening to the servants yet beneficial to all the ladies		
请				maintaining the ladies' rights to freedom by mitigating the imposing force of the request	

Miss–Maid (Lin Daiyu-Zijuan)

Miss-maid relations naturally determine the relative power of a young lady over her maid. Yet there is an exception to the relation type between Lin Daiyu and her maid, Zijuan. In Zijuan's words, "偏生他又和我极好，比他苏州带来的还好十倍，一时一刻我们两个离不开。" Zijuan knows Daiyu much better than anybody else does. She tends to Daiyu with enormous care and consideration. Such seeming miss-maid but actual sister-sister relations make possible a generally literal way of speaking between the two girls except on special occasions.

Example 50:

这里林黛玉还自立于花阴之下，远远的却向怡红院内望着，只见李宫裁、迎春、探春、惜春并各项人等都向怡红院内去过之后，一起一起的散尽了，只不见凤姐儿来，心里自己盘算道："如何他不来瞧宝玉？便是有事缠住了，他必定也是要来打个花胡哨，讨老太太和太太的好儿才是。今儿这早晚不来，必有原故。"一面猜疑，一面抬头再看时，只见花花簇簇一群人又向怡红院内来了。定眼看时，只见贾母搭着凤姐儿的手，后头邢夫人王夫人跟着周姨娘并丫鬟媳妇等人都进院去了。黛玉看了不觉点头，想起有父母的人的好处来，早又泪珠满面。少顷，只见宝钗薛姨妈等也进入去了。忽见紫鹃从背后走来,说道："姑娘吃药去罢，开水又冷了。"黛玉道："你到底要怎么样？只是催，我吃不吃，管你什么相干！"紫鹃笑道："咳嗽的才好了些，又不吃药了。如今虽然是五月里，天气热，到底也该还小心些。大清早起，在这个潮地方站了半日，也该回去歇息歇息了。"一句话提醒了黛玉，方觉得有点腿酸，呆了半日，方慢慢的扶着紫鹃，回潇湘馆来。 (*DRM*, Chap. 35: 954)

But just then, raising her head, she caught sight of a gaily dressed group proceeding in that direction. Looking more closely she could recognize the Lady Dowager on Xifeng's arm, then Lady Xing and Lady Wang, with Concubine Zhou and some maids bringing up the rear. Together they entered the court. Daiyu nodded and tears ran down her cheeks as she reflected wistfully how good it was to have parents. A little later she saw Baochai enter with Aunt Xue, and then Zijuan came up suddenly behind her.

"Do go and take your medicine, miss, before the boiled water gets cold," she urged.

"Must you always be hurrying me?" protested Daiyu. "Whether I take it or not is none of your business."

"You shouldn't stop taking medicine just because your cough's beginning to be better. Although it's the fifth month and the weather's warm, you still ought to be careful. You've been standing here in the damp since first thing this morning. It's time to go back now and rest."

Daiyu realized then that she was indeed rather tired, and after some hesitation she walked slowly back to Bamboo Lodge on her maid's arm. (*DRM*, Chap. 35: 955)

All the influencing factors are shown in Table 22.

Table 22   Specification of all the influencing factors

Interactional roles	Miss-Maid (Lin Daiyu-Zijuan)
Rapport orientation	Zijuan's rapport maintenance with Lin Daiyu
Message content	The weather, medicine and rest
Communicative activity	Talking about the weather, persuading Lin Daiyu to take medicine and have a rest
Cost-benefit consideration	Making the message most beneficial to Lin Daiyu

Regarding the present miss-maid relations, rapport orientation is supposed to be that of maintenance. Both the message content and communicative activity are for Zijuan to wait on Lin Daiyu by talking her into taking the medicine and having a rest. By nature such a request is costly and threatening to Daiyu. But with the particle "罢" following the request Zijuan seems to maintain Lin Daiyu's equity rights by modulating the imposing force of her message. The moment Zijuan asks Daiyu to take the medicine she does not know that self-pity has already put this sentimental and melancholy young lady in a bad mood. That's why Daiyu feels irritated with a protest when she replies "你到底要怎么样？只是催，我吃不吃，管你什么相干！"

Having waited on her for so long, Zijuan immediately realizes that Daiyu is not in mood. Now she begins to speak in a euphemistic manner in order to maintain Lin Daiyu's association rights: "咳嗽的才好了些，又不吃药了"，"如今虽然是五月里，天气热，到底也该还小心些" and "大清早起，在这个潮地方站了半日，也该回去歇息歇息了". In this way the tone of imposition is mitigated and Lin Daiyu's equity rights are maintained.

Besides, this euphemistic way of advising helps maintain Daiyu's association rights in terms of her entitlements to concerns. Finally, Daiyu takes Zijuan's advice and goes back to have a rest. In this sense, the rapport-maintenance outcome meets the rapport-maintenance orientation to a great extent.

It is noteworthy that the euphemisms in this example are largely situational. The management of Lin Daiyu's rights is thus shown in the table below.

Table 23 Euphemisms used by Zijuan for Lin Daiyu's rights

Interactional roles		Face Management		Sociality Rights Management	
Miss-Maid (Lin Daiyu-Zijuan)		Quality face (personal/ independent perspective)	Identity face (social/ interdependent perspective)	Equity rights (personal/ independent perspective)	Association rights (social/ interdependent perspective)
Euphemisms					
Conventional euphemisms	Situational euphemisms				
	罢			maintaining Lin Daiyu's rights to freedom by mitigating the imposing force of the request	
	咳嗽的才好了些，又不吃药了。				maintaining Lin Daiyu's rights to care and consideration from other people
	如今虽然是五月里，天气热，到底也该还小心些。			maintaining Lin Daiyu's rights to freedom by mitigating the imposing force of the request	maintaining Lin Daiyu's rights to care and consideration from other people
	大清早起，在这个潮地方站了半日，也该回去歇息歇息了。			maintaining Lin Daiyu's rights to freedom by mitigating the imposing force of the request	maintaining Lin Daiyu's rights to care and consideration from other people

5.5 Summary

Considering the complexity of the social hierarchy and intricate vertical line of the family relationships in *DRM*, this chapter has examined the strategic use of euphemisms in terms of power, one of the influencing factors in rapport management. As a major variable, power is further studied from two perspectives: social power relations and familial power relations. At the same time, all the other related factors such as rapport orientation, message content, social/interactional roles and communicative activity are taken into account and analyzed in detail. Examples of euphemisms in the character utterances are discussed in terms of face and rights, two core components of Spencer-Oatey's theory of rapport management. The demonstration analysis in this chapter indicates that euphemisms used by the characters in their utterances have, by and large, facilitated the maintenance or even enhancement of rapport in a variety of power-based contexts.

Chapter Six

Discussions

· 6.1 Introduction

In Chapter Four euphemisms in the character utterances of *DRM* are described and categorized into conventional and situational euphemisms. Examples are provided to suffice the description and categorization. Then Chapter Five is focused on a demonstration analysis of the euphemisms in light of Spencer-Oatey's theoretical framework of rapport management. With regard to the complexity of relationships characteristic of hierarchy in the feudal society and the big aristocratic family, power is taken as a variable that influences the option and use of euphemisms. Meanwhile, equal attention is paid to all the other related influencing factors, such as interactional role, rapport orientation, message content, communicative activity and cost-benefit consideration. The demonstration analysis naturally leads to discussions in Chapter Six, which is encapsulated as follows.

First of all, this chapter focuses on the relationship between euphemisms in *DRM* and Spencer-Oatey's theory of rapport management. The discussions are two-fold: how euphemisms are used as a language strategy to facilitate the management of rapport in the novel and how the theory of rapport management is capable of accounting for the option and use of euphemisms in the character utterances of the novel.

Then what follows is a tentative study in which the previously revisited theories and principles are further compared and contrasted in reference to both Spencer-Oatey's theory of rapport management and euphemism. Such related theories and principles are known as Grice's CP and CI, Leech's PP, Brown and Levinson's face theory as well as Gu Yueguo's PP.

In addition, a couple of examples of non-use of euphemisms in *DRM* are presented and interpreted to testify to the fact that in a power-based context, a person with a relative power of one kind or another is generally not expected to use euphemisms because he/she does not have to.

Finally, the Chinese concept of politeness is traced historically and culturally to complement the study of euphemisms and rapport management in the novel.

6.2 Rapport Management and Euphemisms in *DRM*

The theory of rapport management is basically composed of the management of face (quality face and identity face) and the management of sociality rights (equity rights and association rights). Within this theoretical framework, quality face and equity rights are deemed personal whereas identity face and association rights social. Based on the demonstration analysis in Chapter Five, this part is designed to discuss how (in what way) rapport management is realized with the help of euphemisms and why (out of what consideration) euphemisms are used for the management of rapport. In other words, the present study focuses on how quality face, identity face, equity rights and association rights are verbally maintained or even enhanced by means of euphemisms. Conversely, the study is also aimed at investigating how the theory of rapport management is capable of accounting for the option and use of euphemisms of various kinds in the novel.

6.2.1 Quality Face and Euphemisms

Quality face is personal for its close relatedness to one's personal qualities such as competence, abilities and appearance, which largely concern his/her self-esteem either positively or negatively. It is found that both conventional and situational euphemisms in the novel contribute to one's quality face, particularly in terms of his/her moral standing, disposition and the like.

On the one hand, related conventional euphemisms in the novel are generally negative. Such negative euphemisms are varied: low moral standing and unpleasant disposition such as "不干净" and "性子不好", jealousy such as "争风吃醋", illegitimate sex and prostitution such as "爬灰" and "偷鸡摸狗". All of them sound, by nature, unpleasant to the ear even though they are euphemisms. However, in a maintenance-oriented rapport where such euphemisms are particularly addressed to a superior, they are assumed to help maintain his/her quality face by not making him/her feel much too ashamed or offended.

On the other hand, in order to maintain one's quality face, related situational euphemisms are supposed to operate in a certain context. For example, hedges like "未免" can be used in front of some quality-related expressions to mitigate the tone of threat or criticism so that the addressee's quality face can somehow be maintained.

In general to maintain other's (a superior in particular) quality face, a speaker (an inferior in particular) may opt for euphemisms demonstrated in Figure 5.

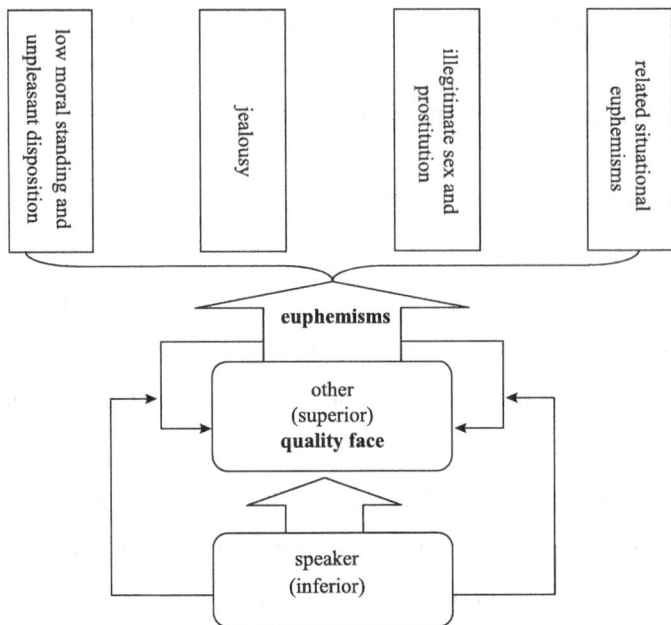

Figure 5   Euphemisms for maintenance/enhancement of quality face

Conversely, the following figure shows how the notion of quality face is capable of accounting for the variety of euphemisms available to the characters in the novel. According to Figure 5, low moral standing and unpleasant disposition, jealousy as well as illegitimate sex and prostitution are indicative of undesirable or distasteful qualities of a person. A starkly straightforward or explicit verbal expression in relation to any of such topics is, by nature, threatening to his/her sense of personal self-esteem. Instead, a roundabout or implicit way of expression may sound at least not so embarrassing. Now euphemisms may come in handy. Euphemisms that fall into this category are in effect concerned with what Spencer-Oatey terms as quality face. Being inherently negative, they are not capable of satisfying one's desire to be evaluated positively in terms of his/her particular personal qualities. Yet they can help avoid the possible loss of quality face by euphemistically replacing those dispreferred expressions so that the addressee may not feel much too embarrassed or ashamed.

Therefore, such euphemisms can be grouped into one category under the management of an individual's quality face. Figure 6 shows how quality face is capable of accounting for the strategic use of such euphemisms.

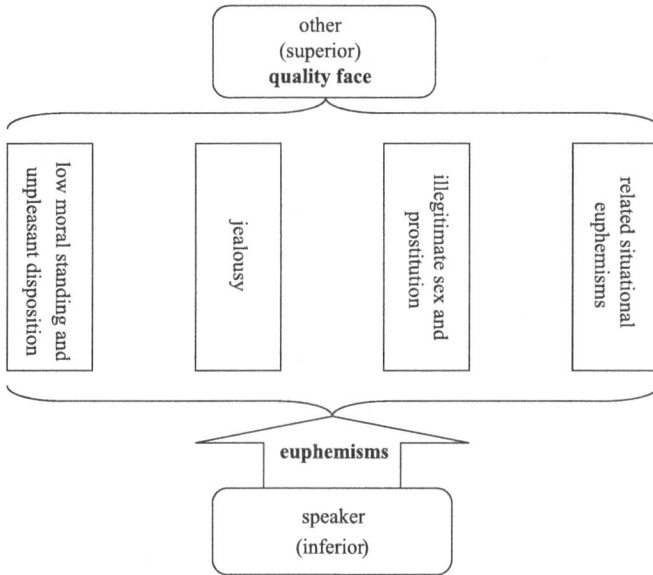

Figure 6　Euphemisms explicated by the maintenance of quality face

6.2.2　Identity Face and Euphemisms

Identity face is social for its close relatedness to one's sense of public worth. It is usually realized in terms of his/her social identity or group role either positively or negatively.

The demonstration analysis in Chapter Five reveals that an individual's identity face is mainly realized with the help of a number of honorifics and self-denigrating terms.

According to the description and categorization of euphemisms in Chapter Four, honorifics in *DRM* are "老爷", "老太太", "太太", "先父", "令亲大人", "大爷", "先生", "西宾", "尊兄", "世兄", "老兄", "老先生", "尊夫人" and "尊府". On the contrary, self-denigrating terms or self-effacing terms are "寒族", "在下", "敝友", "贱荆", "贱内", "小女", "晚生", "晚晚生", "弟", "小弟", "小的" and "小的们".

To be more specific, the demonstration analysis in Chapter Five indicates that in power relations when addressing other (a superior in particular), a speaker (an inferior in particular) tends to make use of a number of honorifics, which are targeted at acknowledging or upholding the addressee's social identity or group role. It turns out that they sound highly respectful by maintaining or even enhancing his/her identity face. Yet it is also noteworthy that very frequently an inferior is inclined to use self-denigrating terms. Such terms are generally deemed risky and undesirable, for they are likely to jeopardize the speaker's own identity face by humbling or belittling him/herself. In effect the frequent use of self-denigrating terms is like a double-edged sword, threatening the inferior's own identity face but deviously benefiting the superior in terms of his/her identity face otherwise. And the truth is that it is usually the latter's identity face that matters. This often takes place in a power-based context that is oriented towards rapport maintenance or even enhancement. Figure 7 shows how other's (a superior in particular) identity face is maintained or even enhanced by means of the following euphemisms.

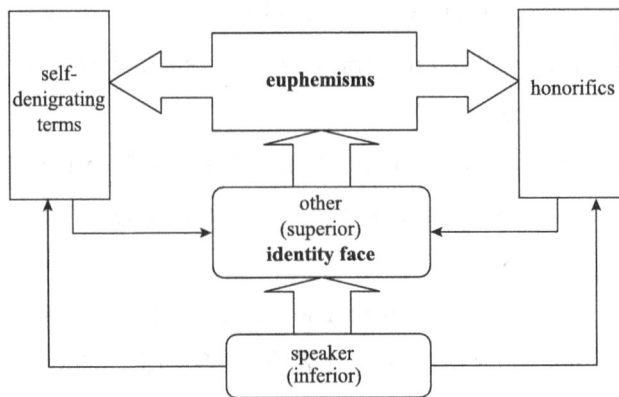

Figure 7　Euphemisms for maintenance/enhancement of identity face

The following figure shows how the notion of identity face is capable of accounting for the variety of euphemisms available to the characters in the novel. Such a category is mainly composed of honorifics and self-effacing terms. On the one hand, honorifics are intended to show a speaker's respect for other by magnifying his/her social status or group role. On the other hand, self-denigrating terms are targeted at belittling the speaker him/herself but stand as a foil to the very importance of other's social identity or group role. In that sense, both types of euphemisms are meant to acknowledge other's sense of public worth or group influence in relation to the rest. This happens to comply with what Spencer-Oatey terms as identity face. In other words, the notion of identity face is capable of interpreting the use of such euphemisms as honorifics and self-denigrating terms.

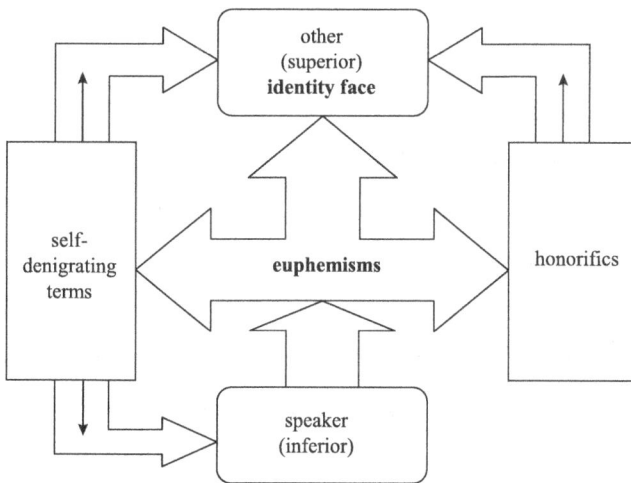

Figure 8   Euphemisms explicated by maintenance/enhancement of identity face

6.2.3 Equity Rights and Euphemisms

Like quality face, equity rights are personal in that they are closely associated with one's entitlements to personal consideration from others. The ingredients of equity rights are: the notion of cost-benefit and the issue of autonomy-imposition. Fairness and independence stand at the core of equity rights.

It is noteworthy that the notion of fairness and independence seems to repel orders, requests, suggestions, advice or invitation which may sound, in varying degrees, threatening to a person's equity rights in terms of cost-benefit or autonomy-imposition. To strike balance between benefit and cost or autonomy and imposition one of the best ways is to euphemize orders, requests, suggestions, advice or invitation. The demonstration analysis in Chapter Five reveals that equity rights are maintained mainly in euphemized orders, requests, suggestions, advice or invitation. In point of fact, to modulate the tone of cost or compulsion the characters in the novel may start their orders, requests, suggestions, advice or invitation with such face markers as "望", "祈" and "请". Besides, other linguistic devices are available: rhetorical questions with "岂不", particle "罢", hedges such as "少不得", and adverbs such as "也" and "还" preceding verbs such as "该". What's more, a variety of euphemized sentences are found actively at work. Such sentences have no resort to syntactical devices, yet they are semantically euphemistic and practically context-dependent.

In a power-based context, when imposing utterances are addressed to other (a superior in particular) the above-mentioned situational euphemisms may be put to good account in that the tone of imposition can be modulated to a certain extent and equity rights thus maintained. Figure 9 shows how one's equity rights can be maintained by means of euphemisms.

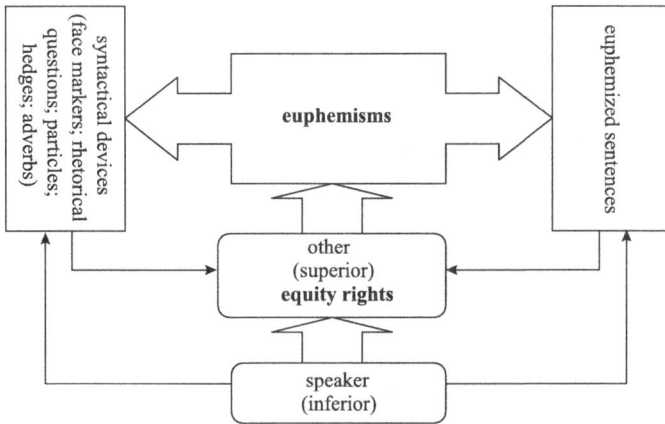

Figure 9   Euphemisms for maintenance of equity rights

The following figure shows how the notion of equity rights is capable of accounting for the variety of euphemisms at the characters' disposal in the novel.

It is evident that such euphemisms are virtually situational, for they are composed with the help of face markers, rhetorical questions, particles, hedges, adverbs and euphemized sentences. In general they are intended to tone down imposition in orders, requests, suggestions, advice or invitation, which are supposed to have much to do with what Spencer-Oatey refers to as equity rights in terms of one's personal entitlements to freedom or independence. In that sense, the idea of equity rights justifies such a variety of euphemisms. Figure 10 shows the explicability of the notion of equity rights.

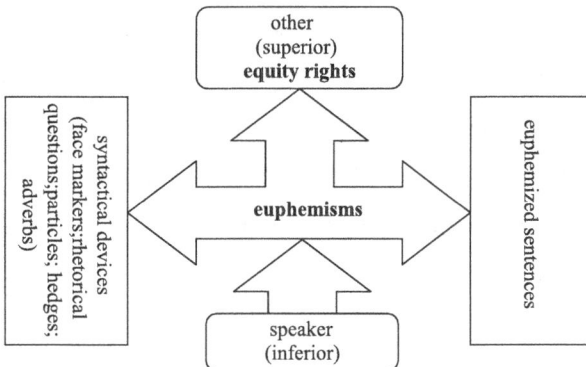

Figure 10   Euphemisms explicated by maintenance of equity rights

6.2.4 Association Rights and Euphemisms

Like identity face, association rights are social in that they are related to one's entitlements to relationship with others. The ingredients of association rights are interactional association-dissociation and affective association-dissociation. Relational involvement and spiritual share are of the essence to association rights.

According to the demonstration analysis in Chapter Five association rights are mainly realized by means of a great majority of conventional euphemisms and a number of situational euphemisms. Categories in the conventional euphemisms are about devil and disaster such as "撞客" and "走水"; death and funeral affairs such as "归西" and "寿木"; disease and ill health such as "见喜" and "欠安"; sex such as "风月" and "怜香惜玉"; excreta and secretion such as "小恭" and "月信"; pregnancy and birth such as "喜" and "落草"; ageing such as "有了春秋" and "上了年纪"; love and affection such as "儿女私情" and "缠绵"; marriage and concubinage such as "出阁" and "收房"; servants and housemaids such as "家里人" and "小子"; names regarded as taboos such as "密" for "敏"; low moral standing and unpleasant disposition such as "不干净" and "性子不好"; and Buddhist practice and practitioner such as "入空门" and "出家人". Situational euphemisms are varied. Some are characterized with semantic fuzziness such as "事" and "东西", some resort to syntactical devices (hedges and negation such as "暂且" and "不爽快", and question words such as "怎样"). In addition, some are euphemized sentences such as "你快给你娘跪下, 你说太太别委屈了……". The categorization of euphemisms for the maintenance of association rights is shown in Figure 11.

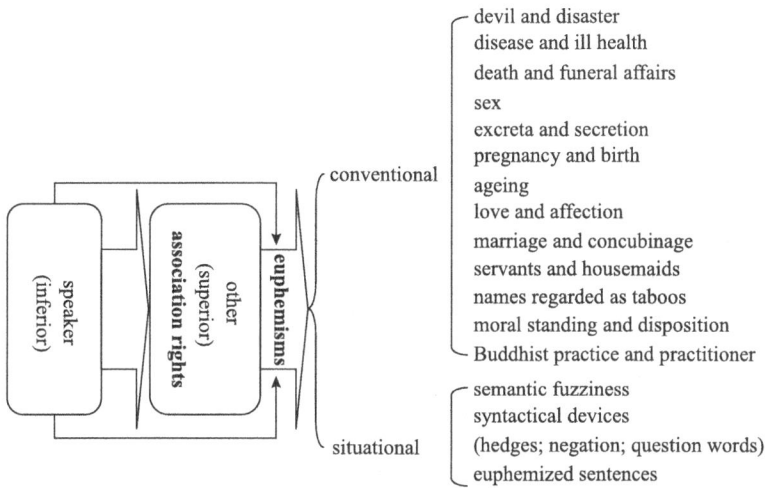

Figure 11 Euphemisms for maintenance of association rights

The following figure shows how the notion of association rights is capable of accounting for such a large variety of euphemisms. The euphemisms in point fall into two categories: conventional euphemisms and situational euphemisms. Both types help diminish embarrassment, shame or shock so that the speaker's concerns about other can tactfully be conveyed. euphemisms. Such euphemisms are verbal expressions of care about what Spencer-Oatey terms as association rights, or one's entitlements to concerns or sympathy from others. In other words, the notion of association rights is capable of interpreting the strategic use of the following euphemisms.

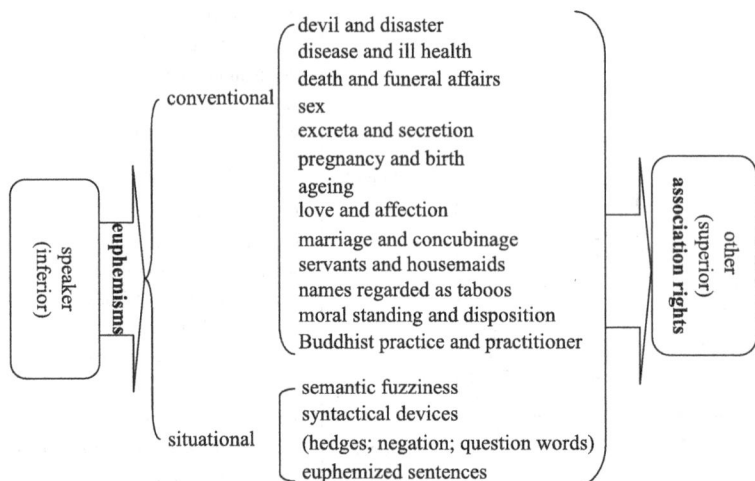

conventional
- devil and disaster
- disease and ill health
- death and funeral affairs
- sex
- excreta and secretion
- pregnancy and birth
- ageing
- love and affection
- marriage and concubinage
- servants and housemaids
- names regarded as taboos
- moral standing and disposition
- Buddhist practice and practitioner

situational
- semantic fuzziness
- syntactical devices
- (hedges; negation; question words)
- euphemized sentences

speaker (inferior) — euphemisms — other (superior) association rights

Figure 12   Euphemisms explicated by maintenance of association rights

Based on the categorization and demonstration analysis in Chapters Four and Five, this part summarizes the relationship between euphemisms in the character utterances of *DRM* and Spencer-Oatey's theory of rapport management. On the one hand, to maintain or enhance rapport euphemisms can be put into effective use. On the other hand, the option and use of euphemisms can also be explicated by the theory of rapport management. Therefore, the discussion may safely be brought to a conclusion: Spencer-Oatey's theory of rapport management has a controlling force and explanatory power over the option and use of euphemisms of various kinds in the character utterances of *DRM*.

·❯❯ 6.3   A Comparative and Contrastive Analysis of Related Theories and Principles

In order to complement the present study a comparative and contrastive analysis will be made between the theories and principles revisited in Chapter Two and Spencer-Oatey's theory of rapport management in relation to euphemism. Such theories and principles include Grice's CP and CI, Leech's PP, Brown and Levinson's face theory as well as Gu Yueguo's PP. Similarities and differences will be explored in the following part.

6.3.1　Grice's CP & CI and Spencer–Oatey's Rapport

Based on his observation that people tend to comply with certain principles in talk exchanges, Grice identifies four maxims as guidelines for an efficient cooperative use of language that jointly compose a general cooperative principle. These maxims are: Quantity, Quality, Relation and Manner. Such conversational maxims at work specify what interlocutors must do in order that the talk exchange can be fulfilled in a maximally efficient, rational and cooperative way. That is, while providing adequate information, participants should speak sincerely, relevantly and clearly.

Yet Grice also notices that interactants frequently do not adhere to the CP and "communicate more than what they actually say" (Blakemore, 1992: 26). As a result, a flout of any of the maxims may give rise to what he terms as 'implicature'. "To imply is to hint, suggest, or convey some meaning indirectly by means of language" (Thomas, 1995: 57). Therefore, the four maxims are also perceived as a set of regulations that govern the generation and interpretation of conversational implicature with regard to the non-observance of these maxims. Conversely, conversational implicature is realized by means of flouting one or more maxims. For the sake of clarity, examples from the collection of euphemisms in *DRM* will be given under each maxim.

1) Maxim of Quantity

Make your contribution as informative as is required (for the current purpose of exchange).

Do not make your contribution more informative than is required.

(cf. Example 45, Chap. 5):

贾政还欲打时，早被王夫人抱住板子。贾政道："罢了，罢了! 今日必定要气死我才罢！"

王夫人哭道："宝玉虽然该打，老爷也要自重。况且炎天暑日的，老太太身上也不大好，打死宝玉事小，倘或老太太一时不自在了，岂不事大！"贾政冷笑道："倒休说这话。我养了这不肖的孽障，已不孝；教训他一番，又有众人护持；不如趁今日一发勒死了，以绝将来之患！" (*DRM*, Chap. 33: 916)

Before his father [Jia Zheng] could beat him [Baoyu] any further, Lady Wang seized the rod with both hands.

"This is the end!" roared Jia Zheng. "You're determined to be the death of me today."

"I know Baoyu deserves a beating," sobbed Lady Wang. "But you mustn't wear yourself out, sir. It's a sweltering day and the old lady isn't well. Killing Baoyu is a small matter, but should anything happen to the old lady that would be serious."

"Spare me this talk." Jia Zheng gave a scornful laugh. "I've already proved an unfilial son by begetting this degenerate. When I discipline him all of you protect him. I'd better strangle him now to avoid further trouble." (*DRM*, Chap. 33: 917)

As mother Lady Wang has a mind to spare Baoyu from his father's deathly corporal punishment. But as wife she is in no position to physically stop Jia Zheng. So preferably she has to talk Jia Zheng out of beating Baoyu by giving a couple of excuses："老爷也要自重"；"况且炎天暑日的，老太太身上也不大好"；"倘或老太太一时不自在了，岂不事大". Such lengthy remarks are about Jia Zheng's health, the hot weather and the Lady Dowager's ailment. The euphemisms in Lady Wang's utterances are intended to maintain the association rights of both Jia Zheng and the Lady Dowager in terms of their entitlements to care and concerns from other people. In other words, Lady Wang has to make her message most beneficial and acceptable to Jia Zheng and the Lady Dowager so that there might be hope of forgiveness of their son.

But notice that although such utterances are intended to show Lady Wang's worries and care about her husband and her mother-in-law in terms of their association rights, obviously they have little to do with what she truly cares about: Baoyu's life that is now put at stake. She has said too much. It is found that her utterances have flouted the maxim of quantity for providing more than enough information. In this case, Lady Wang's flout of the maxim of quantity is actually targeted at false maintenance of the association rights of Jia Zheng and the Lady Dowager with the help of euphemisms. The implicature thus generated is that the Lady Dowager cannot live without Baoyu. As a filial son, Jia Zheng must take the Lady Dowager's health into consideration. In order not to bother the old lady and compound the matter, he must stop beating his son. So ultimately the whole message boils down to one point: Baoyu must be spared.

However, Jia Zheng is wise enough to know what Lady Wang truly means and immediately sees through her trick. That's why in a fit of anger he cuts her short with a sneer and calls for a rope to strangle Baoyu.

2) Maxim of Quality

Do not say what you believe to be false.

Do not say that for which you lack adequate evidence.

Now look again at Example 45 for what Lady Wang says: "打死宝玉事小, 倘或老太太一时不自在了, 岂不事大!" With such words, Lady Wang appears to make slight of Baoyu' death and maintain the Lady Dowager's association rights by showing deep concerns for her health. In effect, everyone is in the know that the Lady Dowager and Baoyu are on intimate grandmother-grandson terms. The two are closely tied and not to be separated. In this case, when Lady Wang says "打死宝玉事小" she has flouted the maxim of quality for saying what is believed to be false. The implicature thus generated is that killing Baoyu is starkly no small matter. Death of Baoyu means end of the Lady Dowager. Therefore, Baoyu must be spared.

3) Maxim of Relation

Be relevant.

Example 51:

贾母因问黛玉念何书。黛玉道："只刚念了《四书》。"黛玉又问姊妹们读何书。贾母道："读的是什么书，不过是认得两个字，不是睁眼的瞎子罢了！"(*DRM*, Chap. 3: 80)

Then her grandmother asked Daiyu what books she had studied.

"I've just finished the *Four Books,*" said Daiyu. "But I'm very ignorant." Then she inquired what the other girls were reading.

"They only know a very few characters, not enough to read any books." (*DRM*, Chap. 3: 81)

When Daiyu asks what books other girls have read, the Lady Dowager does not reply directly by telling her the names of those books that they have read. Instead, she merely says they only know a few characters, not enough to read any books. In fact, almost all the girls in the Jia Family and their kin are well-educated. Quite a few of them are talented and even scholarly. The point is that since Daiyu is quite new here, the Lady Dowager really wants to make her feel at ease among the girls. By flouting the maxim of relation the Lady Dowager intends to maintain Daiyu's quality face in terms of her talent and learning and, her association rights in terms of her entitlements to consideration and sympathy from other people. The implicature thus generated is that Daiyu is superior to other girls because she is intelligent and well-bred.

4) Maxim of Manner

Avoid obscurity of expression.

Avoid ambiguity.

Be brief.

Be orderly.

(cf. Example 47, Chap. 5):

"我正进来要告诉你：方才冯紫英来看我，他见我有些抑郁之色，问我是怎么了。我才告诉他说，媳妇忽然身子又好大的不爽快，因为不得个好太医，断不透是喜是病，又不知有妨碍无妨碍，所以我这两日心里着实着急。" (*DRM*, Chap. 10: 276)

"What I was going to tell you is that Feng Ziying called just now. He asked why I looked so worried. I told him I was upset because our daughter-in-law isn't well but we can't find a good doctor to tell whether she's ill or pregnant, and whether there's any danger or not." (*DRM*, Chap. 10: 277)

The message content is about Qin Keqing's illness. When mentioning his daughter-in-law's poor health, Jia Zhen is careful enough not to speak in a straightforward way. Instead, he uses euphemisms such as "不爽快", "喜" and "有妨碍无妨碍", which are all semantically ambiguous. In this case, the use of such euphemisms has flouted the maxim of manner. Yet in fact it can be interpreted as intentional avoidance of taboos (illness and danger). "不爽快", "喜" and "妨碍" are all euphemisms for such taboos as "illness", "pregnancy" and "danger". The implicature thus generated is that Qin Keqing is seriously ill and there's little hope of recovery.

It is found that when talking about Qin Keqing's illness, Jia Zhen is cautious enough not to speak in a straightforward way even in her absence. She is the third party that the conversation mainly involves but she still deserves due care and sympathy. Any word that sounds costly and threatening to Qin Keqing is undesirable. So by flouting the maxim of manner with euphemisms, Jia Zhen attempts to maintain Qin Keqing's association rights in terms of her entitlements to concerns and consideration from other people.

The above analysis shows that Grice's CP and CI are related to Spencer-Oatey's rapport management and the use of euphemisms. A flout of the CP that gives rise to the CI is verbally realized by euphemisms that are intended to maintain rapport. This is shown in the following figure.

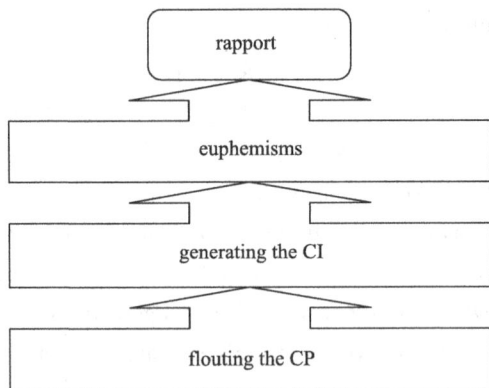

Figure 13　Grice's CP&CI, Spencer-Oatey's rapport and euphemisms

6.3.2　Leech's PP and Spencer–Oatey's Rapport

Leech believes that interlocutors sometimes infringe one or more maxims of the CP for the sake of politeness, which is usually realized in an indirect or roundabout way. He argues that when the CP fails to sufficiently explain indirectness in a conversation the PP may be put into operation. So he assigns politeness and its related notion of "tact" a crucial role in explaining "why people are often so indirect in conveying what they mean" and in "rescuing the Cooperative Principle from serious trouble" (Leech, 1983: 80). In that sense, politeness can satisfactorily account for exceptions to and deviations from the CP.

Leech develops politeness into the Politeness Principle and its six maxims are translated into Tact, Generosity, Approbation, Modesty, Agreement and Sympathy. To be specific, the PP can be stated as follows: Other things being equal, minimize the expression of beliefs that are unfavorable to the hearer and at the same time (but less important) maximize the expression of beliefs which are favorable to the hearer. In other words, the core of the PP is to minimize the expression of impolite beliefs and maximize the expression of polite beliefs.

Leech emphasizes the imbalanced importance within each pair of twinned maxims—Maxims (I) & (II), Maxims (III) & (IV) and sub-maxims. It is found that Maxims (I) and (III) take into account other's benefits and losses whereas Maxims (II) and (IV) pays respect to self's benefits and losses. Besides, there is no apparent relation between Maxims (V) and (VI). Yet generally speaking, Leech's PP is, by and large, more oriented towards other.

Considering its relatedness to the present study, four of the maxims will be discussed in the comparative and contrastive analysis, namely, Tact, Approbation, Modesty and Sympathy.

1) Tact Maxim (in impositives and commissives)

a. Minimize the cost to other   [b. Maximize the benefit to other]

Tact maxim in impositives (minimize the cost to other) will be discussed only because it bears some relation to Spencer-Oatey's equity rights (an individual's entitlements to personal consideration in terms of autonomy and freedom). Impositives are quintessentially deemed costly to other and especially so to a superior in a power-based context. In the present study of euphemisms in *DRM*, face markers such as "望", "祈" and "请", and particle "罢" are supposed to lend a euphemistic tone to impositives, which in turn, may minimize cost to other by modulating the force of compulsion to a certain extent.

> (cf. Example 36, Chap. 4):
> 黛玉笑回道："舅母爱恤赐饭，原不应辞，只是还要过去拜见二舅舅，恐领了赐去不恭，异日再领，未为不可。望舅母容谅。"(*DRM*, Chap. 3: 72, 74)
>
> "Thank you very much, aunt, you're too kind," said Daiyu. "Really I shouldn't decline. But it might look rude if I delayed in calling on my second uncle. Please excuse me and let me stay another time." (*DRM*, Chap. 3: 73, 75)

In declining her aunt's (Lady Xing) invitation, Daiyu tells her why she cannot stay for dinner and begs her pardon by politely saying "望舅母容谅". In this case, the imposing tone of the request is mitigated. In other words, Daiyu is in an attempt at minimizing cost of imposition in her request so as to maintain Lady Xing's equity rights that she is not to be ordered about or imposed upon.

2) Approbation Maxim (in expressives and assertives)

a. Minimize dispraise of other   [b. Maximize praise of other]

Approbation maxim in expressives and assertives is targeted at minimizing dispraise of other and maximizing praise of other. This partly goes along with Spencer-Oatey's maintenance or enhancement of face in rapport management. In the present study of *DRM* honorifics and the like are a type of euphemism and serve to elevate one's sense of self-esteem or public worth. To be more exact, in a power-based context, by minimizing dispraise of other and maximizing praise of other, a speaker is supposed to maintain or even enhance other's quality face and identity face by resorting to such euphemisms.

(cf. Example 43, Chap. 5):

……至密室，侍从皆退去，只留门子服侍。这门子忙上来请安，笑问："老爷一向加官进禄，八九年来就忘了我了？"雨村道："却十分面善，只是一时想不起来。"那门子笑道："老爷真是贵人多忘事，把出身之地竟忘了，不记当年葫芦庙里之事了？"（*DRM*, Chap. 4: 96）

Back in his private office he dismissed everyone but the attendant, who went down on one knee in salute, then said with a smile:

"Your Honour has risen steadily in the official world. After eight or nine years, do you still remember me?"

"Your face looks very familiar, but I can't place you."

The attendant smiled. "High officials have short memories," he said.

"So you've forgotten the spot you started from, Your Honour, and what happened in Gourd Temple?" (*DRM*, Chap. 4: 97)

Jia Yucun is now quite different from what he used to be. He has been working up from a pitiful penniless guy to prefect of Yingtian. Considering his current social status and relative power, the humble attendant means to enhance or at least maintain their rapport for prospective promotion on his own part. The message content is mainly two-fold: their acquaintance in the old days and his flattery to Jia Yucun. The attendant addresses Jia Yucun with an honorific "老爷" to maintain his identity face in terms of his social role. By euphemistically saying "老爷一向加官进禄" the attendant means to maintain Jia Yucun's quality face and identity face in terms of both his individual competence and sense of public worth.

Generally speaking, the attendant flatters Jia Yucun with "老爷" and "一向加官进禄" by means of maximizing praise of other (Jia Yucun). Even in his slight complaint of Jia Yucun's forgetfulness, the attendant intentionally uses "贵人多忘事" to maintain Jia Yucun's quality face by minimizing dispraise of other (Jia Yucun).

3) Modesty Maxim (in expressives and assertives)

a. Minimize praise of self   [b. Maximize dispraise of self]

Modesty maxim in expressives and assertives is intended to minimize praise of self and maximize dispraise of self. This resonates in part with Spencer-Oatey's notion of face maintenance or enhancement in rapport management. Euphemisms with a note of modesty and self-denigration bear much relation to an individual's quality face and identity face. According to the present study of the novel, it is deemed desirable that individuals uphold modesty as one of the virtues and practice it in their everyday life and interactions. One of the ways to show one's modesty is to verbally minimize praise of self and maximize dispraise of self. And a speaker may bring into play self-effacing terms and the like in aid of the maintenance or even enhancement of other's quality face or identity face in a roundabout way.

(cf. Example 19, Chap. 4):

如海道："天缘凑巧，因贱荆去世，都中家岳母念及小女无人依傍教育，前已遣了男女船只来接，因小女未曾大痊，故未及行。"(*DRM*, Chap. 3: 58)

"What a lucky coincidence!" exclaimed Ruhai. "Since my wife's death my mother-in-law in the capital has been worried because my daughter has no one to bring her up. She has sent two boats with male and female attendants to fetch the child, but I delayed her departure while she was unwell." (*DRM*, Chap. 3: 59)

Two self-depreciatory euphemisms are used here: "贱荆" and "小女". "贱荆" refers to Lin Ruhai's late wife, Jia Min whereas "小女" refers to his daughter, Lin Daiyu. By minimizing praise of self and maximizing dispraise of self, Lin Ruhai means to elevate other in terms of face management.

4) Sympathy Maxim (in assertives)

a. Minimize antipathy between self and other

[b. Maximize sympathy between self and other]

Sympathy maxim in assertives is to minimize antipathy and maximize sympathy between self and other. This consideration accords partially with Spencer-Oatey's management of association rights (an individual's entitlements to affective share of concerns, feelings or interests).

The present study of *DRM* reveals that a number of euphemisms are used for the purpose of maintaining other's association rights. More often than not such euphemisms are negative indicating things that are dispreferred or distasteful. In this sense, sympathy is desirable whereas antipathy undesirable so that one's association rights can maximally be maintained in a euphemistic way. Besides, plenty of situational euphemisms are found actively at work and they also contributed to the management of one's association rights.

(cf. Example 44, Chap. 5):

谁知凤姐之女大姐儿病了，正乱着请大夫来诊过脉。大夫便说：

"替夫人奶奶们道喜，姐儿发热是见喜了，并非别病。" (*DRM*, Chap. 21: 582)

"I am happy to inform Her Ladyship and Madam Lian that the little girl's fever is simply due to smallpox." (*DRM*, Chap. 21: 583)

The doctor means to maintain rapport with the Jias. The message content is about a medical check on Dajie and the communicative activity is for the doctor to report the result. Report of the illness with straightforward expressions is certainly not preferred, for it is supposed to be costly to the patient or the hearer. Disease, like death, is verbally prohibited and substituted with euphemisms. "见喜" euphemistically means "to have smallpox". Wang Xifeng's daughter has smallpox, but this is not to be directly mentioned. Rather, "见喜" is commonly accepted as a negative euphemism and used for the sake of good luck. It is meant to maintain Dajie's association rights in terms of her entitlements to appropriate consideration and sympathy from other people. And when making a medical report to Lady Wang and Wang Xifeng, the doctor uses "见喜", another euphemism for a disease. This is done totally for the sake of maintaining Lady Wang and Wang Xifeng's association rights to consideration and sympathy rather than shock and displeasure. By means of maximizing sympathy between self and other, the doctor's euphemistic report on Dajie's illness can easily be accepted so that nobody may feel embarrassed or offended.

It must be pointed out that Leech's PP bears much relation to Spencer-Oatey's rapport management. In Spencer-Oatey's (2007) words, "Leech's (1987) approbation and modesty maxims could be seen as addressing quality face concerns; and his tact and generosity maxims could be seen as addressing concerns over equity rights" (40). The comparative analysis indicates that Leech's approbation and modesty maxims can also be seen as addressing identity face concerns. It is evident that Spencer-Oatey's rapport management is rapport-oriented and built upon face and politeness. Leech's

PP is definitely politeness-oriented and accordingly the maxims are stipulated for the sake of politeness. The relatedness of Leech's PP to Spencer-Oatey's rapport can be interpreted as follows: To manage rapport, politeness should be taken into account and put into effect. Figure 14 shows that politeness can be realized with a number of maxims that might be verbally euphemistic for the sake of rapport management.

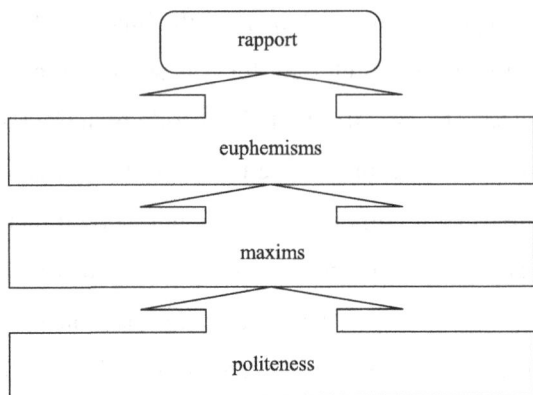

Figure 14   Leech's PP, Spencer-Oatey's rapport and euphemisms

6.3.3 Brown & Levinson's Face Theory and Spencer-Oatey's Rapport

Very frequently Brown and Levinson's (1987) theory of linguistic politeness is identified as the "face-saving" theory of politeness for the reason that they base their theory upon Goffman's (1967) notions of face.

Brown and Levinson (1987) assume that every individual of a society has (and knows each other to have) "face", which, in their words, is "the public self-image that every member wants to claim for himself" (61).

It is found that although both theories are built upon Goffman's notions of face, Brown and Levinson's classification of face is different from that of Spencer-Oatey. They classify "face" into two types: positive and negative.

Positive face is an individual's desire that his/her wants be appreciated and approved of in social interaction, whereas negative face is the desire for freedom of action and freedom from imposition. In this sense, politeness strategies are intended to maintain or enhance the addressee's positive face (positive politeness) and avoid transgression of the addressee's freedom of action and freedom from imposition (negative politeness).

However, face, according to Spencer-Oatey's theory of rapport management, is associated with personal/social value, dignity, honor, reputation as well as competence and is concerned with people's sense of worth, personal/social expectancies and so on. Here face is classified into two types: quality face and identity face. Quality face is an individual's desire that his/her personal qualities be positively evaluated. Identity face is an individual's desire that his/her social identities or roles be acknowledged or acclaimed. In this sense, Spencer-Oatey's quality face is personal whereas identity face social.

A comparative analysis shows that Brown and Levinson's notion of positive face generally overlaps with those of Spencer-Oatey's quality face and identity face. However, their "concept of "negative face" is not treated as a face need but rather as a sociality right" (Spencer-Oatey, 2007: 15) in her rapport management. To be more exact, their negative face accords with Spencer-Oatey's equity rights (an individual's entitlements to personal consideration from others for the purpose of fair treatment).

Yet the comparative and contrastive analysis also indicates that Spencer-Oatey's notion of association rights is absent in Brown and Levinson's theory. And the very absence of association rights in Brown and Levinson's theory is quintessentially central to the Chinese context. Association rights, according to Spencer-Oatey, are an individual's entitlements to interactional association (an individual's involvement with others) or affective association (an individual's share of concerns, feelings or interests with others). In

Chinese culture that generally features collectivism, individuals' association rights are highlighted in rapport. Joining others in an activity is interactionally relational whereas having a share of concerns, feelings or interests from others is deemed affectively relational.

This is best demonstrated in Figures 11 and 12 of the chapter at issue. In the present study, the large variety of euphemisms that contribute to the management of association rights confirm a want of entitlements to association in the Chinese context. So it is self-evident that the component void in Brown and Levinson's face theory finds a full explanation in Spencer-Oatey's theory of rapport management. In other words, while Brown and Levinson's face theory may fail to account for such a large stock of euphemisms in the novel, Spencer-Oatey's rapport management is capable of handling them with a strong explanatory power (see Figure 15).

Brown and Levinson's conceptualization of face   Spencer-Oatey's rapport

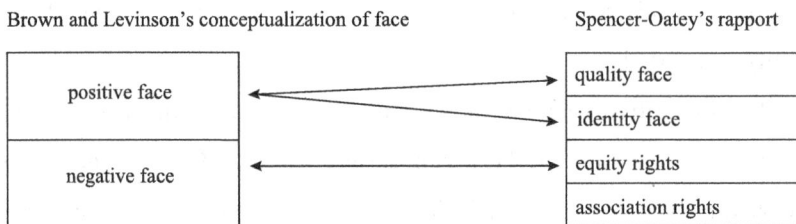

Figure 15   **Brown and Levinson's conceptualization of face and Spencer-Oatey's rapport**

6.3.4   Gu Yueguo's PP and Spencer–Oatey's Rapport

Having his study closely based on the origin of the notion of Chinese politeness and critically adopting Leech's maxims of politeness with some reservations, Gu Yueguo postulates the politeness principle in Chinese culture and identifies a set of maxims of politeness different from those of Leech's PP yet virtually characteristic of the Chinese setting.

Gu Yueguo's (1990) politeness principle is "a sanctioned belief that an individual's social behavior ought to live up to the expectations of respectfulness, modesty, attitudinal warmth and refinement" (245). These four essential notions are believed to be well-established in the Chinese conception of politeness. They are developed into the politeness principle and its maxims. These maxims are: the Self-denigration Maxim, the Address-term Maxim, the Refinement Maxim, the Agreement Maxim and the Virtues-words-deeds Maxim.

In view of their relatedness to the present study three of the maxims will be discussed in the comparative and contrastive analysis. They are the Self-denigration Maxim, the Address-term Maxim and the Refinement Maxim.

1) The Self-denigration maxim

a. Denigrate self   b. Elevate other

According to the self-denigration maxim, generally the speaker is expected to denigrate him/herself out of respectfulness and modesty. Breach of either maxim is likely to make the speaker appear rude or self-conceited.

The core of this maxim is first and foremost lexicalized with the help of a number of self-denigrating or self-effacing address terms. Such address terms are euphemisms, which, according to the analysis in Chapters Five and Six (see Figures 7 and 8), are intended to maintain or even enhance the identity face of the hearer. Secondly, if the speaker denigrates his/her own competence, ability or appearance in a euphemistic way, he/she might be in an attempt at elevating the hearer's personal qualities otherwise. In this sense, the hearer's quality face can be maintained or even enhanced. Of course, the lexicalization of this maxim is inherently threatening or costly to the speaker him/herself, yet a power-based context may predeterrmine the speaker's consideration of most benefit/least cost to the hearer and define venture of most cost/least benefit to him/herself. Table 24 shows Gu Yueguo's summary of some spheres of politeness in which the self-denigration maxim usually operates with corresponding terms as a result of its lexicalization.

Table 24　Lexicalization of the self-denigration maxim (Gu Yueguo, 2010: 302)

Sphere of politeness	Self-denigration Denigrative use	Other-elevation Elevative use
Person	鄙人	您
Surname	敝姓、贱姓	尊姓，贵姓
Profession	卑职	尊职
Opinion	愚见	高见
Writing	拙作	大作
Wife	内助	夫人
House	寒舍	贵府
School	敝校	贵校
Visit	拜访	赏光

It is found that most of the self-denigrating terms and other-elevating terms in the table fall into the category of address terms for interpersonal relations, which have already been discussed in Chapter Four. Gu Yueguo's self-denigrating terms accord with those that are referred to as self-denigrating terms or self-effacing terms in Chapter Four and his other-elevating terms are, in point of fact, a number of honorifics in that chapter.

2) The Address Maxim

Address your interlocutor with an appropriate address term.

According to the address-term maxim, the speaker is supposed to address the hearer in a proper way out of the consideration of "respectfulness and attitudinal warmth" (ibid. 304).

The maxim connotes two aspects: "(a) S's recognition of H as a social being in his specific social status or role, and (b) S's definition of the social relation between S and H. It helps establish or maintain social bonds, strengthen solidarity, and control social distance" (ibid. 304).

With breach of the maxim the speaker is likely to run the risk of appearing rude. At the same time, the failure tends to be seen as "a signal of a breakdown of established social order" (ibid. 304).

Gu Yueguo's elaboration on the maxim focuses on the social relations between the speaker and the hearer, in which the hearer's social status or group role is estimated or defined by the speaker so that he/she can opt for an address term most appropriate to the social identity of the hearer. This happens to comply with Spencer-Oatey's management of identity face. In her opinion, identity face is social and relates to one's sense of public worth. It is usually realized in relation to one's social status or group role.

In a power-based context, if the speaker recognizes the hearer as a superior in terms of his/her social status or group role and believes that the current social bond should be maintained or even enhanced, language strategies are deemed necessary and instrumental. As a type of address term, honorifics are, in a sense, verbal recognition of a person's social status or group role. Naturally they are also categorized as euphemisms targeted at maintaining or enhancing one's identity face.

3) The Refinement Maxim

Use refined language, including the use of euphemisms and indirectness, and avoid foul language.

Euphemisms are, by nature, indirect, refined and polite language as against straightforward, vulgar and rude language. At the same time, they are indicative of an individual's self-cultivation and due respect for other people. That's why as a language strategy euphemisms assume a role of lubricating interpersonal relations and maintaining the face of interactants. In essence, the refinement maxim accords with the use of euphemism for rapport management in interpersonal communication.

In conclusion, with the help of euphemisms, Gu Yueguo's self-denigration maxim may be targeted at maintaining other's quality face and identity face, and his address maxim maintaining other's identity face. Besides, to manage face and rights in all cases the refinement maxim may be realized with the help of euphemisms in a maximally desirable and efficient way. The relations are shown in Figure 16.

Gu Yueguo's PP

Spencer-Oatey's rapport

self-denigration maxim	quality face
address maxim	identity face
refinement maxim	equity rights
	association rights

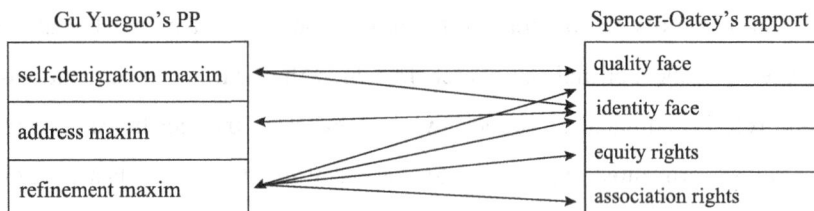

Figure 16　Gu Yueguo's PP and Spencer-Oatey's rapport

➤➤ 6.4　Non-use of Euphemisms

The previous chapters have revealed the fact that in a power-based context, a speaker (an inferior in particular) tends to make use of euphemisms of various kinds for the purpose of managing rapport with other (a superior in particular). To be more exact, as a linguistic strategy such euphemisms have turned out to be in active aid of maintaining or even enhancing what Spencer-Oatey identifies as quality face, identity face, equity rights or association rights in her theory of rapport management. Conversely, the theory has also proved to be capable of explicating why euphemisms are perceived as one of the best linguistic strategies in interpersonal communication and rapport management.

To complement the present study, some examples of non-use of euphemisms are selected from the character utterances of *DRM*, showing occasions on which euphemisms may fall idle.

Example 52:

贾妃亦嘱"只以国事为重，暇时保养，切勿记念"等语。(*DRM*, Chap. 18: 484)

Then it was Yuanchun's turn to urge her father to devote himself to affairs of state, look after his health and dismiss all anxiety regarding her. (*DRM*, Chap. 18: 485)

This remark is given to Jia Zheng by the Worthy and Virtuous Consort (Jia Yuanchun) at the Grand View Garden after he greets her. It essentially carries a message of care and concern from the Imperial Consort. However, as an impositive that sounds grave, formal and void of such linguistic mitigating devices as euphemism, her remark can be taken for a threat to Jia Zheng's equity rights: an individual is not to be ordered about or imposed upon. But on this grand occasion Jia Zheng will by no means feel offended in terms of his entitlements to freedom from any imposition. Instead, as a subject he will deem it a privilege and favour to be spoken to like that by a royal member. In this case, the relative power dominates familial relations and euphemism seems virtually unnecessary.

Example 53:
那贾政喘吁吁的，直挺挺坐在椅子上，满面泪痕，一叠声"拿宝玉！拿大棍！拿索子捆上！把各门都关上！有人传信往里头去，立刻打死！"众小厮们只得齐声答应，有几个来找宝玉。(*DRM*, Chap.33: 912, 914)

Then Jia Zheng, panting hard, his cheeks wet with tears, sat stiffly erect in his chair.

"Bring Baoyu in!" he bellowed. "Fetch the heavy rod! Tie him up! Close all the doors. Anyone who sends word to the inner apartments will be killed on the spot."

The servants had to obey. Some pages went to fetch Baoyu. (*DRM*, Chap. 33: 913, 915)

This happens after Jia Zheng has had the news of Jinchuan's suicide. Full of disappointment with Baoyu, he inclines to trust whatever Jia Huan slanders against Baoyu, whom he then decides to be guilty. In father-son relations, a father is supposed to have both absolute coersive power and legitimate power. With such power, the father is entitled to prescribe what his son should do and what he should not. Besides, he has control over the negative outcomes by exercising punishment. What's more, as far as obligation-right is concerned, the more obligation, the more right. Scolding and beating are taken-for-granted practices in old times. Against such background and power consideration, Jia Zheng is justified in giving Baoyu a good beating.

As master of the family, Jia Zheng now issues a series of orders to the servants: 拿宝玉—拿大棍—拿索子捆上—把各门都关上—立刻打死. All these orders are impositives, which sound threatening to the servants' equity rights of freedom from compulsion. However, in the feudal society, servants, as possessions of their master, are totally deprived of right and fully resigned to mastership in all circumstances. In this sense, orders are not deemed right-threatening, nor are euphemisms imperative in any respect.

Example 54:

一面说，一面又至一间房前，只见炕上有个纺车，宝玉又问小厮们：“这又是什么？”小厮们又告诉他原委。宝玉听说，便上来拧转作耍，自为有趣。只见一个约有十七八岁的村庄丫头跑了来乱嚷：“别动坏了！”众小厮忙断喝拦阻。宝玉忙丢开手，陪笑说道：“我因为没见过这个，所以试他一试。”那丫头道：“你们那里会弄这个，站开了，我纺与你瞧。”(*DRM*, Chap. 15: 380, 382)

Strolling into an outhouse, he was still more intrigued by a spinning-wheel on the *kang*. His pages told him this was used to weave yarn. He had just climbed up on the *kang* to turn the wheel for fun when in came a peasant girl of seventeen or eighteen. She ran over crying:

"Don't! You'll break it!"

She was shouted at by his pages, but Baoyu had already let go of the wheel.

"I've never seen one before," he explained with a smile. "I just wanted to have a try."

"How could you people know how?" said the girl. "Get out of my way and I'll show you." (*DRM*, Chap. 15: 381, 383)

During a halt in Qin Keqing's funeral procession, Baoyu walks around a farmhouse and gets curious about a spinning wheel on the *kang*, for he has never seen one like that before. The moment he turns the wheel for fun he is stopped by a girl of almost his age. Not knowing who he is the girl speaks in a straightforward manner.

She shouts orders to Baoyu: 别动坏了—站开了. Such orders are threatening and costly to Baoyu's equity rights that an individual is not to be ordered about. However, since the girl is supposed to be the owner of the farmhouse, she is entitled to exercise legitimate power over those outsiders like Baoyu. In this case, she does not have to use euphemisms. Furthermore, she says "你们那里会弄这个", which is meant to threaten the quality face of Baoyu and his pages in terms of their inability to handle the spinning wheel.

The above examples of non-use of euphemisms indicate that in a power-based context a person with relative power of one kind or another is generally not inclined to use euphemisms because he/she is not under an obligation to maintain or even enhance rapport. Instead, owing to his/her superiority in power relations, he/she tends to have more options in types of wording and ways of speaking.

6.5 *Li* and Politeness

Politeness is one of the major social constraints on human interaction regulating participants' communicative behavior by constantly reminding them to take into consideration the feelings of others (He Ziran, 2003).

There is no such Chinese equivalent to the English word "politeness". The most approximate one is *limao* (礼貌), which is believed to have evolved historically from the old Chinese notion *li* (礼). Like "face", the notion of *li* also finds its origin in the ancient Chinese philosopher and thinker, Confucius, who lived in a time of decayed slavery system, constant wars, shattered aristocratic social hierarchy and irremediable chaos shrouding the land. According to

Confucius, one of the best policies to settle such predicament was to restore *li*, which had nothing to do with politeness but referred to social hierarchy and order instead that were strictly exercised in the Zhou Dynasty. The restoration of *li* necessitated *zhengming* (正名), i.e. rectifying names. To be more exact, to rectify names meant to put each individual in his/her place according to his/her social position. At the same time, the restoration of *li* required appropriate speech in line with the speech user's social status. It was not until two or three hundred years later that the word *li* denoting politeness became well established in usage. The very usage of *li* meaning *limao* is well exemplified in the book *On Li* (《礼记》) compiled by Dai Sheng in the West Han Dynasty. "Speaking of *li* [i.e. politeness], humble yourself and show respect to other" can be found in its opening lines and has remained the core of the Chinese conception of politeness. So diachronically *li* (politeness) is born out of *li* (social hierarchy), articulates and buttresses *li* (social hierarchy and order).

Over the years *Li* has evolved into "social appropriacy by way of self-denigrating and other-respecting. It has ever since become an essential feature of the Chinese notion of politeness and has remained at the core of politeness in the Chinese culture" (He Zhaoxiong, 1995: 3-4). Gu Yueguo rightly observes that there are four notions that underlie the Chinese concept of politeness. They are "respectfulness, modesty, attitudinal warmth, and refinement" (Gu Yueguo, 1990: 245).

Now it is seems unfair not to take notice of the Chinese concept of face, which is equally long-standing and far-reaching. The characteristics of face indicate that it has long been held dear by every member of the Chinese society and has permeated in all most all spheres of people's daily life. To maintain face of interactants, politeness is usually deemed one of the best policies and strategies. Pointing out a close bond between the notion of politeness and politeness-bound literary works such as *DRM*, Hu Wenbin (2005) notes, "*A Dream of Red Mansions* is one of the carriers of ancient

Chinese *li* culture. *Li* culture penetrates all aspects of the novel, in which the delineation of *li*, *li*-related terms and *li*-related behaviour constaints abound in almost all the details of life" (《红楼梦》是中国古代礼文化载体之一。礼文化在这部小说中可以说渗透到各个方面，几乎每一个生活细节中无不有礼的描写、礼的专门用词、礼的行为约束。) (648). Likewise, it is found that in *DRM* in order to manage rapport euphemisms are used in the character utterances as verbal realization of face and politeness. As a means to maintain face, *li* is strategic and instrumental. As restraints of human speech and conduct, *li* is normative. Here He Zhaoxiong (1995) draws an incisive conclusion to *li*, saying "politeness can at once be understood as a social phenomenon, a means to achieve good interpersonal relationship, and a norm imposed by social conventions. So it is phenomenal, instrumental and normative by nature" (2).

6.6 Summary

In this chapter investigation is conducted on the relationship between euphemisms in the character utterances of *DRM* and Spencer-Oatey's theory of rapport management. In general, Spencer-Oatey's theory of rapport management suggests more of a balance between self and other. The discussion reveals that in order to maintain or enhance rapport euphemisms can be put into effect. The use of euphemisms in interpersonal interation can be explicated by the theory of rapport management. That is, Spencer-Oatey's theory of rapport management has a controlling force and explanatory power over the use of euphemisms of various kinds in the character utterances of *DRM*.

Still the discussion shows that euphemisms and Spencer-Oatey's theory of rapport management at issue bear much relation to such theories and principles as Grice's CP and CI, Leech's PP, Brown and Levinson's face-saving theory as well as Gu Yueguo's PP. A comparative and contrastive analysis indicates that there exist overlaps, similarities and differences. The result reveals that both Brown and Levinson's face theory and Spencer-Oatey's theory of rapport management are goal-directed. Besides, Brown and Levinson's concept of positive face overlaps with Spencer-Oatey's notion of face and their concept of negative face coincides with Spencer-Oatey's notion of equity rights. It is equally noteworthy that Grice's CP and CI, Leech's PP and Gu Yueguo's PP, compared with Spencer-Oatey's theory of rapport, tend to be instrumental. That is, to manage face and rights referred to in Spencer-Oatey's theory of rapport, Grice's CP and CI, Leech's PP and Gu Yueguo's PP can be put into use with the assistance of euphemisms.

To complement the present study, three examples of non-use of euphemisms are presented and interpreted, underlining the fact that in a power-based context, a person with a certain kind of relative power of one kind or another is generally not expected to use euphemisms for the simple reason that as a superior in the power relations he/she does not have to maintain or even enhance rapport with other (his/her inferior).

Finally, the Chinese notions of *li* and politeness are traced historically and culturally. The review delineates the complicated evolvement of politeness from *li*. In the Chinese context, great importance has long been attached to politeness, which unarguably assumes a significant role mainly in the following three aspects. As a social phenomenon politeness permeates almost every sphere of human life. As a social norm it regulates people's speech and conduct, thus it is taken as a mirror image of an individual's self-cultivation and refinement. As a principle of communication it serves to facilitate interpersonal relationship.

Built upon the politeness theory, Spencer-Oatey's theory of rapport management addresses the ubiquitously fundamental face and right concerns as its core components. The present study shows that the management of face and rights bears much relation to politeness and can be verbally realized with the assistance of euphemism.

Chapter Seven

Conclusion

7.1 Introduction

On the basis of an extensive literature review of euphemism and a full exposition of Spencer-Oatey's theory of rapport management, euphemisms in the character utterances of *A Dream of Red Mansions* are exemplarily described and categorized in Chapter Four. What follows in Chapter Five is a demonstration analysis of euphemisms in concert with Spencer-Oatey's theory of rapport management. The discussions in Chapter Six prove that euphemisms can effectively help maintain rapport and conversely, Spencer-Oatey's theory of rapport management is applicable to the pragmatic analysis of the strategic use of euphemisms in the character utterances of the novel. In other words, the theory of rapport management has a strong controlling force and explanatory power over the option and use of euphemisms under study.

In addition, the theories and principles revisited in Chapter Two are comparatively and contrastively discussed in reference to Spencer-Oatey's theory of rapport management and euphemisms. Similarities and differences are found and related conclusions are tentatively drawn. Then a couple of examples of non-use of euphemisms are presented and interpreted, pinpointing the fact that being entitled to a relative power of one kind or another in a power-based context, a person is generally not expected to use euphemisms to other unless he/she has a mind to show self-cultivation and politeness. Finally, the Chinese concept of politeness is traced historically and culturally to complement the study of euphemisms.

The following two sections delineate respectively the findings and implications of the present study. Then limitations so far are revealed. Finally friendly suggestions are made for further related research.

7.2 Findings

The findings of the study are, by and large, intended to answer the questions in Introduction (See 1.3). More elaboration will be focused on Question Eight in terms of the controlling force and explanatory power of Spencer-Oatey's theory of rapport management over the use of euphemisms. The findings are as follows:

1) Euphemisms in the character utterances of *A Dream of Red Mansions* are generally classified into conventional euphemisms and situational euphemisms.

Conventional euphemisms are largely an inventory of negative euphemisms because they are traditionally substitutes for taboos. This testifies to the origin and nature of euphemism. Conventional euphemisms in the collection are primarily concerned with everyday topics and activities: devil and disaster, death and funeral affairs, disease and ill health, sex, excreta and secretion, pregnancy and birth, ageing, love and affection, marriage and concubinage, jealousy, address terms for interpersonal relations, servants and housemaids, names regarded as taboos, moral standing and disposition as well as Buddhist practice and practitioner. It should be pointed out that some types of euphemisms are positive because they are used to camouflage the dispreferred by virtue of semantic inflation and magnification.

Besides, honorifics are also categorized as positive euphemisms.

Situational euphemisms, on the other hand, are heavily context-dependent. They are formed by resorting to semantic fuzziness and syntactical devices. Syntactical devices, including negation, hedges, face markers, rhetorical questions, particles and question words, seem to be much more complicated. They have all proved to help mitigate the tone of unpleasantness, imposition or threat.

2) In *DRM* the characters' option of euphemisms as a linguistic strategy helps attest the availability of Spencer-Oatey's theory of rapport management.

As the nature of euphemism is avoiding offence and giving face in interpersonal interaction, euphemisms in the character utterances of the novel are largely intended to maintain or enhance rapport.

To maintain other's quality face (a superior in particular), negative euphemisms that indicate personal qualities may come in handy. It turns out euphemisms implicating a person's low moral standing and distasteful disposition that go against the established values or social code of conduct help maintain his/her sense of personal self-esteem.

Very frequently situational euphemisms are also used to soften the tone of criticism or complaint so that other's quality face can somehow be maintained. Such euphemisms are constructed with the help of hedges to tone down the dispreferred expressions. In addition, the speaker can deviously quote other people's comment. This is also taken as a euphemistic way of expression. What's more, hedges equally help maintain one's quality face by creating semantic indistinctness.

To maintain or enhance other's (a superior in particular) identity face, honorifics are commonly used in terms of his/her sense of public worth either socially or familially. At the same time, it is found that self-denigrating terms have an equal footing. They are, by nature, threatening to the speaker's own identity face. However, in a power-based context where communication is usually oriented towards the maintenance or enhancement of rapport the speaker (supposedly an inferior in the power relations) may take the risk of sacrificing his/her own sense of public worth and resort to self-denigrating terms merely for the purpose of deviously elevating other's sense of public worth, namely, identity face.

To maintain other's (a superior in particular) equity rights, that is, his/her entitlements to personal consideration from people, situational euphemisms constructed with face markers such as "望", "祈" and "请" are usually found at work with orders or requests so that the tone of imposition can be mitigated. Besides, euphemizing devices such as approximators and particles help tone down the cost or compulsion in varying degrees for the purpose of maintaining other's equity rights. Furthermore, euphemisms in the form of rhetorical questions serve to help make suggestions or requests sound mild so that other may not feel coerced into doing anything.

To maintain other's (a superior in particular) association rights, that is, his/her entitlements to involvement with others or share of concerns, negative euphemisms play an active part in substituting for the unpleasant or dispreferred expressions and thus maintaining his/her association rights. It is noteworthy that hedges can also help soften the tone of complaint or disapproval for the purpose of maintaining other's association rights.

3) In *DRM* as a variable power exerts a great influence on the characters' option and use of euphemisms. To be more exact, the complexity of social hierarchy and familial network in the novel highlights the truth that power is a major factor that people must take into consideration if they want to appropriately handle such issues as face and rights. As a result, euphemisms are tailored to the management of rapport.

In the present study the power relations are categorized into two major types: social power relations and familial power relations. Then they are further divided into the absolute royal power, power relations between social unequals, power relations between familial unequals and power relations between master and servant.

The study reveals that it is usually an inferior that aims to maintain or even enhance rapport with a strategic use of euphemisms.

In pairs of unequal social relations, a superior is entitled to one or more kinds of power: reward power, coercive power, legitimate power or expert power, which is certainly nonreciprocal to an inferior. So usually the goal of interaction for an inferior is to maintain or strengthen rapport by virtue of euphemisms, which frequently and emphatically address the superior's identity face, quality face and occasionally association rights. What merits attention is that the absoluteness of royal power corners the option of euphemisms to extremity. That means euphemisms used by an inferior on such occasions carry an extreme sense of rigidity and formality, which on other occasions are deemed embarrassingly inappropriate.

The unequal familial relations also ensure that a senior or a superior enjoys a certain nonreciprocal type of power over a junior or an inferior: reward power, coercive power, legitimate power or expert power. Honorifics, self-denigrating terms and other address terms for interpersonal relations are primarily used as euphemisms to maintain the superior's identity face in terms of his/her sense of public worth in the family. Negative euphemisms are frequently used because they are closely associated with people's daily life. Such euphemisms cater mostly for the purpose of maintaining a senior's or superior's association rights or quality face. Besides, situational euphemisms are found in extensive use on such occasions.

4) The study demonstrates that generally the degree of indirectness is positively correlated with power relations. When addressing himself/herself to a royal member, an inferior is inclined to opt for a limited number of extremely devious, frozen and rigid euphemisms in concert with the royal

supremacy and inaccessibility. As far as the familial relations and master-servant relations are concerned, formality of indirectness is also found remarkable and prevalent to a certain extent but with much less rigidity. It should be pointed out that there are exceptions of non-use of euphemisms in such relations. That is, occasionally a junior or an inferior may not use euphemisms owing to his/her intimacy with a senior or a superior. In such cases, another contextual variable "distance" is found at work, which is not addressed in the present study.

5) There are some types of euphemisms that an inferior tends to use when he/she interacts with his/her superior.

When interacting with his/her superior, an inferior usually intends the communication to be oriented towards the maintenance or enhancement of rapport. In fact, power relations largely determine his/her way of speaking. The greater relative power a superior has over him/her, the more indirect his/her speech is expected to be.

The study shows that more often than not first consideration is given to the maintenance or enhancement of a superior's identity face with regard to his/her sense of public worth either socially or familially. The maintenance of identity face as a top priority in interactions rightly explains the traditional Chinese concerns over one's public image. That is, importance is first and foremost attached to how an individual is looked upon in public. To this end, honorifics and self-denigrating terms may be taken as expediencies.

In addition, to maintain the equity rights of a superior, both negative and situational euphemisms are extensively used in terms of his/her entitlements to personal consideration. An inferior is not in a position to give an order to his/her superior. He/She may make a request or suggestion, which is usually euphemized with face markers such as "望", "祈" and "请" to mitigate the tone of imposition so that the superior's equity rights can be maintained.

6) It is noteworthy that when interacting with a person of lower social

or familial status a superior occasionally uses euphemisms when he/she does not have to. The types of euphemisms available to him/her seem to be quite limited. Besides, the degree of indirectness is not so remarkable. This might largely be attributable to the traditionally upheld idea of being humble, modest, polite and elegant that every individual is expected to live up to. Two such cases are worth mentioning. In one case it is found that a superior is inclined to use honorifics to seemingly address an inferior's identity face. However, he/she may not truly mean so. The other case shows that despite the fact that a superior is presumably in a position to give orders, occasionally he/she may use face markers such as "请" and "望". However, this may not be interpreted as due care of the inferior's equity rights. So the two cases demonstrate that when a superior uses euphemisms in his/her interactions with an inferior, he/she may not be taking seriously such issues as the inferior's face and rights. Rather, it is merely a refined way of speaking to show off politeness and self-cultivation on his/her own part.

7) The salient emphasis on the "socialness" of "face" and "rights" in Spencer-Oatey's theory of rapport management has proved to be well exemplified in the characters' choice of euphemisms in *DRM*. According to Spencer-Oatey, identity face and association rights are the social components of rapport. In fact, it is found that a top priority is given to these two aspects in the novel. This, by and large, complies with the Chinese context of collectivism that highly values the idea of socialness.

The study shows that in *DRM* identity face is usually realized by means of honorifics or self-denigrating terms, which are both taken as euphemisms. Besides, negative euphemisms have a lot to do with association rights in terms of appropriate share of concerns, feelings or even interests so that other may not feel embarrassed, offended or shocked. In effect, the euphemisms that are put under investigation in the present study are mostly used to maintain or strengthen other's identity face and association rights. In that sense, the "socialness" of face and rights highlighted in the theory of rapport management is adequately exemplified and well tested in the characters' strategic use of euphemisms.

8) The theory of rapport management proves to have a remarkable controlling force and explanatory power over the characters' option and use of euphemisms in that it provides a detailed framework for explaining the euphemisms in terms of rapport orientation, face and rights, influencing factors as well as rapport outcome.

Stressed and upheld in the Chinese context are relations in which people make every effort to maintain each other's face and establish harmonious rapport. Cao Yingzhe (2004) rightly observes,

> Ever since ancient times the Chinese people have been striving, in every aspect of their life, for integrity with nature and have deemed harmony the supreme realm. In interpersonal relations and speech acts, the Chinese people are inclined to achieve and maintain harmonious and integral social relations and create an intimate atmosphere (自古以来，中国人在各个生活侧面都力求与自然统一，视和谐为最高境界。反映在人际交往和言语行为中，中国人也倾向于实现和维系一种 "和合" 的社会关系和制造一种亲密无间的和睦气氛。) (106).

It so happens that Spencer-Oatey's rapport management has a nice ring to the traditional Chinese value of rapport that can be verbally realized. Furthermore, in order for rapport to be properly managed and for message to come across in an appropriate manner, euphemisms are frequently found alternatively desirable. The applicability and explicability of the theory are elaborated in the following with regard to the components of rapport management: quality face, identity face, equity rights and association rights.

Firstly, quality face is personal for its close relatedness to an individual's personal qualities such as competence, abilities and appearance, which are supposed to contribute to his/her sense of self-esteem. The present study shows that both conventional and situational euphemisms are related to one's quality face. On the one hand, since quality face is concerned with a person's competence, ability, appearance and the like, related euphemisms are generally positive. However, there are also negative euphemisms regarding particular aspects of quality face. The study in Chapter Four shows that negative euphemisms are concerned with an individual's low moral standing and undesirable disposition such as "不干净" and "性子不好", jealousy such as "争风吃醋", illegitimate sex and prostitution such as "爬灰" and "偷鸡摸狗". These euphemisms, by nature, are threatening to one's quality face even though they are euphemistic. However, in a certain context that is oriented towards rapport maintenance such negative euphemisms are assumed to maintain one's quality face by not making him/her feel much too ashamed or offended. On the other hand, in order to maintain one's (a superior in particular) quality face, situational euphemisms can be put into operation in a certain context. Hedges like "未免" can be put in front of some quality-related negative euphemisms and they together mitigate the tone of disapproval so that quality face is maintained.

Secondly, identity face is social for its close relatedness to an individual's sense of public worth. It is generally recognized in terms of his/her social and group roles. The demonstration analysis in Chapter Five indicates that a superior's identity face can be realized by means of a number of honorifics and self-denigrating terms.

According to the description and categorization of euphemisms in Chapter Four, honorifics in *DRM* are "老爷", "太太", "先父", "令亲大人", "大爷", "先生", "西宾", "尊兄", "世兄", "老兄", "老先生", "尊夫人" and "尊府". Self-denigrating terms or self-effacing terms are "寒族", "在下", "敝友", "贱荆", "贱内", "小女", "晚生", "晚晚生", "弟" and "小弟". The demonstration analysis reveals that when addressing a superior (other or the third party) in power relations, an inferior has a variety of honorifics at his/her disposal, which are by nature targeted at acknowledging or upholding the superior's social identity or group role. As a result, they sound fairly beneficial to the superior by virtue of maintaining or even enhancing his/her identity face. It is also noteworthy that very frequently an inferior is inclined to use self-effacing terms at the risk of humbling him/herself with regard to his/her own identity face. To be more exact, self-denigrating terms are threatening to the inferior's own identity face. However, in a power-based context that is oriented towards rapport maintenance or even enhancement, self-effacing terms are like a double-edged sword, threatening the inferior's own identity face but at the same time deviously benefiting the superior in terms of his/her identity face.

Thirdly, like quality face equity rights are personal in that they are associated with one's entitlements to personal consideration from others. The ingredients of equity rights are the notion of cost-benefit and the issue of autonomy-imposition. Fairness and independence stand at the core of equity rights. The demonstration analysis in Chapter Five shows that equity rights are mainly realized by means of euphemized orders, requests, suggestions, advice or invitation. In most cases, they are used together with face markers "望", "祈" and "请", rhetorical questions with "岂不", particle "罢", hedges such as "少不得", adverbs such as "也" and "还" preceding verbs such as "该". Orders, requests, suggestions, advice or invitation usually sound threatening to a superior's equity rights in terms of cost-benefit or autonomy-imposition. However, in a power-based context, when such imposing utterances have to be made to a superior, the above-mentioned situational euphemisms are readily at an inferior's disposal. Correspondingly, the tone of imposition can be appropriately modulated and the superior's equity rights thus maximally maintained.

Finally, like identity face, association rights are social in that they are associated with one's entitlements to relationship with others. The ingredients of association rights are interactional association-dissociation and affective association-dissociation. Relational involvement and spiritual share are the core of association rights.

Association rights in the demonstration analysis of Chapter Five turn out to have a lot to do with most of the conventional euphemisms and a number of situational euphemisms. Categories in the conventional euphemisms are about devil and disaster such as "撞客" and "走水", death and funeral affairs such as "归西" and "寿木", disease and ill health such as "见喜" and "欠安", sex such as "风月" and "爬灰", excreta and secretion such as "小恭" and "月信", pregnancy and birth such as "喜" and "落草", ageing such as "有了春秋" and "上了年纪", love and affection such as "儿女私情" and "缠绵", marriage and concubinage such as "出阁" and "收房", servants and housemaids such as "家里人" and "小子", names regarded as taboos such as "密" for "敏", low moral standing and distasteful disposition such as "不干净" and "性子不好", and Buddhist practice and practitioner such as "入空门" and "出家人". Situational euphemisms are constructed with the help of semantic fuzziness such as "事" and "东西", syntactical devices (negation such as "不爽快", hedges such as "暂且" and question words such as "怎样"). Euphemized sentences are not few. One of the many examples is, "你快给你娘跪下，你说太太别委屈了……".

The above discussion on the relationship between rapport and euphemisms has proved that Spencer-Oatey's theory of rapport management is equal to account for the strategic use of euphemisms in the novel. In other words, the theory of rapport management is capable of governing and interpreting the use of euphemisms in the character utterances of *DRM*.

9) The one single puzzle that remains with the theory of rapport management so far seems to be its inability to account for the question of equity rights when occasionally a superior gives an order to an inferior in a euphemistic way. For example, at times a superior is likely to start an order

with a face marker such as "请". In appearance a euphemized order helps maintain the inferior's equity rights. However, in such a context of feudal society where a superior claims authority and order whereas an inferior is taught to habituate him/herself to submission, a euphemized order is not necessarily meant to maintain the inferior's equity rights of autonomy by means of mitigating the tone of imposition. A possible interpretation of the case is the superior's show of self-cultivation. To be more exact, to an inferior, the so-called imposition under such circumstances is by no means imposing or threatening in terms of freedom or cost-benefit consideration. That is why no examples have been found truly for the maintenance of the equity rights of an inferior. On the contrary, when an inferior makes a request to a superior, the face markers are usually indications of his/her effort to maintain the superior's equity rights.

10) In Chapter Six, a comparative analysis is conducted in reference to euphemisms, Spencer-Oatey's theory of rapport management, Grice's CP & CI, Leech's PP, Brown and Levinson's face theory and Gu Yueguo's PP.

The analysis indicates that Grice's CP and CI bear some relation to Spencer-Oatey's theory of rapport management and euphemisms in the novel. A flout of the CP that gives rise to the CI is verbally realized by euphemisms that are intended to maintain rapport.

Leech's PP has a lot to do with Spencer-Oatey's theory of rapport management. His approbation and modesty maxims can be seen as addressing Spencer-Oatey's quality face and identity face concerns, and his tact and generosity maxims addressing Spencer-Oatey's concerns over equity rights. In addition, Spencer-Oatey's rapport management is rapport-oriented and grounded in the notions of face and politeness. Leech's PP is of course politeness-oriented with its maxims stipulated for the purpose of realizing politeness. It is thus interpreted that to manage rapport, politeness must be taken into account and can be realized with the help of a number of maxims that are rendered verbally euphemistic.

Brown and Levinson's conception of positive face generally overlaps with that of Spencer-Oatey's quality face. However, their idea of negative face complies with the notion of sociality rights in her rapport management. To be more exact, their negative face can be put on a par with Spencer-Oatey's equity rights (an individual's entitlements to personal consideration from others for the purpose of fair treatment). In addition, the comparative analysis reveals that Spencer-Oatey's association rights are not found in Brown and Levinson's theory. Yet the very absence of association rights in their theory turns out to be central to the Chinese context. Association rights, according to Spencer-Oatey, are an individual's entitlements to interactional association (an individual's involvement with others) or affective association (an individual's share of concerns, feelings and interests with others). Rapport, in Chinese culture, has much to do with individuals' association rights: joining others in an activity is interactionally relational whereas having a share of concerns, feelings or interests with others is deemed affectively relational. In the present study, the wide varieties of euphemisms that contribute to the management of association rights confirm generally grave concern about entitlements to interpersonal association in the Chinese context. So it is self-evident that the component of association rights absent in Brown and Levinson's face theory finds a full explanation in Spencer-Oatey's rapport management. In other words, while Brown and Levinson's face theory may fail to account for such a large stock of euphemisms, Spencer-Oatey's theory of rapport management is capable of handling them with a strong explanatory power.

The comparative and contrastive study also indicates that with the help of euphemisms, Gu Yueguo's self-denigration maxim can be targeted at maintaining other's quality face and identity face, and his address maxim maintaining other's identity face, too. In respect of both face (quality face and identity face) and rights (equity rights and association rights), the refinement maxim, with the help of euphemisms, can assist with the management of rapport in a maximally desirable and efficient way.

Still the comparative and contrastive analysis reveals that in general Spencer-Oatey's theory of rapport management, like Brown and Levinson's face theory, is goal-directed. In addition, the theory proves comparatively practical and comprehensive owing to its full consideration and inclusion of face and rights as well as salient emphasis on their "socialness" in the framework of rapport. However, what Leech's PP, Brown and Levinson's face theory and Gu Yueguo's PP noteworthily share in common is that they all boast a number of concise principles or maxims as guidelines by which face or politeness can be managed. In effect, this is what seems absent in Spencer-Oatey's theory of rapport management. Therefore, it is desirable that her theory be complemented by formulating a number of maxims or principles of its own so that face and rights can be appropriately managed.

7.3 Implications

Guided by Helen Spencer-Oatey's theory of rapport management, euphemisms in the character utterances of *A Dream of Red Mansions* have been tentatively studied. At the same time, the feasibility of the theory of rapport management has been explored and tested. It is assumed that the study has both theoretical and practical implications.

There is no denying that Grice's CP & CI, Leech's PP, Brown and Levinson's face theory and Gu Yueguo's PP have proved applicable to the study of euphemisms. A new theory, "a modified framework for conceptualizing face and rapport" (Spencer-Oatey, 2007: 13) by drawing on "social pragmatics, politeness theory and face theory" (ibid. 6), has also proved worth trying. The present work has endeavored to conduct a pioneering study of euphemisms in the character utterances of *DRM* by taking rapport management as its theoretical framework, which is relatively new yet challenging in pragmatically studying euphemisms. The findings of the study support the feasibility and applicability of the theory of rapport management to the Chinese context. The theory has proved to have a controlling force over the characters' option of euphemisms as against other ways of expression. At the same time, the theory is strong in its explanatory power over the euphemisms in the novel.

A tentative study has been conducted on the character utterances, in which euphemisms are put in a dynamic context with power as a major variable influencing the strategic use of euphemisms. The result of the pragmatic investigation of euphemisms in the character utterances of *DRM* is expected to supplement and enrich the unremitting nationwide and even worldwide academic studies of the novel, namely, Redology.

As euphemisms are extensively used in interpersonal communication, more often than not they are context-dependent. The variables governing the use of euphemisms are also deemed primary concerns of pragmatics. So the findings of the present study may help verify and enrich the related theories and principles in the field of pragmatics.

The present study has taken *A Dream of Red Mansions* as its text and tentatively analyzed euphemisms in the character utterances of the novel in light of Spencer-Oatey's theory of rapport management. The theory has proved to be capable of governing and interpreting the euphemisms in the character utterances of the novel. It is thus argued that this theory can also be applied to the pragmatic analysis of other texts in both English and Chinese languages.

Language is both universal and culture-bound. As a part of language, euphemism reflects yet is constrained by cultural traditions and national mentality. Hopefully the findings of the present research may have some implications to culturology and ethnography.

7.4 Limitations and Suggestions

The present study suffers two major limitations, which call for considerable attention and appeal to further improvement.

For one thing, heavily based on observation, the present study has mainly attempted a qualitative approach to the discussion and analysis of euphemisms in the character utterances of *DRM*. In spite of a large collection of euphemisms from the novel, the research cannot claim to be quantitative in its true sense. Hence it is desirable that a quantitative approach be simultaneously adopted to jointly work with the qualitative approach for the sake of a more objective bird's-eye view of the pragmatic use of euphemisms in the character utterances of the novel.

For another, there is still much room for improving the description and categorization of euphemisms in Chapter Four. It seems impossible to categorize the situational euphemisms in an exhaustive way. Besides, judgment of situational euphemisms may differ from person to person. Therefore, more attention should still be drawn to the classification and illustration of situational euphemisms, which have proved dynamic and significant to the analysis of euphemisms in the forthcoming chapters.

The existing problems and limitations with the present study are awaiting settlement and improvement by related studies, so further attempts are encouraged, for which friendly suggestions are made in the following three aspects.

Firstly, the contextual variable "power" has been taken as a major influencing factor in the pragmatic study of the euphemisms in the novel. Significant conclusions are drawn in terms of the strategic use of euphemisms for the maintenance or enhancement of rapport on the one hand and the explanatory power of rapport over the strategic use of euphemisms on the other. Now it is suggested that one or more influencing factors other than "power" in the theory of rapport management, such as "distance", be taken as major variables in investigating the pragmatic use of euphemisms for the management of rapport and interpreting the strategic use of euphemisms by virtue of the theory of rapport management.

Secondly, a joint approach can also be taken of both Spencer-Oatey's theory of rapport management and Gu Yueguo's PP. Spencer-Oatey's theory of rapport is well-grounded in the notions of face and politeness whereas Gu Yueguo's PP is closely based on the origin of the Chinese notion of politeness and critical adoption of Leech's maxims of politeness with some reservations. In that sense, Spencer-Oatey's theory of rapport might be taken as goal-oriented and Gu Yueguo's PP instrumental. The two might be operating as a complementarily combined means-end approach to the analysis of euphemisms in the character utterances of *DRM*.

Thirdly, Spencer-Oatey's rapport management is theoretically goal-oriented yet void of its own corresponding maxims that may assume the role of guiding the enhancement, maintenance, neglect or challenge of face and rights. Therefore, an attempt seems most worthwhile to complement the theory of rapport management by formulating a set of maxims in its own right so that a truly means-end model of rapport management might be built with face and rights appropriately managed.

Bibliography

[1]   Adler, M. *Naming and Addressing: A Sociolinguistic Study* [M]. Hamburg Germany: Helmut Buske Verlag Hamburg, 1978.

[2]   Allan, K. *Linguistic Meaning* (vol. 1) [M]. London: Routledge & Kegan Paul, 1986.

[3]   Allan, K., Burridge, K. *Euphemism & Dysphemism: Language Used as Shield and Weapon* [M]. Oxford: Oxford University Press, 1991.

[4]   Allan, K., Burridge, K. *Forbidden Words: Taboo and the Censoring of Language* [M]. Cambridge: Cambridge University Press, 2006.

[5]   Aronoff, M., Rees-Miller, J. (eds.). *The Handbook of Linguistics* [C]. Oxford: Blackwell, 2001.

[6]   Austin, J. L. *How to Do Things with Words* [M]. Oxford: Oxford University Press, 1962.

[7]   Ayto, J. *Euphemisms* [M]. London: Bloomsbury Publishing Limited, 1993.

[8]   Barron, C., Bruce, N., Nunan, D. (eds.). *Knowledge and Discourse: Towards an Ecology of Language* [C]. Harlow: Pearson Education Limited, 2002.

[9]   Bertram, A. *NTC's Dictionary of Euphemisms* [Z]. Lincolnwood, Illinois: NTC Publishing Group, 1998.

[10]   Blakemore, D. *Understanding Utterances: An Introduction to Pragmatics* [M]. Oxford: Blackwell Publishers, 1992.

[11]   Bloomer, A., Griffiths, P., Merrison, A. J. (eds.). *Introducing Language in Use: A Coursebook* [M]. London and New York: Rougledge, 2005.

[12]   Blum-Kulka, S. You don't touch lettuce with your fingers: parental politeness in family disourse [J]. *Journal of Pragmatics*, 1990 (2): 259-288.

[13] Bolinger, D. *Aspects of Language* [M]. New York: Harcourt, Brace & World, Inc., 1968.

[14] Bolinger, D., Sears, D. A. *Aspects of Language* [M]. New York: Harcourt Brace Jovanavich Inc., 1981.

[15] Brown, R., Gilman, A. Pronouns of power and solidarity [A]//T. A. Sebeok (ed.). *Style in Language* [C]. Cambridge, MA: MIT Press, 1960/1972: 253-276.

[16] Brown, P., Levinson, S. C. *Politeness: Some Universals in Language Usage* [M]. Cambridge: Cambridge University Press, 1987.

[17] Burns, L. C. *Vagueness* [M]. London: Kluwer Academic Publishers, 1991.

[18] Carroll, D. W. *Psychology of Language* [M]. Beijing: Foreign Language Teaching and Research Press, 2000.

[19] Chang, H., Holt, R. A Chinese perspective on face as inter-relational concern [A]//S. Ting-Toomey (ed.). *The Challenge of Facework: Cross-Cultural and Interpersonal Issues* [C]. Albany: State University of New York Press, 1994: 95-132.

[20] Chen, R. Responding to compliments: a contrastive study of politeness strategies between American English and Chinese speakers [J]. *Journal of Pragmatics*, 1993 (20): 49-75.

[21] Cheng, C. The concept of face and its Confucian roots [J]. *Journal of Chinese Philosophy*, 1986 (13): 329-348.

[22] Chi, R., Hao, Y. Euphemism From Sociolinguistics Perspective [J]. *Studies in Sociology of Science*. 2013 (4): 45-48.

[23] Clark, H. H. *Using Language* [M]. Cambridge: Cambridge University Press, 1996.

[24] Culpeper, J. *Language and Characterisation: People in Plays and Other Texts* [M]. Harlow: Pearson Education, 2001.

[25] Cupach, W. R., Metts, S. *Facework* [M]. CA: SAGE, 1994.

[26] Dascal, M. *Pragmatics and the Philosophy of Mind I: Thought in Language* [M]. Amsterdam: John Benjamins, 1983.

[27] Enright, D. J. *Fair of Speech—the Use of Euphemism* [M]. Oxford: Oxford University Press, 1985.

[28] Fauconnier, G. *Mental Spaces: Aspects of Meaning Construction in Natural Language* [M]. Cambridge: Cambridge University Press, 1994.

[29] Fetzer, A. (ed.). *Context and Appropriateness* [M]. Amsterdam: John Benjamins Publishing Company, 2007.

[30] Filllmore, C. Pragmatics and the description discourse [A]//P. Cole (ed.). *Radical Pragmatics*. New York: Academic Press, 1981: 143-166.

[31] Fraser, B. Acquiring social competence in a second language [J]. *RELC Journal*, 1978, (9): 1-26.

[32] Fraser, B., Nolen, W. The Association of deference with linguistic form [J]. *The International Journal of the Sociology of Language*, 1981 (27): 93-109.

[33] Fraser, B. Perspectives on politeness [J]. *Journal of Pragmatics*, 1990 (14): 219-236.

[34] French, J. R. P., Raven, B. The bases of social power [A]//D. Cartwright & A. Zander (eds.). *Studies in Social Power*. Ann Arbor: University of Michigan Press, 1959. 150-167.

[35] Gadlin, H. Conflict resolution, cultural differences and the culture of racism [J]. *Negotiation Journal*, 1994, (10): 33-48.

[36] Goffman, E. *Interaction Ritual: Essays on Face-to-Face Behavior* [M]. Garden City, New York: Anchor Books, 1967.

[37] Goffman, E. *Interaction Ritual: Essays on Face-to-Face Behavior* [M]. Harmondsworth: Penguin, 1972.

[38] Goffman, E. *Forms of Talk* [M]. Oxford: Basil Blackwell, 1981.

[39] Green, J. *Neologisms: New Words since 1960* [M]. London: Bloomsbury Publishing Limited, 1991.

[40] Grice, H. P. Logic and conversation [A]//P. Cole & J. L. Morgan (eds.). *Syntax and Semantics* (Vol. 3). New York: Academic Press, 1975: 41-58.

[41] Grice, H. P. *Studies in the Way of Words* [M]. Cambridge, MA: Harvard University Press, 1989.

[42] Gu, Y. G. Politeness phenomena in modern Chinese [J]. *Journal of Pragmatics*, 1990 (14): 237-257.

[43]   Günthner, S., Knoblauch, H. Culturally patterned speaking practices: the analysis of communicative genres [J]. *Pragmatics*, 1995, (5): 1-32.

[44]   Hartwell, P., Robert, H. B. *Open to Language: A New College Rhetoric* [M]. Oxford: Oxford University Press, 1982.

[45]   Ho, D.Y. On the concept of face [J]. *American Journal of Sociologist*, 1976, (81): 867-884.

[46]   Holder, R.W. *The Faber Dictionary of Euphemisms (rev.)* [Z]. London: Faber and Faber, 1989.

[47]   Holder, R. W. *Oxford Dictionary of Euphemisms* [Z]. Oxford: Oxford University Press, 1995.

[48]   Holder, R. W. *How Not to Say What You Mean: A Dictionary of Euphemisms* [Z]. Oxford: Oxford University Press, 2003.

[49]   Holder, R. W. *Oxford Dictionary of Euphemisms: How Not to Say What You Mean* [Z]. New York: Oxford University Press, 2007.

[50]   Hornby, A. S. *Oxford Advanced Learner's English-Chinese Dictionary* [Z]. Oxford: Oxford University Press, 1997.

[51]   Hu, H. C. The Chinese concepts of "face" [J]. *The American Anthropologist*, 1944 (46): 45-50.

[52]   Huang, Y. *Pragmatics* [M]. Beijing: Foreign Language Teaching and Research Press, Oxford University Press: 2009.

[53]   Hymes, D. Competence and performance in linguistic theory [A]//R. Huxley & E. Ingram (eds.). *Language Acquisition: Models and Methods*. London: Academic Press, 1971: 3-28.

[54]   Hymes, D. Models of the interaction of language and social life [A]//J. Gumperz & Hymes (eds.). *Directions in Sociolinguistics* [C]. New York: Holt, Rinehart and Winston, 1972: 35-71.

[55]   Ide, S. Introduction: linguistic politeness I [J]. *Multilingua*, 1988 (7): 371-374.

[56]   Ide, S. Formal forms and discernment: two neglected aspects of universals of linguistic politeness [J]. *Multilingua*, 1989 (2/3): 223-248.

[57]   Kramsch, C. *Language and Culture* [M]. London: Oxford University Press, 1998.

[58]   Kramsch, C. *Language and Culture* [M]. Shanghai: Shanghai Foreign Education Press, 2000.

[59]   Lakoff, G. Hedges: A study in meaning criteria and the logic of fuzzy concepts [J]. *Journal of Philosophical Logic*, 1972 (4): 458-508.

[60]   Lakoff, G. The logic of politeness: or, minding your p's and q's [A]//C. Corum et al. (eds.). *Papers from the Ninth Regional Meeting of the Chicago Linguistic Society*. Chicago: Chicago Linguistic Society, 1973: 292-305.

[61]   Lakoff, R. *Language and Woman's Place* [M]. New York: Harper and Row Publishers, 1975.

[62]   Lee-Wong, S. M. *Politeness and Face in Chinese Culture* [M]. Frankfurt: Peter Lang, 1999.

[63]   Leech, G. N. *Explorations in Semantics and Pragmatics* [M]. Amsterdam: John Benjamins Publishing Company, 1980.

[64]   Leech, G. N. *Principles of Pragmatics* [M]. London: Longman, 1983.

[65]   Leech, G. N. Politeness: is there an East-West divide? [J]. *Journal of Foreign Languages*, 2005 (6): 3-31.

[66]   Levinson, S. C. *Pragmatics* [M]. Cambridge: Cambridge University Press, 1983.

[67]   Lim, T. S., Bowers, J. W. Facework: solidarity, approbation, and tact [J]. *Human Communication Research*, 1991 (3): 415-450.

[68]   Lim, T. S. Facework and interpersonal relationships [A]//S. Ting-Toomey (ed.). *The Challenge of Facework: Cross-Cultural and Interpersonal Issues* [C]. Albany: State University of New York Press, 1994: 209-229.

[69]   Linfoot-Ham, K. The linguistics of euphemism: a diachronic study of euphemism formation [J]. *Journal of Language and Linguistics*, 2005, (2): 227-243.

[70]   Mao, L. R. Beyond politeness theory: 'face' revisited and renewed [J]. *Journal of Pragmatics*, 1994 (5): 451-486.

[71]   Martin, B., Ringham, F. *Dictionary of Semiotics* [Z]. London and New York: Cassell, 2000.

[72] Matsumoto, Y. Reexamination of the universality of face: politeness phenomena in Japanese [J]. *Journal of Pragmatics*. 1988 (4): 403-426.

[73] Mencken, H. L. *The American Language: An Inquiry into the Development of English in the United States* (4th ed.) [M]. New York: Alfred A. Knopf, 1936.

[74] Miller, G. A., Johnson-laird, P.N. *Language and Perception* [M]. Cambridge: Harvard University Press, 1976.

[75] Mish, F. C. (ed.). *Webster's Word History* [M]. Springfield, Massachusetts: Merriam-Webster Inc., Publishers, 1989.

[76] Neaman, J. S., Silver, G. C. *Kind Words: A Thesaurus of Euphemisms* (rev.) [M]. New York, Oxford, Sydney: Facts on File, 1983.

[77] Neaman, J. S., Silver, G. C. *Kind Words: A Thesaurus of Euphemisms* [M]. New York: Facts on File, 1990.

[78] Neaman, J. S., Silver, G. C. *In Other Words: A Thesaurus of Euphemisms* (rev.) [M]. London: Angus & Robertson, 1991.

[79] Onions, C. T. (ed.). *The Oxford Dictionary of English Etymology* [Z]. Oxford: Clarendon Press, 1982.

[80] Pan, Yuling. *Politeness in Chinese Face-to-Face Interaction* [M]. Stamford, CT: Ablex Publishing Corporation, 2000.

[81] Partridge, E. *Shakespeare's Bawdy* [M]. London: Routledge, Kegan and Paul, Ltd., 1968.

[82] Penman, R. Facework and politeness: multiple goals in courtroom discourse [J]. *Journal of Language and Society*, 1990 (1-2): 15-38.

[83] Penman, R. Facework in communication: Conceptual and moral challenges [A]//S. Ting-Toomey (ed.). *The Challenge of Facework: Cross-Cultural and Interpersonal Issues*. Albany: State University of New York Press, 1994: 15-46.

[84] Rawson, H. *A Dictionary of Euphemisms and Other Doubletalk* [Z]. New York: Crown Publishers, 1981.

[85] Sapir, E. *Language: An Introduction to the Study of Speech* [M]. Beijing: Foreign Language Teaching and Research Press, 2002.

[86]   Scollon, R., Scollon, S. W. Face parameters in East-West discourse [A]//S. Ting-Toomey (ed.). *The Challenge of Facework: Cross-Cultural and Interpersonal Issues* [C]. Albany: State University of New York Press, 1994: 133-158.

[87]   Scollon, R., Scollon, S. W. *Intercultural Communication: A Discourse Approach* [M]. Oxford: Blackwell, 1995.

[88]   Scollon, R., Scollon, S. W. *Intercultural Communication: A Discourse Approach* [M]. Beijing: Beijing Foreign Language Teaching and Research Press, Blackwell Publishers Ltd, 1995.

[89]   Searle, J. R. (ed.). *Expression and Meaning* [M]. Cambridge: Cambridge University Press, 1979.

[90]   Searle, J. R. (ed.). *Expression and Meaning: Studies in the Theory of Speech Act* [M]. Beijing: Beijing Foreign Language Teaching and Research Press, 2001.

[91]   Spencer-Oatey, H. Reconsidering power and distance [J]. *Journal of Pragmatics*. 1996 (26): 1-24.

[92]   Spencer-Oatey, H. Unequal relationships in high and low power distance societies: a comparative study of tutor-student role relations in Britain and China [J]. *Journal of Cross-Cultural Psychology*. 1997 (3): 284-302.

[93]   Spencer-Oatey, H., Xing, J. Relational management in Chinese-British business meetings [A]//S. Hunston (ed.). *Language at Work*. Clevedon: British Association for Applied Linguistics in Association with Multilingual Matters Ltd, 1998.

[94]   Spencer-Oatey, H. (ed.). *Culturally Speaking: Managing Rapport through Talk across Cultures* [C]. London: Continuum, 2000.

[95]   Spencer-Oatey, H. (ed.). *Culturally Speaking: Managing Rapport through Talk across Cultures* [C]. Shanghai: Shanghai Foreign Language Education Press, 2007.

[96]   Spencer-Oatey, H. (ed.). *Culturally Speaking: Culture, Communication and Politeness Theory* (2nd ed.) [C]. London ; New York: Continuum, 2008.

[97]   Sperber, D., Wilson, D. *Relevance: Communication and Cognition* [M]. Oxford: Basil Blackwell Ltd., 1986.

[98]   Thomas, J. Cross-Cultural Pragmatic Failure [J]. *Applied Linguistics*, 1983 (4): 91-112.

[99] Thomas, J. *Meaning in Interaction: An Introduction to Pragmatics* [M]. Harlow: Pearson Education, 1995.

[100] Ting-Toomey, S. Intercultural conflicts: a face-negotiation theory [A]//Y. Y. Kim & W. Gudykunst (eds.). *Theories in Intercultural Communication*. Newsbury Park, CA: SAGE, 1988. 213-235.

[101] Ting-Toomey, S., Cocroft, B. A. Face and facework: theoretical and research issues challenges [A]//S. Ting-Toomey (ed.). *The Challenge of Facework: Cross-Cultural and Interpersonal Issues*. Albany: State University of New York Press, 1994. 307-340.

[102] Ting-Toomey, S., Kurogi, A. Facework competence in intercultural conflict: an updated face-negotiation theory [J]. *International Journal of Intercultural Relations*, 1998 (2): 187-225.

[103] Tracy, K., Coupland, N. (eds.) *Multiple Goals in Discourse* [C]. Clevedon & Philadelphia: Multilingual Matters Ltd., 1990.

[104] Tracy, K., Baratz, S. The case for case studies of facework [A]//S. Ting-Toomey (ed.). *The Challenge of Facework: Cross-Cultural and Interpersonal Issues* [C]. Albany: State University of New York Press, 1994: 287-306.

[105] Trudgill, P. *Sociolinguistics: An Introduction to Language and Society* [M]. England: Penguin Books, 1986: 31.

[106] Verschueren, J. et al. (eds.). *Handbook of Pragmatics* [C]. Amsterdam: John Benjamins Publishing Company, 1995.

[107] Verschueren, J. *Understanding Pragmatic*s [M]. Beijing: Beijng Foreign Teaching and Research Press, Edward Arnold (Publishers) Limited, 2000.

[108] Volkema, R. J. The mediator as face manager [J]. *Mediation Quarterly*, 1988 (22): 5-15.

[109] Waldron, R. A. *Sense and Development* (2nd ed.) [M]. London: André Deutsch Ltd., 1979.

[110] Warren, B. What euphemisms tell us about the interpretation of words [J]. *Studia Linguistica*, 1992 (46): 128-172.

[111] Watts, R. J. *Politeness* [M]. Cambridge: Cambridge University Press, 2003.

[112] Winkler, E. G. *Understanding Language* [M]. New York: Continuum, 2007.

[113] Yang, H. Y., Yang, G. (trans.). *A Dream of Red Mansions*. Beijing: Foreign Languages Press, 1978.

[114] Zhan, K. *The Strategies of Politeness in the Chinese Language* [M]. Berkeley CA: Institute of East Asian Studies, 1992.

[115] 曹雪芹，高颚. 红楼梦 [M]. 北京：人民文学出版社，1982.

[116] 曹雪芹，高颚. 红楼梦 [M]. 杨宪益、戴乃迭译. 北京：外文出版社，长沙：湖南人民出版社，1999.

[117] 曹颖哲. 礼貌现象的英汉语用对比 [J]. 黑龙江社会科学，2004 (6)：103-106.

[118] 陈科芳. 修辞格翻译的语用学探解 [M]. 上海：复旦大学出版社，2010.

[119] 陈林华. 语言学导论 [M]. 长春：吉林大学出版社，1999.

[120] 陈融. 面子、留面子、丢面子 [J]. 外国语，1986 (4)：16-21.

[121] 陈融. 英语的礼貌语言 [J]. 现代外语，1989 (3)：5-14.

[122] 陈望道. 修辞学发凡 [M]. 上海：上海教育出版社，2002.

[123] 陈维昭. 红楼梦精读 [M]. 上海：复旦大学出版社，2009.

[124] 陈原. 社会语言学 [M]. 上海：学林出版社，1983.

[125] 陈原. 社会语言学 [M]. 北京：商务印书馆，2000.

[126] 戴聪腾. 汉英委婉语的跨文化研究 [J]. 福建师范大学学报，2003 (1)：93-96.

[127] 邓炎昌，刘润清. 语言与文化：英汉语言文化对比 [M]. 北京：外语教学与研究出版社，1989.

[128] 冯其庸. 红楼论要——解读《红楼梦》的几个问题 [J]. 红楼梦学刊，2008 (5)：9-39.

[129] 冯庆华主编. 红译艺坛——红楼梦翻译艺术研究 [M]. 上海：上海外语教育出版社，2006.

[130] 冯庆华. 母语文化下的译者风格——《红楼梦》霍克斯与闵福德译本研究 [M]. 上海：上海外语教育出版社，2008.

[131] 顾曰国. 礼貌、语用与文化 [J]. 外语教学与研究，1992 (4)：10-17.

[132] 顾曰国. 顾曰国语言学海外自选集 [M]. 北京：外语教学与研究出版社，2010.

[133] 郭锦桴. 汉语与中国传统文化 [M]. 北京：中国人民大学出版社，1993.

[134] 郭尚兴. 中国儒学史 [M]. 上海：上海外语教育出版社，2011.

[135] 贺阿莉. 委婉语的社会语言学研究 [D]. 重庆：西南师范大学，2002.

[136] 何善芬. 英汉语言对比研究 [M]. 上海：上海外语教育出版社，2002.

[137] 何永康主编. 红楼梦研究 [M]. 苏州大学出版社，2002.

[138] 何兆熊. Study of Politeness in Chinese and English Cultures [J]. 外国语，1995 (5)：2-8.

[139] 何兆熊，梅德明主编. 现代语言学 [M]. 北京：外语教学与研究出版社，1999.

[140] 何兆熊，俞东明等. 新编语用学概要 [M]. 上海：上海外语教育出版社，2000.

[141] 何兆熊. 语用学文献选读 [M]. 上海：上海外语教育出版社，2003.

[142] 贺又宁. 修辞学：言语行为之视野 [M]. 北京：民族出版社，2008.

[143] 胡文彬. 红楼梦与中国文化论稿 [M]. 北京：中国书店，2005.

[144] 胡文炜. 《红楼梦》欣赏与探索 [M]. 北京：北京图书馆出版社，2006.

[145] 胡文仲主编. 交际与文化 [M]. 北京：外语教学与研究出版社，1994.

[146] 黄清贵. 从语言到语用：理论与实践 [M]. 厦门：厦门大学出版社，2009.

[147] 黄雅颖. 转喻视角下的委婉语生成 [J]. 安徽工业大学学报 (社会科学版)，2014 (5)：52-54.

[148] 黄衍. 语用学[M]. 北京：外语教学与研究出版社，2009.

[149] 金惠康. 跨文化交际翻译 [M]. 北京：中国对外翻译出版公司，2003.

[150] 蓝纯. 语用学与红楼梦赏析 [M]. 北京：外语教学与研究出版社，2006.

[151] 蓝纯，赵韵. 《红楼梦》中跨等级道歉的语用研究 [J]. 当代修辞学，2010，158 (2)：77-84.

[152] 李国南. 英语语言中的委婉语 [J]. 外国语，1989，(3)：23-27.

[153] 李国南. 英汉修辞格对比研究 [M]. 福州：福建人民出版社，1999.

[154] 李国南. 辞格与词汇 [M]. 上海：上海外语教育出版社，2001.

[155] 李军. 话语修辞理论与实践 [M]. 上海：上海外语教育出版社，2008.

[156] 李军华. 关于委婉语的定义 [J]. 湘潭大学学报 (哲学社会科学版)，2004 (4)：162-165.

[157]　李军华. 汉语委婉语研究 [M]. 北京：中国社会科学出版社，2010.

[158]　连淑能. 英汉对比研究 [M]. 北京：高等教育出版社，1993.

[159]　梁红梅. 委婉语的语用分析 [J]. 天津外国语学院学报，2000 (1)：30-34.

[160]　梁扬，谢仁敏. 《红楼梦》语言艺术研究 [M]. 北京：人民文学出版社，2006.

[161]　林兴仁. 《红楼梦》的修辞艺术 [M]. 福州：福建教育出版社，1984.

[162]　刘纯豹. 英语委婉语词典 [Z]. 南京：江苏教育出版社，1993.

[163]　刘金保. 《红楼梦》中死亡委婉语翻译研究 [J]. 安徽工业大学学报 (社会科学版)，2013 (3)：66-71，82.

[164]　刘倩. 委婉表达新论——语言研究的心智哲学视角 [D]. 开封：河南大学，2013.

[165]　刘越莲. 委婉语与禁忌语的家族相似性研究 [J].《外语教学》，2010，(6)：10-13.

[166]　卢兴基，高鸣鸾. 红楼梦的语言艺术 [M]. 北京：语文出版社，1985.

[167]　罗纳德·斯考伦，苏珊·王·斯考伦. 跨文化交际：话语分析 [M]. 北京：社会科学文献出版社，2001.

[168]　彭文钊. 委婉语——社会文化域的语言映射 [J]. 外国语，1999 (1)：66-71.

[169]　钱大昕. 潜研堂文集 [M]. 上海：上海古籍出版社，1989.

[170]　钱冠连. 语言学自选集：理论与方法 [M]. 北京：外语教学与研究出版社，2008.

[171]　任显楷，柯锌历.《红楼梦》四种英译本委婉语翻译策略研究：以死亡委婉语为例 [J]. 红楼梦学刊，2011 (6)：73-85.

[172]　邵军航，樊葳葳. 也谈委婉语的构造原则 [J]. 山东师范大学学报，2002 (2)：32-34.

[173]　邵军航，曹火群. 对委婉语"语用原则"的批判分析 [J]. 孝感学院学报，2006，26 (2)：39-43.

[174]　邵军航. 委婉语研究 [D]. 上海外国语大学，2007.

[175]　邵志洪. 英汉语研究与对比 [M]. 上海：华东理工大学出版社，1997.

[176]　束定芳. 现代汉语中的委婉语 [J]. 汉语学习，1989 (2)：34-38.

[177]　束定芳. 委婉语新探 [J]. 外国语，1989 (3)：28-34.

[178] 束定芳. 试论Geoffrey Leech的语言观和人际交际修辞理论 [J]. 外语研究, 1990 (4)：1-8.

[179] 束定芳, 王虹. 言语交际中的扬升抑降与礼貌原则 [J]. 外国语, 1993 (3)：7-13.

[180] 束定芳, 徐金元. 委婉语研究：回顾与前瞻 [J]. 外国语, 1995 (5)：17-22.

[181] 束定芳主编. 中国语用学研究论文集 [C]. 上海：上海外语教育出版社, 2001.

[182] 孙爱玲.《红楼梦》对话研究 [M]. 北京：北京大学出版社, 1997.

[183] 孙汝建. 修辞学的社会心理分析 [M]. 上海：上海外语教育出版社, 2006.

[184] 索振羽. 语用学教程 [M]. 北京：北京大学出版社, 2000.

[185] 田九胜. 委婉语的语用分析 [J]. 福建外语, 2001 (2)：18-21.

[186] 王春艳, 刘素华. 英汉委婉语的语用分析 [J]. 西南民族大学学报 (人文社科版), 2007 (12)：96-98.

[187] 王德春、李月松主编. 修辞学论文集 (第十集) [C]. 上海：上海外语教育出版社, 2006.

[188] 王冬梅. 委婉语的概念隐喻分析 [J]. 江西师范大学学报 (哲学社会科学版), 2010, (6)：132-136.

[189] 王国栋、甘世安、周春艳. 认知语境观与英语委婉语的认知范式 [J]. 西北大学学报 (哲学社会科学版), 2011, (6)：164-166.

[190] 王国凤.《红楼梦》与 "礼"：社会语言学研究 [M]. 杭州：浙江大学出版社, 2011.

[191] 王海龙. 曹雪芹笔下的少女和妇人 [M]. 上海：上海文艺出版社, 2010.

[192] 王海明. 新伦理学 [M]. 北京：商务印书馆. 2001.

[193] 王秋香, 郎佳. 委婉语生成机制的心智视角分析 [J]. 中北大学学报 (社会科学版), 2015 (3)：88-91.

[194] 王守元, 郭鸿, 苗兴伟. 文体学研究在中国的进展 [C]. 上海：上海外语教育出版社, 2004.

[195] 王希杰. 修辞学通论 [M]. 南京：南京大学出版社, 1996.

[196] 王雅军. 委婉语应用辞典 [M]. 上海：上海辞书出版社, 2011.

[197]　王永忠. 从语言模糊性看委婉语的交际功能 [J]. 外国语, 2001 (4)：27-30.

[198]　吴礼权. 试论汉语委婉辞格的历史文化背景 [J]. 修辞学习, 1987 (6)：43-44.

[199]　吴礼权. 论委婉修辞生成与发展的历史文化缘由 [J]. 河北大学学报, 1997a (3)：56-60.

[200]　吴礼权. 论委婉修辞的表现形态与表达效应 [J]. 湘潭大学学报 (哲学社会科学版), 1997b, 21 (3)：94-97.

[201]　吴礼权, 邓明以. 中国修辞学通史：当代卷 [M]. 昆明：吉林教育出版社, 2001.

[202]　吴礼权. 修辞心理学 [M]. 云南人民出版社, 2002.

[203]　吴礼权. 现代汉语修辞学 [M]. 上海：复旦大学出版社, 2006.

[204]　吴礼权. 委婉修辞研究 [M]. 济南：山东文艺出版社, 2008.

[205]　伍铁平. 从委婉语的机制看模糊理论的解释力 [J]. 外国语, 1989 (3)：16-22.

[206]　伍铁平. 模糊语言初探 [J]. 外国语, 1979, (4)：41-46.

[207]　徐海铭. 委婉语的语用学研究 [J]. 外语研究, 1996, (3)：21-24, 47.

[208]　徐莉娜. 跨文化交际中的委婉语解读策略 [J]. 外语与外语教学, 2002, (9)：6-9.

[209]　徐莉娜. 委婉语翻译的语用和语篇策略 [J]. 中国翻译, 2003, (6)：15-19.

[210]　徐鹏等. 修辞和语用——汉英修辞手段语用对比研究 [M]. 上海：上海外语教育出版社, 2007.

[211]　徐盛桓. 礼貌原则新拟 [J]. 外语学刊, 1992 (2)：1-7.

[212]　徐宜良. 委婉语的语境制约与解读 [J]. 西南民族大学学报 (人文社科版), 2007 (7)：200-203.

[213]　俞东明主编. 文体学研究：回顾、现状与展望 [C]. 上海：上海外语教育出版社, 2010.

[214]　张发祥, 康立新, 赵文超. 话语分析：理论与案例 [M]. 北京：科学出版社, 2009.

[215]　张拱贵. 汉语委婉语词典 [Z]. 北京：北京语言文化大学出版社, 1996.

[216]　张瑞娥, 董杰. 多维视角下二元翻译因素的并置与转换——以《红楼梦》判词的英译为例 [J]. 天津外国语学院学报, 2010 (2)：35-41.

[217] 张宇平，姜艳萍，于年湖. 委婉语 [M]. 北京：新华出版社，1998.

[218] 赵蓉晖. 语言与性别：口语的社会语言学研究 [M]. 上海：上海外语教育出版社，2010.

[219] 周建民主编. 修辞学论文集 (第十一集) [C]. 北京：中国社会科学出版社，2008.

[220] 周振甫. 中国修辞学史 [M]. 南京：江苏教育出版社，2006.

[221] 朱建，孟建国. 委婉语的翻译原则——以《红楼梦》部分原句的委婉语翻译为例 [J]. 新疆大学学报 (哲学·人文社会科学版)，2011 (6)：151-153.

[222] 朱永生，严世清. 系统功能语言学多维思考 [M]. 上海：上海外语教育出版社，2001.